A Sugarplum Promise

Other Books by C. L. Fails

A Spoonful of Sugarplums

Where Sugarplums Shimmer

So Okay...Treasured Stories from the Life of James M. Robinson, Sr.

My Magical Story Journal

The Secret World of Raine the Brain Series

The Ella Books Series

The Christmas Cookie Books

A Sugarplum Promise

A Novel

LaunchCrate Publishing
Kansas City, KS

C.L. Fails

A Sugarplum Promise is a work of fiction. Names, characters, places, and incidents are either the productions of the author's imagination or are used fictitiously. Any resemblance to actual persons, living or dead, events, or locales is entirely coincidental.

A Sugarplum Promise
Written by C. L. Fails

LaunchCrate Publishing
Kansas City, KS
info@launchcrate.com
www.launchcrate.com

Ordering Information:
Quantity sales. Special discounts are available on quantity purchases by corporations, associations, and others. For details, contact the publisher at the email address above. Orders by U.S. trade bookstores and wholesalers.

Library of Congress Control Number: 2021920129

Hardcover ISBN: 978-1-947506-23-7
Paperback ISBN: 978-1-947506-89-3

Printed in the United States of America
10 9 8 7 6 5 4 3 2 1

First Edition

For those of you in search of seeds of hope, may you find them, plant them, and water them to create a garden for others to discover along their path.

"I felt like I was everything I wanted to be in that moment. I was enough. He was enough. We were enough, and we were about to step beyond any place we'd ever been before, and then it all changed in the blink of an eye."

CONTENTS

Contents

A Sugarplum Promise

Chapter 1
Mother's Day

Dr. Chris:

He was everything that I wanted in a partner. He was everything that I needed. And I - I felt like I was everything I wanted to be in that moment. I was enough. He was enough. We were enough, and we were about to step beyond any place we'd ever been before, and then it all changed in the blink of an eye.

The dream I'd had on the day before my birthday had just come true and I didn't see any of it coming. I was sitting beside Charlie, at a table full of our family, in a place where the celebration, I thought, was intended to honor my mother. They were all in on it; his family, my family, everyone. I must have missed all the signs because I was completely caught off guard.

The last time I'd seen Charlie, I asked for some time apart. It took more than a notion for me to relax and allow the waves of emotion to come and go instead of reaching out to him like I wanted to. But I had no idea that the next time I would see him, he would bend down on one knee and ask if he could marry me. Not if I would marry him. "Will you allow me to marry you, Chris?"

I locked my knees and nearly fainted. He was the best person I knew and he asked if I would allow him to share our lives with each other, which spoke volumes about his character. I loved him deeply and thought about all of this as the two of us sat side by side, Charlie with his arm draped behind my chair, listening to our family celebrate the two of us after we ate.

"So, when's the wedding?" his Dad joked. I beamed with joy as those words wove their way through my brain.

"Dad, we haven't seen each other in a month. Can we just be for a moment?" Charlie asked his father.

"Well I'm sorry son. I assumed that you had a plan since you decided to propose the first time you laid eyes on your bride after a month of separation!"

Charlie's mom tapped her husband on the hand. "Leave him alone, Bub." He nodded.

I rested my head on the inside of Charlie's shoulder and allowed his frame to hold the weight of my relief. Both moms, mine and his, smiled at the sight of their children reconnecting in love. I wasn't sure what could make this moment any better than it was. I was content. I was hopeful. I was elated. I was full and completely engrossed in the moment. Before I could realize what was happening, Charlie held up a phone in front of my face. I tilted my head to the side, confused at the face I saw on the screen.

A voice chirped out, "Hi friend!" I found myself looking at Marlo through the wave of tears that were quickly welling in my eyelids. Sensing the rise of my emotions, Charlie leaned in to tenderly kiss my temple before handing me the phone and wiping away some tears of his own with the back of his index finger. Marlo and I were still, neither of us knowing quite where to find the words to describe the moment.

"So, you're with him again. I can only assume that means he proposed to you," he finally spoke through words that were caught in the back of his throat.

"Did you know he was going to propose?"

"The last time I spoke to Charlie he told me that the next time he saw you, he was going to propose. He said it didn't matter where you were or who was nearby."

I gazed at Charlie, who shrugged his shoulders and nodded his head. "Did you plan this?" I asked him directly.

He raised a hand in resignation, "I had no idea that everybody would be here today. I only thought I was meeting you."

"So you said yes, right, Chris?" Marlo asked exuberantly.

I nodded and chuckled through more tears as I looked around the room at the number of people who were invested in our contentedness. My niece and nephew both smiled in our direction before Corwin decided to stand and pointedly walk towards us, his strides full of purpose. I thought he was going to stop at me, instead he tapped Charlie on the shoulder I was nestled in. "Uncle Charlie?" he softly spoke.

Charlie removed his arm from the back of my chair and sat up enough to turn his body in Corwin's direction. "What's up buddy?" he asked as he patted him on the back.

"Did Corwin just call him Uncle Charlie?" Marlo asked from the phone.

"He's been calling him that since New Year's eve," I told Marlo.

"Oh wow!" Marlo exclaimed. I shrugged.

"Uncle Charlie, does this mean you're gonna have babies with Aunt Chris?" I froze, unwilling to turn my head in Charlie's direction. Marlo tried his best to keep his mouth closed, but despite his efforts, his face still contorted in joyful discomfort. Thankfully not a peep left his mouth.

Charlie was very matter of fact as he opened his mouth to answer Corwin. "If, God wants us to raise awesome children like you and your sister, then yes."

"I want a boy cousin! Can you do that?" Corwin asked emphatically. I couldn't see my own face, but I know that my eyes bugged. Marlo snickered. I tried not to move.

"I'll see what I can do, Corwin," Charlie gently replied which prompted Corwin to squeeze between the two of us to drape a loving embrace over him. I could barely take it. I finally turned my head in their direction and watched as Corwin leaned his head onto the same shoulder I had just been resting on.

Corwin whispered exactly what was on his mind. "I love you, Uncle Charlie."

"I love you too Corwin," Charlie responded, tilting his head onto the top of Corwin's. Before I knew it, Christina had leaned in for a hug from Charlie too. I looked over at my sister Vonne, who placed one palm over her own heart and wiped away tears from her eyes with the other hand. I didn't know love to wash over you in multiple waves, but that's exactly how I would describe it.

"I'm so happy for you, Chris," Marlo whispered through tears of his own. "I knew he was a fit when I saw how excited you were about this mystery man," he continued. "There's never been anyone you've spoken so highly about. And I do mean never, and you know how far back we go."

The only thing I could do was nod as I acknowledged exactly what Marlo was getting at. Charlie was my person. He was the one I had waited patiently for. He was the "better" that I knew existed. He was the human whose heart I wanted to hold through whatever transformations life took us through. I told Marlo that I would call him later. I had a strong desire to stay present in this moment. It was almost like my mind wanted to protect and preserve the joy that was present. Maybe it was a subconscious attempt at overriding the lingering fear that this inexplicable "thing" between us could have been too good to be true. I was still learning to trust myself again after my last love.

Charlie:

Everyone I loved dearly was with us on the day I asked to share my life with her. I didn't know how they managed to pull it off and surprise both of us, but there we were nonetheless and before I knew it I was hugging her niece and nephew like they were my own. I reached out for Dr. Chris' hand and pulled her in to hug them as well. The twins wriggled out from between us and forced us to hug each other by jumping on their aunt's back. She didn't even flinch.

Since we were so close, it felt like the perfect time to whisper in her ear, "I love you so much, Sugarplum. This day is perfect."

Her words tickled my ear, "I love you deeply, Charlie. Always have and always will." Never in my life did I think I would find contentment like this. So I took it all in. The sound of each of our family members in conversation with each other. The laughter, presumably at our expense. The cooing of my mother as she watched the two of us canoodling with children on our backs. The sound of Corwin and Christina's hearty laughter that pierced the air with joy. The rise and fall of Dr. Chris, resting across my chest again. She was back in the nook of my arm, but her soul it seemed, was already connected to mine. *This woman.*

How the two of us had a complete conversation without using words is beyond me. But I didn't question it. In our time apart, I had learned not to question much of anything when it came to our relationship. Instead I'd decided to lean on our experience together. She was a phenomenal woman and I felt so lucky that she was willing to share our lives with each other.

Brunch turned into an afternoon gathering at Dr. Chris' parents' house. Vonne and her family had something else planned to celebrate her on that day, but everyone else made it to their split level house. I loved watching the way our families co-mingled with each other. It reminded me of the world I had created for future me as a child. Being an only child, I used to think about how MY family would look; not only a wife and children, but an extended family that loved my parents like family. I never wanted to marry into a family that didn't like me. I always dreamed of people who would bring me into the fold like I was a long lost family member they were welcoming home.

Dr. Chris and I had the chance to snag a moment to ourselves as we slipped from the basement where everyone gathered, up to the kitchen to refresh the snacks. She quietly eyed me as she grabbed a sleeve of crackers and artfully arranged them on the platter. I wanted to ask what was on her mind but instead I opted to intermittently return her intense gaze as I began to slice the cheese into more manageable bites. We were in the middle of a silent tango as we navigated around the kitchen replenishing the nosh.

"Charlie," she began.

"Dr. Chris," I replied.

"You had the ring in your pocket with you today. What did they say to get you to the restaurant?"

"My Mom and your Dad told me that they'd find a way to get you to the restaurant so the two of us could talk. The only thing I was told is that you would be there at 11:00 this morning. So my job was to show up and to ask for the reservation that was supposed to be in my name. I had no idea they were all going to be there too."

"Oh. But the ring..."

"It's been in my pocket since the Friday before your birthday. I was originally going to propose to you on that weekend, at the surprise party. Then we were watching that stupid movie and you made the comment about how the guy was strong-arming the woman into accepting his proposal and I didn't know what to do. I only knew that proposing to you in front of your family was no longer an option." I laughed nervously at the thought of me proposing in front of her family anyway.

"But then you proposed in front of my family today!" She laughed at the absurdity of my comment as well. All I could do was shrug my shoulders and allow the moment to be what it was, unapologetically awkward.

"I told myself if I was lucky enough to see you again and if you were receptive to my apology that I'd tell you what happened and how I truly felt about you. I wasn't expecting everyone else to be there, but I knew that I needed to apologize first. How did you feel my words?"

"I'm not sure, but it was just like the dream I had."

"The dream?"

"Yeah. On my birthday, when you woke me up for breakfast I'd just finished dreaming about exactly what happened today. I wasn't sure how it was even possible or if it was going to happen, but I was hopeful."

"This is wild, huh?"

"What's wild?"

"We haven't seen each other in a month and now we've committed to share our lives together forever."

"It is pretty wild when you put it like that, Charlie. Wait, you said you had the ring since February."

"Mmm hmm."

"February, Charlie?"

I smiled at her surprise and watched her face droop as I began to speak. "The day that you asked for space, I tried to place it in your hand and you wrapped my hand around it without even looking at it."

"I did what?!"

"I called your name as I reached in my pocket and you wouldn't hear me out. I didn't want to propose to you in that way, but the way that conversation was headed I wasn't sure I was going to get to see you again."

"I thought you were trying to hand me the key," she said as I shook my head in reply. "So you mean I turned down this beautiful ring?" I nodded in the affirmative. "Oh, Charlie."

"This was probably better for us anyway. It's okay. I don't think I would have taken the time to figure out what and who was important to me if it weren't for the space you asked for," I said as she smiled. I could feel the warm energy filling my gut and before I could stop myself, my mouth spewed exactly what was on my mind. "I've missed your face, Chris."

She stood in front of me and lovingly stared into my soul. "I've missed yours too, Charlie." Her hand raised to the side of my face and stroked the outline of my beard. I wanted to kiss her, but I didn't want to ruin the moment. It was intimate. The two of us stealing away from the family and creating our own place of peace. She was home, wherever we were and that last month had definitely been a trying time for me. I wouldn't trade it for the world though. I was a better person for it.

In the distance I heard the door to the basement open and heavy footsteps as they ascended the stairs. Dr. Chris laid a quick peck on my lips as I tried to maintain my composure, knowing that someone was on their way to see where we had disappeared to. Her Dad cleared his throat on the way up the stairs, I'm guessing to let us know that he was present. I grabbed the platter of cheese and crackers, raised my eyebrows at Dr. Chris and turned to head towards the basement stairs.

"Is everything okay up here?" Mr. James asked with a grin spread wide on his face.

"Yes, sir," I replied. "Just taking this cheese and crackers downstairs to everyone."

"I thought I saw you getting a little sugar in the kitchen!" he chided.

"You'll have to talk to your daughter about that, sir."

"Dad."

"Dad."

"I told you she missed you, didn't I?"

"You did indeed."

"Welcome to the family, Son."

I couldn't muster any words, only a smile and a shallow nod.

Dr. Chris:

I was outdone by the fact that Charlie had been carrying around the ring, waiting for the right time to propose to me. I was so stuck in my own version of what was going on that I neglected to see what was going on with Charlie. I knew I had to do better and I felt grateful that I had the rest of my life to learn how to grow in that area with him.

We stayed at my parents house until late that evening. I needed to rest for the next day of work and so did Charlie, but neither of us wanted to leave the other's side.

After his parents and grandparents headed towards his house for the night, the two of us lingered in the driveway, hand in hand - our fingers intertwined and dancing with each other.

"So, I guess I'll give you a call tomorrow if that works for you," he said.

"I mean we are engaged now you could just greet me with 'good morning' when we wake up together tomorrow."

"There is that. That's definitely an option." He paused, his lip tucked inside his mouth as he hesitated for a second before asking his next question. "Do I still have clothes at the condo?"

I smiled. "You do, but I was kind of hoping to spend a bit more time with your family. Last time they were in town I didn't get to and you promised me that I could the next time they were here."

"I did say that, didn't I?" he asked just as his phone rang. "It's Mom. Do you mind if I take this?" I shook my head incredulously, confused that it was even a question he'd pose to me. All I could hear was his end of the conversation.

"Yes ma'am. It's in the same space. But I. Mom, I. We did talk about it. She wants to spend time there with all of you. Okay, I'll tell her. I'll tell her. Do you want to tell her? I need to swing by to grab my work bag tonight but I'll be quiet since you're all going to bed. I'll see you after work tomorrow. I love you too. Bye."

Charlie's Mom had been my biggest supporter since I met her that Christmas Eve, and the puzzled look on his face as he ended the call suggested that she might have caught her son off-guard during that conversation.

"So Mom basically told me that she would disown me if I spent the night in my own house. She said she loves you dearly and she's so excited that you're joining the family. I need to swing by to grab my bag for work but I'll meet you back at the condo if that's okay with you."

"I love your mom so much, Charlie." I cheesed. Excited that we'd be together that evening after a month apart, I leaned in and placed my forehead on his. I spoke softly, "Be careful on your way to the condo. I'll tell Ralph that you're coming."

His mouth curled up into a smile, our fingers danced together again. "I'll see you shortly, Sugarplum." He kissed my temple before we parted and my insides flipped.

My breathing shallowed as I ended my intercom call with Ralph. I was anxious to greet Charlie at the door. I'd grown so accustomed to doing it before that I think I took it for granted. But seeing him through the peephole was a welcome site. I wasn't sure why he didn't use his key, as he had never returned it, but I opened the door for him nonetheless. He tipped a single red carnation in my direction.

"Charlie, where did you get this flower from at this hour?"

"I was optimistic in thinking that you would be receptive to my apology, so I picked one up yesterday."

I shook my head at my future husband and just how

well he actually knew me, then leaned in for a quick kiss after ushering him inside.

"Can I get you anything, Sweetheart?"

He shook his head and ran a hand across the back of his head, dragging it forward and smoothing his hair, before running it down his face and reaching for my hand. "It's pretty late and I'm a bit outdone after today."

I led him into the living room, pausing near the couch. "So you're ready to turn in for the night?"

"I am. Is that okay with you?"

"Charlie, you don't need my permission to go to sleep." I yawned.

"Someone else looks sleepy too."

"I am. Your toothbrush is still in the bathroom and I can grab some pajamas for you to wear."

He turned around to face me, after sitting his bag on the couch and opened up his arms slightly to request a hug. A request I gladly fulfilled.

His arms were safe. The last hug I received from him before requesting space was such a heavy embrace. I wasn't sure I'd see him again, even though I wanted to. I hoped that the space would be good for both of us, but I remember holding on to him and simultaneously feeling safe and at home, and sad at the thought that it might be the last hug we'd have.

So there we were again, in a full body embrace. Him welcoming me back into his life, and me gladly doing the same for him. The feeling of home was still present and I could feel myself letting go of every relationship driven stressor that I thought I had already dealt with. I was even lighter than I had already been told I appeared. With every passing second I leaned harder into him, my weight shifting from my own two feet into his sturdy chest and solid arms. The more I let go, the more I leaned, the harder he squeezed. The harder he squeezed, the more I felt loved. And the more love I felt him pour into me, the more I leaned. It was a gentle cycle of love.

"I could fall asleep right here in your arms," I grumbled through a contented sigh.

Charlie placed his cheek atop my forehead, a move I had grown to anticipate as part of our hugs. Though I didn't anticipate his newly formed strength, which was on full display as he dipped me backwards, sweeping my feet off the floor before rocking in the other direction and cradling me in his arms. This was new. Good new, but new. I'm almost certain that I yelped, which spawned a chuckle from Charlie as he buried his lips in my neck.

"Is your room in the same place?" He joked.

"It's only been a month, Charlie," I said as he began to walk through the living room.

"So that's a yes?" He laughed as he carried me down the hallway to the bedroom, pausing at the door and gazing into my eyes - such a piercing stare. Without breaking our connection I reached down for the doorknob, opening the door for him since his hands were full. A single eyebrow raised on his face and I couldn't hide the smile from my own. "No ma'am." He chuckled again as he slowly entered the room and lowered me back to my feet.

"What, Charlie?" I giggled.

A semi-permanent grin graced his face. "You already know what. I don't need to answer that. I'm not even sure why you asked me."

I straightened my clothes and walked to his drawer, pulling out the t-shirt and shorts I'd washed with my last load of clothes, tossing them in his direction. He caught them close to his chest and raised them to his nose, taking a whiff of their scent and suppressing a smile. He disappeared from the bedroom as he went to clean up in the bathroom across the hallway. By the time he returned to the doorway to lean in and tell me that the bathroom was free, I had changed into my own pajamas and was working on rearranging the bedding.

"You don't have to do that, Chris," he said as he entered the room.

"It's okay, Charlie. I want to make sure you're comfortable tonight."

I could smell the minty toothpaste on his breath as he neared. "I don't think we'll need that anymore." His eyebrow raised again. Maybe it was subconscious. I'm not sure.

"What do you mean, Charlie?"

He paused near the hamper and pointed to it, both eyebrows raising in question. I nodded. He dropped in his clothes and answered my question. "We're not dating anymore. I'm your fiancé. Soon to be your life partner. That's a little different than dating to learn more about each other, don't you think?"

I couldn't argue with him. Being a fiancée was new to me. Like, hours new. I didn't know what that meant. But I did understand what he was saying. So, together we remade the bed. I watched Charlie take great care in tucking in the excess sheet on his side of the bed and smoothing the top of both sides before pulling the comforter up. I knew we were about to go to sleep, but that didn't seem to factor into the way he chose to make the bed. I loved that about him. He took great care to give his best when he put his mind to it. The love in my heart surfaced as a smile in his direction from across the bed and he shook his head at me.

Charlie:

She kept making eyes at me all night. She did it when I carried her into the bedroom, so I put her down on her feet instead of gently on the bed like I had planned. She did it as I sniffed my freshly laundered clothes. She did it when I came back from brushing my teeth, then again when I made the bed. Each and every time tested my strength, and each and every time I felt so lucky to get to spend the rest of my life with someone who looked at me the way she did. I didn't realize how much I'd missed those glimpses until I saw them again. Then my heart melted, all over again, just like it did when she looked up at me as I caught her in the coffee shop. That surge of warm energy was back and it was coursing all throughout my veins - all of them. I was relieved when she stepped out to brush her teeth and I took that time to redirect my thoughts into a prayer of thanksgiving. That day was one for the memory books, that's for certain.

I was already in the bed when she returned. I'd heard her walk down the hallway to turn out the rest of the lights in the condo before slowly creeping back into her room. She smiled in my direction and hopped on top of the covers.

"Thank you for today, Charlie," she said while stretching out on her stomach.

"Thank YOU for today, Dr. Chris."

Her already bright smile widened, "What are you thanking me for?"

"Everything. Being you. Saying yes, and not making me look like a fool."

"Was there any doubt that I'd say yes?"

"Honestly, yes. I hadn't seen or spoken with you in over a month, and things ended so abruptly and not on very good terms. I wasn't sure if you'd accept my apology, let alone a proposal of marriage."

"I can see that. But honestly, Charlie."

"Yeah?"

She climbed underneath the covers and the words rolled off her tongue so nonchalantly. "You could've asked me at any point in our relationship and I probably would've said yes."

"What?" I didn't believe her.

"Yep. You could have asked me jokingly in the coffee shop line and I would've jokingly said yes."

"How about at the Jubilee?"

"Yes."

"When we got snowed in?"

"Yes."

"Carriage ride?"

"Absolutely."

"How about on Easter Sunday?" I asked as I opened my arm for her to snuggle in beside me.

"I would've felt bad about second guessing things, but I would've said yes." She curled up in the nook of my arm.

I ran my fingers across the babyhair that framed her edges. "Wow. I should've just blurted it out."

"It wouldn't have been nearly as memorable as today."

"Oh, I think that would've been pretty memorable. Don't you?"

She made eyes at me again. "Yeah, but this was a different type of memory."

I nodded, thinking back on what was just a few hours ago but seemed like a full week. She hadn't even been back in my life for half a day and already I felt more at peace. My sense of calm had returned and my purpose, it seemed, had been restored. I went to sleep that night with her head resting on my chest, protecting my most vulnerable organ. *My heart.*

CHAPTER 2

NOW WHAT?

Dr. Chris:

I woke up to the sound of his heartbeat pumping directly underneath my ear. His warm breath tickled my ear and his arm wrapped softly around my back. I lifted my left hand from his chest and gazed at the ring he chose for me to wear forever. I hadn't really given it much of a look the day before, as he and I really were more focused on reconnecting and staying in the moment than anything else. The weight of it on my finger was noticeable because I wasn't used to having anything on my hand at all. But to look at this masterpiece was something different entirely. It wasn't just the beauty of the ring itself but the beauty of what it represented more than anything that captivated my attention. My mind continued to circulate on the fact that this man wanted to grow with me, forever. He wanted to laugh with me, forever. He wanted to face all of the scary unknown stuff, with me, forever. And after all of these thoughts circulated on repeat moment after moment, it felt like this day was the true start of the rest of our lives together. I know that was technically supposed to be whatever day we actually got married, but asking the question meant he was ready to commit to that. So holy crap, there we were - about to live life together. I could and couldn't wrap my head around it. My heart, was fully on board though. I didn't know what time it was, but I knew it was too early to have such a philosophical conversation with myself.

I know it had to be fairly early in the morning because the sun hadn't yet started to rise and his alarm hadn't yet sounded. I thought I had laid still enough to not wake him, but despite my best effort, I failed.

He inhaled sharply. His voice extra deep in the early morning hours. "Do you like it?" He must've caught me looking at the ring.

"This thing on my finger?"

"This thing. Yes, this thing on your finger," he said through a deep rumbly laugh.

"I love it, Charlie. I'm sorry I woke you."

"It's okay. I love that I got to wake up to you."

"Did I move too much?"

"Your breathing shifted and I woke up to see if you were okay."

"I'm okay. My breathing shifted?"

"Yeah, you breathe a certain way when you sleep - like deeper than normal. It's not quite a snore, but it's deeper than when you're awake."

"What?"

"Mm hmm."

"So how long have you been awake?"

"Since your breathing shifted. I've just been quietly laying here watching you look at the ring and smile, then wander off in thought, then look at it again and smile, then do some more thinking."

"Why didn't you say anything, Charlie?"

"Because it was cute. You weren't saying anything out loud so I didn't feel like I was eavesdropping. I probably would've cleared my throat if that was the case."

"I feel so exposed." I laughed.

"Well this is what I'll probably be doing for the rest of our days, so you might want to get used to it."

"You mean you'll be creeping on me?" I joked.

"Not creeping. Just admiring."

"Okay, Charlie."

"So, my alarm is going to go off in a few minutes and we didn't have the chance to talk about how today would look for each of us before sleep knocked us out. What's on your calendar?"

"A few follow-up appointments and one surgery."

"Light work," he joked.

"Totally," I replied. "How about you? Any end of year things coming up for you?"

"Not this week, but next. This week is basically the last round of testing and next week is full of the fun stuff."

"Do they still do field day?"

"They have a modified version of it."

"Got it. All the safety precautions are probably ramped up and the fun dialed down a notch?"

"Pretty much," he snickered.

"So just a regular day today then?"

"Yes ma'am. So I'm probably gonna go to work and then I'll head to my house to hang with my family. I'm not sure how long they're in town, honestly."

"Okay. I can call you when I'm back at the Condo after work."

"Or you can give me a call when you're on your way home to me."

I liked the sound of that, but I couldn't let him know.

I probably should have told him, but it made me all too giddy to hear.

"Or I can give you a call when I'm on my way home." I had turned my head to rest my cheek back on his chest at that point, so I couldn't see his face anymore. But, I know I heard a smile. "What are you smiling about, mister?"

"You think you always know when I'm smiling?"

"Don't I?"

"I suppose so," he said while lightly rubbing my back, a move he used to quiet me back to sleep.

"Well..."

"Anyway, I just love the sound of that. I've always loved the way you distinguished between our two spaces, Chris."

"Charlie...you're so chatty at 4 in the morning!" I joked.

He tickled my side as he laughed. "Was that your way of telling me to shut up?"

"Nope. That was my way of telling you that I appreciate your honesty this early in the morning."

"I'm gonna be quiet now."

I nudged him to try to get him to say something. Anything. But he was sticking to his word. I loved this man, more than I knew how to express to him, but I knew better than to not even attempt to try.

"Charlie, I love you deeply. You know that," I said as he squeezed my shoulder - still not speaking. "I appreciate you more than you know. I'm excited to have these conversations with you at 4 in the morning, or midnight, or in the evening, or whatever time. I feel closer to you every time we speak." There was silence. Then I heard a soft snore coming from Charlie's direction. I wasn't sure how much he heard, but I knew he needed to rise soon so I didn't push it. I whispered softly, "Sleep well, Sweetheart," then closed my eyes.

"You too, Sugarplum," he whispered back.

"You tricky man!"

"Shh...I'm sleeping."

"I'll see you in the morning."

He kissed my temple and rubbed my back again. Before I knew it, I was out like a light.

Charlie:

The alarm on my watch buzzed, waking me gently. I didn't want to get up. I wanted to call in sick. But she had some major appointments on her calendar so we couldn't just play hooky today. I wasn't even going to suggest it as an option. She was still breathing pretty heavily, so I knew she was sleep. I slid out from under her body blanket and slipped out into the hallway to get cleaned up and get breakfast started.

In my mind, when we first had our break, I had envisioned all of my things stored somewhere in a box in the closet, underneath some extra blankets and towels or something. I know it was pretty extreme. But when I went to change and brush my teeth last night, my toothbrush and toothpaste were in the same place as before. As were my brush and comb, and my body wash and lotion. My clothes had been freshly washed and were still in my drawer. She was truly optimistic that I would eventually understand what she needed from me and grow into a stronger human being. If she wasn't, I'm not even sure if my stuff would have still been in there.

I slinked down the hallway to the kitchen to see if she'd made her way to the grocery store recently. She had not. But, there were still enough goods for me to whip up a special "Good morning Fiancee Feast." So I worked as quietly as I could, preparing a few healthy-ish options for her. Just as I was about to wash the dishes, I heard the bedroom door crack. I turned my head towards the hallway and just waited to see her face as she noticed the place setting for two this morning.

"Oh Charlie," she gushed. "Why didn't you wake me? I was hoping to make breakfast for you this morning."

"I wanted you to rest."

"My place. I got you. Remember?"

"That was when we were just dating. Today is the first day of our journey through life together."

She paused. "Did I say that out loud?"

"Say what out loud?"

"That last part?"

"When?"

"This morning when I thought you were sleep and I was looking at my beautiful ring."

"No. You never said anything out loud. Why?"

"Because that's exactly what I remember thinking."

"Come here, Sugarplum." I hugged her good morning and kissed her on the temple. She was truly my favorite person.

Dr. Chris:

I called Charlie on my way home. His family was still there and before we got off the phone he told me that they had a surprise for me. My mind wandered and roamed as I tried to speculate what that surprise could be.

When I got to Charlie's house, I parked on the street because his family was parked in the driveway. Before I could get out of the car, both he and his dad were on their way out with truck keys in hand. Charlie motioned for me to stay in the car and I watched as the two of them moved their pickups around until they were both on the same side of the driveway. Then like synchronized swimmers, they guided me into "my spot" in the driveway.

"Hey Daughter!" Charlie's dad waved as he headed back to the house. His son, on the other hand, came car-side to open the door for me. "You better greet your bride, son!" Mr. Hughes finished before slipping inside the house. I laughed as the two of us hugged in the sun on that warm May evening.

"Hey Sugarplum," he said as he kissed my temple.

"Hey Sweetheart," I said as I absorbed every ounce of his love.

Charlie grabbed my bag and slipped an arm around my waist, guiding me towards the house. It felt like my body was moving without me, almost as though I was having an out of body experience. "How was your day?" he asked me. I heard him say it. But I don't remember if I replied. I only remember wondering how I ended up here, as Charlie's fiancee. It was such a stark difference from my life on Saturday. Even at work that day, people seemed to make a big deal out of what they deemed, "The Planet." Apparently they said it had its own orbit and gravitational pull.

That morning was easy peasy. I waved to Jake, the parking lot attendant with my right hand as usual, then slipped into my office without seeing anyone. Susan had called me to the family room to greet a family and everything seemed fairly normal. Once that appointment was done though, I was met by Susan and a group of nurses with a million and one questions. "Is that ring to throw off the scent of other men?" "Does Charlie know you're wearing an engagement ring?"

"Did the ring come from Charlie?" What-what-what. When-when-when.

I asked what they were all supposed to be doing and they all had the same answer, getting some details from me. So I told them the truth.

"I saw Charlie yesterday for the first time in about a month. He apologized and proposed. I accepted. End of story."

"Wait, how did he propose?" Susan asked.

"On one knee, in front of our families." I tried to keep it brief. They wanted details they just weren't going to get. So I ended up avoiding their questions and listening to them joke about the gravitational pull of my ring all day long. By the end of the day, I slipped out of my office and tried my best to sneak down to the car to disappear without making a scene. Success.

Now, back to reality - there I was with Charlie, my fiancé, walking towards his house where his parents and grandparents were waiting for us. He stopped on the front stoop and passed me a key to unlock the door. It was my key, the one I had handed back to him on Easter Sunday.

"I figured you might want this back," he grinned from ear to ear.

I raised up on my tiptoes and planted a soft kiss on his cheek, then whispered in his ear. "Thank you, Charlie."

"You bet, Sugarplum. I'll get you the spare key for Chief when we get inside."

What? The spare key to his truck? Is that typical? I'd never been someone's fiancee before, but I guess if we were planning on marrying each other then we had to start sharing more than just our meals with each other. So many questions. So many conversations. So many details. What an adventure.

I placed the key in the keyhole and glanced at Charlie, who was grinning from ear to ear.

"What are you cheesing about, mister?"

"I love this."

"You love what?"

"Open the door. You'll see."

Now a little nervous about what was on the other side, I turned the key and slowly pushed the door open.

"Go on in, Sugarplum. Nothing's going to bite you."

I stepped inside with the timidity of an infant tasting new baby food. I became a little more anxious when I didn't see or hear anyone in the house.

I looked back towards Charlie again. "Charlie, I know I just saw your dad. Where did he go?"

"Why don't you call him and see?"

"Mr. Hughes?" I gingerly called out. Before I could say his name again, I heard him laughing in the backyard. I felt Charlie's hand on the small of my back, slightly nudging me towards the back door. My feet were heavy. I wasn't sure what I was walking towards. His hand shifted from my back to my shoulders.

"It's okay, Chris. I promise. Just trust me," Charlie urged, attempting to convince me to walk a little faster.

I stepped out onto the back patio and found Charlie's grandparents smiling with open arms, waiting to welcome me home. Their warm embraces both felt just like home, especially his Grandma Elizabeth. Her hugs were special, in only a way that a grandma's can be. It felt like being cocooned in a cozy blanket on a chilly day with the warmth from a mug of hot cider restoring peace in your soul. While my soul was being restored through Grandma Elizabeth's hug, I turned my head in the direction of a familiar squeak and saw Mr. and Mrs. Hughes comfortably seated in the glider that looked just like the one on the balcony of their house.

"Hi Mom! Hi Dad!" I said as they both waved in my direction.

Charlie's mom stood to her feet to greet me. "Welcome home, Chris."

"Thank you," I said. "I'm so glad you're still in town."

"We are too," she said in reply. "We couldn't leave until we had the chance to bring this to the two of you."

"What's that?" I asked her.

"This," she said, handing me a framed picture. I began to tear up as I looked at the photo of Charlie and I in silhouette, as we sat on the glider Christmas morning.

I was befuddled. "When did you take this?"

"I'd come up to ask if Charlie could show me how to add a contact to my phone and I saw the two of you looking cozy and content out there. So I snapped a picture really fast and just as I was sneaking back out of the room to give you some privacy, I heard you ask Charlie to promise he'd get you a glider for your house. So please consider this an engagement gift from Dad and I."

I was definitely crying now. I could feel the tears warming my cheeks as his mom wrapped me up in her arms. "Thank you so much!"

"It's our pleasure, Sweetheart," she whispered through teardrops of her own.

"So this isn't the one from your house is it?" I asked.

"It most definitely is," Charlie's Dad quickly replied.

"What?"

His mom answered first, "Until today, we hadn't sat on that glider in at least 10 years."

Followed by his Dad, "I couldn't fix the squeak, so we just held onto it because it used to be one of Charlie's favorite places to sit. We hoped he would ask to take it with him when he moved into this house."

"I didn't know that, Dad!" Charlie nearly shouted.

"Yes, son. We probably should have just asked you if you wanted it."

"I think this is much more meaningful, honestly. In fact, I know it is. Thank you again," he said as he man-hugged his Dad.

"You're both very welcome. Just give this glider some love from time to time. I'm sure it'll be a favorite place for the two of you before you know it."

I had a sneaking suspicion his mom was right.

Charlie:

The look on Dr. Chris' face when she saw the photo of the two of us sitting on the glider will be etched in my brain for a while. It was like she saw herself loving me all over again. My parents offered their spots on the glider to the two of us and we both asked that they return to their seats before my Grandpa chimed in.

"Charlie, will you take your bride to her love seat?"

How do you say no that that? You don't. "Yes, Grandpa."

I grabbed Dr. Chris by the hand and opened the palm of my hand towards the glider, encouraging her to sit down first. As I sat down beside her it was reminiscent of our first ride together on the streetcar. I draped my right arm behind her and opened my left palm on her lap. She intertwined her fingers with mine and I was content.

The time away was good for me. It was tough. But it gave me a chance to grow in more ways than one. I certainly didn't imagine the two of us sitting on that glider. She had extended me so much grace within the last 36 hours. I wanted to repay her as often as I could. I wanted to let her know that she was my priority, that she had helped me identify part of my purpose, and that she was my heart.

I loved this woman with everything in me, and when she snuggled up next to me and allowed her head to rest in the crook of my shoulder again, that warmth was back - everywhere. I felt like the scared and excited 10 year old me with a school-age crush. I had a serious case of the collywobbles just being beside her, and the thought that I was going to get to spend the rest of my life with her, made me feel a little bit off balance. I know it sounds bad, but it was probably the most alive I'd felt in a long time.

"Charlie, are you smitten by your bride?" Grandma Elizabeth called to me.

I rested the side of my face against the top of Dr. Chris' head and simply nodded. I couldn't get out any words.

"I think we should give them a minute to greet each other. They haven't seen each other all day," Grandma said through an encouraging smile. They all agreed simultaneously and then slipped back into the house, leaving the two of us alone on the patio together.

"How was your day, Sugarplum?" I asked, without moving.

"It was okay. The appointments went well and the patient from surgery was recovering from their procedure when I left the hospital. So I'm assuming everything went okay with that as well."

"You sound a little bit melancholy."

"Maybe not melancholy, but today was just weird. People are so nosey."

"What do you mean?"

"The ring has a name now because of the ladies at work."

I laughed. "What do they call it?"

"The Planet."

"Oh that's a good one. Gravitational pull?"

"Yep."

"It's not too much is it?"

"The people asking questions?"

"The ring."

"I love my ring, Charlie. I don't necessarily love everyone all up in our business though."

I kissed the top of her head. "I understand," I said before pausing for a moment. "What else made today weird?"

She took in a deep breath and slowly exhaled between her lips. "Knowing that I'm going to get married was a little weird. I've never been engaged before and I don't really know what it means to be someone's fiancée."

"Now that I definitely understand," I told her emphatically.

"How was YOUR day?" she asked me through a chuckle.

"My day was cool."

"Cool?" she asked. "I know it's different for men because you don't go back to work wearing a symbol that you're engaged."

"Not typically, but they could tell that things were different with me."

"Oh yeah?"

"They kept saying I was walking around like I was floating on a cloud. Several of them asked if you were 'back in my life, or something.' I told them that we had the chance to work things out this weekend."

I could feel the pace of her breath quicken. She was concerned about something but wasn't saying anything.

"What's wrong, Sugarplum?"

"Why do you think something's wrong?" she asked

me.

"I can feel it in your breath."

A nervous laugh escaped her nostrils. "Just thinking about some of the teachers up there, probably feeling disappointed that we're back together."

I knew exactly which "some" Dr. Chris was referring to and I was going to confront it head on. "You mean, like Jessica?" Jessica had been an underlying issue before and there was no way I was going to let that continue to linger.

"Mm hmm."

"Yeah, she and I aren't really on speaking terms anymore."

"Why not, Charlie? She's still your co-worker."

"She is, but the day after Easter, I was still a bit raw from our break. So my filter was non-existent when she attempted to ask me all about how my Easter went -"

"Oh no."

"Yeah. No-filter Charlie is pretty ruthless."

"Charlie."

"It was rough, Chris. I was so angry and heartbroken that I didn't know what to do. So she caught it and then decided to stop speaking with me outside of work capacity, which I was okay with."

"Are you okay?"

"I did apologize to her the next week, so there's at least that. But I was just hoping to be saved by love, your love, floating in on the wings of angels."

"That's a bit much, Charlie." She laughed.

"You're right. But I did spend a couple of weeks waiting for love to find me again instead of realizing that I WAS love. Once that clicked, I changed everything. I started working out and meditating. I started allowing love to flow in and out of my heart - first with my students, and then with those I interacted with regularly."

"Wow."

"Yeah. I just wanted to be ready for you whenever the moment, our moment came around again."

"Charlie!"

"You asked for space, not eternity."

"I did."

"And I was resolute in being truly ready for you this time around. I knew what I wanted and I knew that the moment I saw you yesterday..."

"Charlie, I don't know if I can take it."

"I knew you were my bride. I felt like a little kid who had the chance to become friends with someone all over again. Except this someone wasn't just my friend, this someone was my love."

She began to weep in my arms.

"What is it, Chris?"

"I felt like a kid when I sensed your presence standing behind me. It was so surreal. I couldn't even see you. But I knew it was you, and everything aligned with the dream I had. I was nervous, but you have such a calming presence on my life that those nerves just dissipated and it left room for love to come flooding back in. That's what I'm feeling right now."

"Love?"

"Your love, Charlie."

"Our love, Chris."

We sat on the glider in silence, holding onto each other and soaking up our love. I'm not gonna lie. It made me cry too. I was okay with her seeing it, even though she wasn't in a position to at the moment.

Mom stuck her head outside to check on us. Her eyes asked if everything was okay. I closed mine and nodded yes, opening them just in time to see her nod in return and quietly shut the door.

"We're gonna be just fine, you know that right?"

"I do, Charlie."

"She's practicing for the wedding already!" I joked.

She laughed through her tears and I gently wiped her face dry.

"They're going to call us in for dinner soon, I know it. Grandma cooked."

"I better get myself together."

"I don't think they'll mind any of that."

"I know, Charlie. I want to do it for me."

"I sit corrected."

She excused herself to go freshen up in the bathroom and I sat on the glider soaking up the radiant light from the sun and the remnants of Dr. Chris' warmth. *This woman.*

CHAPTER 3
SHATTERED PLANS

Dr. Chris:

More than a month had passed since Charlie and I had reconnected. That time moved swiftly too. We didn't waste any time relearning each other, spending every night on the phone or in each other's presence. Eventually the two of us felt confident enough to set a wedding date. New Year's Eve, 2020.

We had less than half a year to plan for and create a wedding that was fitting of our relationship. I was overjoyed that love had found us again and all was right within my world. I wanted to ensure that our ceremony and reception were reflective of that. So we reached out to our families to share the news of the date.

My parents and sister were elated to expand this year's family tradition to include our wedding. Charlie's family was excited to travel back to Kansas City to share in this new tradition with us. The two of us sifted through the friends, family and colleagues that we knew we wanted to invite to celebrate with us, as well as those we wanted to stand with us. The latter was a no brainer. Vonne as my Matron of Honor, and Sabrina as a Bridesmaid. Steve as Charlie's Best Man, and Marlo as his groomsman. Jax and Corwin as the ring bearer and bell ringer, and my niece Christina as the flower girl. We intended to keep it small, and then our families got involved.

I didn't have a desire to rock the boat. I wanted to preserve my peace. So, whatever our Moms wanted, I agreed to. Whatever Charlie suggested was fine with me, even when none of it was necessarily what I actually wanted. Sifting or bartering my way through a million decisions for just one day wasn't worth risking the pure love that I thought I had with Charlie. So they could have whatever they wanted, even if it didn't necessarily feel like me. The family meetings we had for our wedding were much more easy going because I went with the flow.

The guest list from both sets of parents reached the 200 mark and that was before Charlie and I decided on who we wanted to invite. We'd be feeding a lot of people, but okay. Mom wanted to hold the wedding in the church I grew up in. Sure. Charlie's Mom wanted the two of them to wear matching gowns. Whatever's clever. Vonne suggested matching earrings *in addition* to the matching bridesmaid dresses. Okey dokie, smokey. Charlie and Steve wanted the reception to be held at Arrowhead Stadium. You got it, boss. Our celebration was going to be one big pot of stew, made up of a hodgepodge of ideas from everybody we knew. It was what it was. I just wanted to marry Charlie, who had started to pick up on my newfound indifference.

"It's our wedding, Chris. I want you to ask for what you want."

After I had alluded to the falsehood that everything was fine, Charlie pushed back. We were spending Father's Day in Kansas City and had planned to chat with both sets of families via video call on that Sunday so we could set some boundaries and ground rules.

Charlie and I had already started to bring more of my things home, so I was spending less and less time at the condo, which meant, I would go stretches where I would miss things like mail. My bills were set on autopay, so I didn't worry about those. And I figured anything else wouldn't be major, so I'd let things stack up for a while. I dropped by the condo that morning to grab Dad's gift and picked up a stack full of mail, leaving it on the counter to sort through later. We were in a hurry to get to my parents' house.

Charlie:

I waited downstairs in Chief for her to return with her Dad's Father's Day gift and called Steve to wish him a Happy Father's Day himself. That narrow window of time gave us space to touch base. Jax was out on Summer Break, so I hadn't seen him in a while. I wondered how much taller he was. He seemed to stretch out like taffy every single time I saw him. I had just asked Steve to be my Best Man when Dr. Chris came trotting out towards the truck.

"Of course, man!"

"Thanks, brother. I'll give you a call later. We're headed to the James' house for Father's Day festivities."

"Cool. Tell Chris I said hello!"

"Hi Steve! Tell your wife I'm going to call her later."

"She's right beside me trying to pretend like she's not eavesdropping. Would you like to talk to her now?"

"Sure!"

"Hi, Chris!"

"Hi, Sabrina! How is everyone?"

"We're all doing great here. Celebrating this handsome, strong, and funny father that Jax has."

"Wish him a Happy Father's Day for me, would

you?"

"I sure will."

"Great! So I don't want to keep you long, but Charlie and I were trying to decide who we would be honored to have stand beside us as we join our lives together and I would love it if you would be my bridesmaid."

"Dr. Chris, I'm there!"

"Fantastic! Thank you so much. I love your family as much as I love my own, and we'd love to have Jax join us too if he's interested."

"Jax, come here for a second," Sabrina called to him.

"Hi Mr. Charlie and Dr. Chris!"

"Hi Buddy!"

Charlie took over the conversation, asking his Godson to serve as his ring bearer. "We're trusting you to bring our rings down to us so we can actually get married. It's a super important job and we know that you can handle it. But, I wanted to know if that's something you want to do."

"Do I get to balance them on a pillow or something?"

"Sure. You can balance them on your nose if you want to." Charlie joked.

"I can?!" Jax asked, far more enthusiastically than his mom was interested in.

"No, Jax. But a pillow will work if you're interested in helping them with that."

"I can help with that."

"Thanks, Jax! We're so glad that you're going to help us out."

"Cool."

"Okay Sabrina, well we need to drive to The James' house, and Dr. Chris won't let me chat on the phone while I drive."

She tapped me on the arm. "Ouch," I replied in response. "Okay, I don't like to do it, but we'll call you later with details okay?"

"Sounds good Charlie."

"Thanks and love to all of you!" Dr. Chris exclaimed before they could hang up the phone.

"We love you both!" Sabrina responded.

I put the truck in gear before Ralph could come ask us to move it out of the drive and we headed over to the James' house to relax and celebrate her Dad.

Dr. Chris:

Once we arrived, things moved swiftly. We ate dinner, showered Dad with gifts and enjoyed each other's company. We were nearly tackled by Corwin and Christina once we asked them to be part of our big day. The two of them might have been more excited than Charlie and I were. Vonne was already on board as my matron of honor and had a million questions prepared for me to answer. I didn't have the answer to even half of those, but it helped me to think about all of the detail work that still needed to be done. Charlie and Dad were in a fully involved conversation.

"New Year's Eve will be here before you know it, Charlie. Are you ready?" I heard my Dad ask Charlie.

"I'm as ready as I'll ever be, Dad," he replied.

"Who's gonna stand with you, Charlie?" Dad asked him.

"My friend Steve just agreed to be my Best Man, and I'm going to ask Marlo to be a groomsmen."

"Have you called him recently?" I heard Dad ask with a bit of concern in his voice.

"I was going to give him a call before we came this way, but I ran out of time," Charlie offered.

"You should give him a call now," Dad finished very stoically.

"I can wait until this eve-"

"Call him now. Let's step out into the backyard," Dad said as he slowly ushered Charlie to the backdoor.

I continued to hang out with Vonne, Jason and the kids and waited eagerly for Charlie's return to the house so that he could join the fun. Mom was busy in the kitchen, which had a better view of the backyard, so I offered to "help her out."

The two of us were washing the dishes from dinner when I heard Charlie yelp. It was a sound I'd never heard him make before but I knew instinctively that something was wrong. A trail of suds followed me to the backyard, dripping from my arms as I rushed to see if he was okay. Mom followed me outside with a towel and handed it to me as she also came out to inspect the situation.

Dad was consoling Charlie, who appeared to have been stunned into silence. His mouth agape, the phone in his hand by his side. His eyes were wide open, but his spirit looked distant.

I spoke softly, so as not to jolt him out of this horrifying stupor. "Charlie? What is it, Sweetheart?"

Dad, tapped Mom on the shoulder and told her that we needed some space.

"What is it? What's wrong?" Mom asked Dad as he gingerly ushered her back to the house.

"I'll tell you in the house Cille," he told her as he closed the door behind them.

I reached for Charlie's hand and he held onto it softly as he asked me to sit down on one of the rod iron chairs on the deck. "Charlie, I don't want to sit down." I was adamant. "What's going on?"

He took in a slow, deep breath and closed his eyes. I'll never forget that breath because his was so intentional and cleansing that I took one along with him. An 8 second inhale through my nostrils that took about twice as long for me to exhale slowly through pursed lips.

Charlie:

I asked her to sit down as my mind tried to find ways to stall. Anything I could do to delay sharing what I had just discovered I tried. I inhaled deeply and she did the same. I couldn't wrap my mind around the words that would be appropriate, so I spoke from my heart.

"Chris, I just called Marlo's phone to ask him if he would be a groomsman in our wedding." She looked at me like she knew something was wrong and she was just waiting for the devastating blow. I kept talking, "Janae answered it." Chris nodded as her eyebrows began to gather in the middle of her forehead. "I asked to speak with Marlo and she told me that he didn't make it."

"What do you mean he didn't make it?" Chris asked as a single teardrop jumped from her eye. It was the very same question I had asked Janae myself.

"She said the virus spread too quickly and it overwhelmed his body."

She went limp like a wet rag. I dropped my phone on the deck so I could catch her and cradle her in my arms.

"Is this real, Charlie? This is a dream and I'm going to wake up soon, right?"

I whispered through the lump that had gathered in the back of my throat, "No, Baby. I'm so sorry."

Her body shuddered. She wailed. I poured my love into her heart. Every time she cried out loud, I poured more of my love back into her. I could feel her body tremble and shake as she sobbed through news of the sudden loss of her closest friend. I didn't know what to do except be present. She and Marlo had been friends since they were little. I imagined all of the time they must have spent playing together in that backyard. Imagined what it was like to go to college and med school together, then remembered how it impacted her when he left for Colorado. Marlo was like family, and losing him meant losing a brother. I cried with her, for her heart that I knew was breaking, and for my own that was breaking a little bit too. We stood on the deck for what felt like hours before she spoke. In reality, I think it was only a few minutes. But in moments of grief, time has its own unique measure.

"What happened to him, Charlie?"

"She said he had contracted the virus while he was at work and that it spread rapidly to his lungs and muscles before finding its way to his brain." I paused to catch my own breath. "Have a seat, Sugarplum," I encouraged her to do with my words as I pulled a rod iron chair over for her to rest in. Once I had guided her safely into the seat, I pulled up another chair beside her and sat down, reaching out for her hand. The two of us sat in silence until the sun began to set. Her Mom came outside and brought something for Chris to drink, placing a hand on her shoulder to let her know she was present if needed. A stark contrast from the surge of joy we shared on Mother's Day. In fact, it was almost as poles apart as you could get.

Just a few days later we found ourselves preparing for Marlo's funeral. Dr. Chris was anxious and overwhelmed, yet she somehow found the strength to be unwaveringly solid in the moment. I tried to anticipate her needs and stay one step ahead. The truth was, that it was all a guessing game to me. When I asked what

I could do to help, her answer was, "nothing." When I asked what she needed, it was the same. It didn't feel dismissive at all, but rather that she didn't want to burden me with extra because of what was going on in the moment. What she didn't know, is that this is what I wanted to do. So I did the only thing I knew to do, love her through it the same way she'd loved me through the stress-filled moments in my life. Now, none of those compared to the pain of losing a loved one, but if she could love me through that, I could love her through this. The morning of the funeral she got up early to workout so she could shower and be ready in time for the responsibilities of the day. The night before, I had placed her running shoes, headphones and keys near the door so she wouldn't have to search for them. When she came back from her run, I handed her a fresh-pressed juice to refuel and reenergize her system. The dress that she told me she wanted to wear was hanging for her in the bedroom so she didn't have to search for it. I hung a fresh towel for her in the bathroom. She had so many other things to worry about that day. I didn't want any of the minute details to get in the way.

Dr. Chris:

It was one of the longest weeks of my life. I'm not sure how I would have gotten through it alone. Sunday by all accounts was going to be another typical family gathering where we'd eat, laugh, and enjoy each other's company. We had the added element of wedding planning that was out of the norm. Other than that, it had begun as a typical day with family. But that Father's Day was anything but typical. My peace was shattered. I retreated into a hole that I wasn't sure I wanted to climb out of, even if I had some idea of how to get out.

But there he was, helping me find some sense of normalcy in an abnormal time. He was two steps ahead of me, which kept me going. When I hadn't made up my mind about my morning run, Charlie had placed all of my things near the front door, making it easier for me to choose the route to take. When I wasn't sure if I was hungry, Charlie had prepared a nourishing drink. When it was time for me to get ready to go say goodbye to my friend, Charlie had already steamed the outfit I had planned to wear. When it was time for us to go to the church for the funeral, Charlie had already placed a light red carnation inside my car, which he knew would be easier for me to get in and out of in that dress and those heels. There he was, standing in the gap for me so I wouldn't misstep and fall. I hadn't ever thought about what type of support would be necessary during a time such as this, but he was the light at dusk that I didn't realize was helping me navigate through the looming darkness.

The celebration of life was a blur. I remember people sharing the different ways that Marlo had impacted their lives, and I remember Janae looking dazed. I wondered how on earth she could get through something like this. When you promise to share your life with someone, you imagine the good memories you'll build together. You don't think about the what-if's.

During one of the most tumultuous moments of my life, Charlie was my rock. My thoughts wandered. Someday I might find myself like Janae, or if I went first, Charlie would. It was that thought that broke me. I had been stoic during the days leading up to the funeral and during the funeral itself, especially when I was asked to speak. But graveside, as they began to lower his casket into the earth, when Janae's dazed stare turned into tears of grief and I thought about Charlie or me facing the same fate, my heart was pained so deeply that it changed the way I looked at life. I sobbed alongside Janae, while Charlie held my heart.

Charlie:

How do you bury your best friend? I don't know that anyone ever considers that question unless they have forewarning like a serious illness. That was the thought that stuck with me throughout the entire funeral. I kept watching Dr. Chris pull strength from out of thin air and wondering if I'd be able to do the same if it were my lifelong friend whose life we were celebrating. She seemed super human throughout the service itself and even at the graveside as well. She was strong until she wasn't. I could see her emotions welling inside her leading up to the moment she broke. Her shoulders raised near her ears in one deep inhale and the tears streamed down her face as she slowly exhaled. I placed my right hand on the small of her back and poured my love into her the same way she had on the night before her birthday celebration. I wasn't sure if she could feel it, but it wasn't going to stop me from trying.

As I drove us away from the cemetery, she asked to stop at the condo and I was happy to oblige. Whatever she needed, whatever she wanted was already hers. All she need do was ask. In that moment it was a trip back to her place, which she hadn't spent much time in since Mother's Day. Once we figured each other out again, we began spending more of our time together at home, my home, our home. As the date was set, we started moving her stuff into my place little by little. She went back there to grab an outfit for the funeral, but that only lasted a few minutes. I wasn't sure just how long she wanted to stay in that moment, but I wasn't going to put any limits on anything.

I asked if she wanted me to park her car in the garage or drop her off near the front. She asked me to park it in her spot. I hustled to open her car door before she could get it herself, but Dr. Chris gets antsy and impatient when she's overwhelmed. True to form, she had already gotten out and closed the door before I could get halfway around the car. I locked the doors and made an about face, hustling to meet her back at the elevator. We waited for its arrival in silence, but as soon as it opened its doors to greet us and she discovered we were the only two on board, she sunk into my arms. The entirety of the elevator ride up to R2 was silent. Her frame told me everything I needed to know about where she was emotionally. She didn't want space, and I hoped my arms had provided enough of a temporary shelter to quell some of what overwhelmed her. When the elevator doors opened she didn't move. I tried to shift some of her weight back to her own feet, but I could feel her resist. Not knowing what else to do and slightly concerned that someone else would call for the elevator while we were still inside, I scooped her off her feet and carried her down the hallway and into her apartment, using my key to let us in. Her tears were heavy and persistent, and seemingly uncontrollable. I had a feeling we'd be staying for a while.

"Couch or bed, Sugarplum?" I softly whispered into her ear.

"Wherever you are, Charlie," she sniffled as the tears began to slow and gently trail down her face.

My heart ached, knowing that there wasn't anything I could do to take away the pain she was experiencing. In spite of that I understood that it wasn't my job to remove anything for her, but rather to be present. So that's what I tried to do as I lowered her onto the couch and retrieved the wool blanket from the hall closet and her pillow from the bedroom. I got her a glass of water, handed her the remote and excused myself to go to the bathroom. I had to wash my hands and my face before I headed back out to her, as my own emotions began to surface in the span of just a few quick minutes.

I knew she wasn't going to want anything to eat, but I wanted to ensure that she didn't have to think twice about it, so I ordered some food to be delivered to us before returning to the couch with her. She created a space for me to sit beside her, then placed the pillow in my lap and stretched out underneath the blanket. I ran my fingers across her scalp, over and over, then followed the length of her hair down her back, until it almost felt like a habit. We rested on the couch and stared at the tv together until Ralph called up about our delivery.

"Hello, Charlie. How's our girl doing?" he asked.

"She's holding on, Ralph. Thanks for sending up the food."

"You bet, Charlie. Hold onto her."

"Will do, Ralph," I said, pausing briefly to think about holding onto her every day of our lives together. "Will do."

I opened the door and tipped the driver before returning to the kitchen with some soup and sandwiches from The Fresh Pantry.

"Would you like your soup and sandwich now or later, Sugarplum?" I asked as I unpacked the bag of food at the kitchen island. Realizing I hadn't heard a response from her, I called her name again, "Dr. Chris?" Still nothing. I walked towards the couch and saw her sleeping face. So peaceful. I wasn't going to disrupt what might have been the most peace I'd seen in that week. She was understandably restless every other night leading up to that day, so the soup and sandwich would have to wait.

She slept for hours and I was grateful that she had the chance to do so.

Dr. Chris:

I woke up on the couch, with only very vague bursts of memory to help me understand how I got there. I remember asking Charlie to drive us to the condo and I remember falling into his arms in the elevator. That's where things get foggy. My imaginative mind seems to believe he carried me to the couch and I fell asleep as he ran his fingers through my hair. I thought I overheard a conversation with Ralph, but that might have been a dream. I was more exhausted than I realized, but there he was standing beside me the entire time. I turned my head and caught a glimpse of Charlie underneath what little bit of cover he could get - probably without waking me up, knowing him.

I went to the bedroom to change from these clothes, which I hoped I didn't have a need to wear again anytime soon. I had a few missed calls and voicemails on my phone that I didn't want to check. They were all from my family, probably checking in on me. I slipped into the bathroom, then headed out to the kitchen to refresh my water. There on the kitchen island, I noticed two cartons of soup and some sandwiches, still wrapped, but waiting on plates, presumably for the two of us. Maybe I'd heard Ralph's voice after all.

Not really hungry yet, and not wanting to wake Charlie, I sifted through my stacks of neglected mail while sipping on my water. Lots of bills, ads, political mailers, and one piece of mail from a Colorado address. I held it in my hands, knowing it was probably something I needed to read, but wasn't quite ready to just yet. I set it aside on the counter and filed everything else away in the desk in the guest bedroom. When I returned to the living room, Charlie was awake.

"Hey, Sweetheart," I said, reaching out for his hand over the back of the couch. He held it to his heart before kissing the back of it. "Thank you so much, for ordering some food." He nodded in reply, and groggily sat up as though he had something to take care of.

"I can heat it up if you're ready to eat," his voice rumbled.

"I'm already up, Charlie. I'll take care of it."

"Chris, let me take care of you today," he said, his eyes full of gumption.

"It would help me feel better if I took care of it myself." I told him as I spied the disappointment in his eyes.

He raised his hands in the air in resolve. "You got it."

"I love you deeply, Charlie," I said - leaning in to kiss his cheek.

He nodded in reply.

Charlie had a penchant for finding the most simplistic ways to show me that his love was ever present. It was something I was working on doing more myself as a result of the love that he poured into me. I hoped that serving him the soup that he bought for us would be a good start. As heartbroken as I was to no longer have the physical presence of my good friend, I was tremendously appreciative for all that we had experienced together, and for the new light in which I got to see Charlie. In the toughest part of my life thus far, there he was, quietly standing beside me. Nothing showy, nothing that says, "Hey, here I am, helping you out." He just was. His physical strength helped support me when I wasn't able to stand on my own. Just thinking about it swept me off my feet again. He had asked me to hold his heart until it grew old, and I intended to do so. Charlie was love in action and I could be that for him too, if I got out of my own way.

CHAPTER 4
CHASING SUNSETS

Dr. Chris:

The next couple of weeks moved slowly at work and at home. I was working on pushing through each day, one hour at a time. The more appointments and schedules I had on my calendar the faster the day passed by. The only problem is that I always felt like I missed the day. Because the school year had ended, Charlie had more time to help with the details associated with all things wedding planning. The conversation we were supposed to have with our families on Father's Day had been postponed, but I discovered that Charlie had held separate conversations with all of them, asking them for their top 3 ideas and weaving those into the options that he and I had been considering in our conversations together. I was truly grateful for that.

I'd find myself nearly empty when I got home, but he was just as steady as ever, greeting me in the driveway, grabbing my bag from me and walking me into the house. Sometimes, waiting to surprise me with dinner when I got home. It was overwhelming though, making detailed decisions at work and then coming home to do the same. It felt like I was just existing. We were planning for our wedding, reception, honeymoon, and for our future, but I felt like I was missing the present.

We were chillin on the couch one evening after work when I recalled a thought that had almost escaped me during my break that afternoon. I was overwhelmed and didn't feel like writing anything down. I'm sure the fact that I even remembered to ask is because I was given a nudge from my friend in the great beyond.

"Charlie,"

"Yes, Dr. Chris?"

"Do you remember what you asked me on New Year's Day?"

"I don't. I probably asked you quite a bit."

"You asked me about New Year's Resolutions."

"Oh, yeah, I do remember that. You don't set resolutions."

"Right. But we set a New Year's Promise together instead."

Charlie pulled his phone out of his pocket and nodded.

"Charlie?"

"I'm pulling up the list," he said as he leaned in to kiss my temple.

I smiled and waited patiently. I had no desire to pull out my phone. I had just wanted to veg out during my quick lunch break in the cafeteria, but was reminded of our list when thinking about how different things were from the beginning to the middle of this year.

"So..." he began after studying the list. "Do you want the items we haven't checked off or those that we have?"

"Let's go with haven't."

Charlie let out a lingering whistle that let me know that was the longest portion of the list. "Try a new restaurant."

"Wait, we did that on Mother's Day," I grinned.

"You're right. Let's check that off the list," he paused, marking something on his phone. Okay, let's try that again. Travel."

"Hmm."

"Go horseback riding."

"Well."

"Eat lunch on a blanket in the park."

"No, we did that one!"

"You're right. Check and check."

"That was a good day," I sighed.

Charlie studied my face and reached out for my hand. "Another rough one today?" he asked as I nodded quickly, hoping to let him know that I didn't really want to talk about it. Every day, I thought about Marlo and how I had told him that I would reach out to him soon. I took that time for granted and I didn't have the opportunity to connect with him anymore. I didn't want that to happen with anyone else I loved and cared about. I guess that's why this list was so important to me.

With a firm squeeze of my hand he continued, "Know that I'm here when you feel like talking about it."

"Absolutely. What else is on that list?"

"Let's see. Ropes course, concert, family."

"I think we can check family off the list. Unless of course there was someone specific that you had in mind."

"I didn't. We just said visit family. I think we can check that off. That will probably be a pretty regular thing as we get closer and closer to the wedding."

"You're right."

"Host a small gathering for friends."

"Yeah, we didn't do much from this list did we?" I chuckled.

He laughed. "Not really. I mean we still have plenty of time to adopt a family at Christmas, attend a costume party together, deliver food to a stranger, and go zip-lining."

"We put all of that on the list?"

"We sure did!"

"We were mighty ambitious huh?"

"It sure looks like it."

"Oh my."

"Yep. We still have the last of our Sugarplum list to handle during the holidays too."

"Well, I said I wanted to be more intentional about how I spent my time. I guess I should be careful what I request."

"What if we do some of this on our honeymoon?"

"That's next year."

"You're right," he nodded.

We paused and stared at the list on Charlie's phone in silence.

"One month at a time, Sugarplum," Charlie softly spoke as he lightly rubbed my back. His tender heart was on his sleeve again and I so loved all of it.

"You're right," I nodded.

As spring and all of its new growth and blossoms began to give way to the heat of summer, the two of us reflected on the options that we could tackle immediately. Without a summer yield, there's little to harvest in autumn. I was hoping that the more we tended to our plants in that moment, the more it would pay off in the long run. Charlie and I faced a perfect storm of opportunity and adventure, and the very thought of making the most of our time together, gave me something to look forward to, while simultaneously addressing the fear that resurfaced - the same fear that brought me to tears at Marlo's graveside. Charlie's love was big, and by sheer connection, our love was big as well. It wasn't the type of big that overwhelmed the senses, but it was the type that was evident by all who were near.

The staff at Hope Gardens liked to remind me about the time that Charlie brought lunch for everyone on Valentine's Day, or the time he drove me to the hospital during the snowstorm and stayed to play Santa, or the time he rushed back to the hospital to see me before he, we, left for Arkansas. I'm always reminded of the energy I felt when he caught me. We stood together in line and though we didn't speak much at all, we were still present with each other. That was all Charlie. I tried to hide and he somehow found a way to help me feel better about causing the entire line to tumble. His presence was calming and uplifting from the very moment I met him. And there we were, moving into a new season in life and moving towards a new season in love, and this beautiful human being was more consistent and loving than anyone I'd ever met.

He caught me off guard as I was reveling in my daydreams, "Will you come dance with me?" As I had been in my own little world traveling down memory lane, Charlie had asked his home assistant to play satellite radio. I'm not sure what song was finishing as he asked me, but I'll always accept his hand and an invitation to dance. So I stood to my feet, kicked off my shoes, and Charlie reeled me into his arms.

I looked up into his eyes as the drummer counted in

the song, and Charlie smiled down at me before placing his cheek on the side of my face. I'd never heard the song before, but he knew the lyrics by heart. His gentle voice sang quietly into my ear.

The lyrics were perfectly suited for how I felt in the moment and I began to melt into Charlie's arms yet again. He shouldered my weight and danced us from the living room into the kitchen, while still singing something about turning my gray skies blue.

I tried to ask Charlie who the artist was, but he just gazed deeper into my eyes and kept singing.

I placed my head on his chest and swayed with him as he sang the refrain. Such a big love. *My heart.*

Charlie:

I didn't know what else to do. She'd had so many rough days in a row and she looked like she wanted to break free from another one. She'd never say it directly, but I knew she was overwhelmed with the wedding planning. She didn't even have the energy to go dress shopping with her mom and sister yet. So when she asked about the list, I figured it might be a good distraction from everything that was already weighing heavy on her.

I'd hoped that the two of us could just hop in the truck and chase a sunset tonight, but something told me that we needed to move. We'd been sitting on the couch every single night. So I asked for a little help from the virtual assistant. I had no idea that I'd get an assist from Allen Stone in the form of his song, Give You Blue. I've always loved that song, but it held even more meaning in this moment. The lyrics were spot on.

From the moment, I heard the news about Marlo's passing, the only thing I wanted to do was help brighten

Dr. Chris's world. I could only do what was in my power to do. This song, expressed everything that was in my heart that I was struggling to find the words to say myself. Holding her in my arms, dancing around the house with her, being close to her was one of the ways I could show her my love, and I hoped it was enough to lighten the mood a bit.

We swayed and I twirled her around, and I poured my heart into showing her just how much she meant to me, and that I was here no matter what happened. The way I saw it, the two of us were built to last a lifetime. She had always felt like home to me, so home was wherever we were together, facing whatever came our way. That's what I wanted her to feel.

"Three options."

Her face looked beyond confused. Whatever's just on the other side of confused, is where Dr. Chris was in that moment, "For the wedding?"

"No Sugarplum. Nothing related to the wedding tonight. Let's take a break from that."

Her worry brow relaxed and a smile began to crest her face. "What are my three options, Charlie?" Her smile was so wide that I could see ALL of her teeth.

I couldn't help but smile at the glow on her face. "Three options."

"What are they Charlie?" She giggled.

"Option 1: We can eat dinner."

"Uh huh."

"Option 2: We can continue dancing in the house."

"Hmmm. Okay, and Option 3?"

"Option 3." I cheesed.

"What's Option 3, Charlie?"

"Option 3," I paused again and popped an eyebrow at her.

"Charlie! Are you going to tell me Option 3 or do I

have to choose between what I know and what might be a gamble?"

"Oh, there's a thought!"

"Wait, what?"

"I hadn't thought about that as an option, but it could work."

"No it can't," she said in her best attempt to show me how adamant she was. She couldn't even keep a straight face.

"Oh okay. You sure about that?" I laughed.

"No. No, I'm not." She chuckled at her own failed attempt of coercion.

"Option 3." I paused again.

"Yes?" she asked, her facial expression indicating she was open to whatever came out of my mouth.

I grinned, "Option 3: We can pack up this dinner, hop in Chief and chase the sunset across the city, before dancing under the moonlight."

Her lips found mine and her arms squeezed me tightly. I didn't want to let go. I wanted to stay in that moment for as long as I could, but the sun was already on its descent through the evening sky, which meant we needed to get a move on.

"So was that Option 1, then?"

"Charlie, I love you deeply."

I loved hearing those four words strung together just for me. *This woman.* "Option 2, then?"

"Charlie!"

"I need you to say it, Dr. Chris."

"Option 3, please, Sweetheart."

"Yes, ma'am! As you wish."

I proceeded to pack up the food. While I was in the kitchen, Dr. Chris slipped upstairs for a moment, my guess was to change, since she hadn't done that yet. I placed the bags of food near the front door and carried my bluetooth speaker to the back seat of the pickup truck. By the time I got back to the front door, Dr. Chris was coming out, food in hand.

"Do you need anything else, Charlie?"

She was in shorts, chucks, an old t-shirt from college, and her hair had been pulled up on top of her head. Sunglasses framed her face, which meant she must have put in her contact lenses. I couldn't say anything in reply. No words would exit my mouth. I just gazed at her natural beauty, standing in the doorway of our home, wearing the ring I had given to her, asking me if I needed anything. I had everything I could ever need already.

She rephrased her question, "Was this all, Charlie?"

"Yes, Sugarplum, that's all," I said as I grabbed the food from her hand and kissed her on the temple before locking up the house and walking her to the truck.

I opened the passenger door for her, "Are you in?"

"I am," she replied with an ornery smile.

I handed the food back to her as soon as she was all buckled in, and she secured it on the floor of the truck before I closed the door. I walked around towards my door, wondering how I was so lucky that I got a second chance at ensuring I could show her how much I loved her.

I hopped in the truck and asked my navigator to point the way. We wove through the city until we hit the highway and headed west into Kansas. Because it was just after the Summer Solstice, we had plenty of sunlight, left to chase. We eventually wove our way into a park that overlooked a lake. I backed the truck into a cove where the two of us could watch the sun set from the bed. I asked her to wait in the truck while I got things ready for her. I took one of my blankets and lined the bed of the truck with it, moved some of the throw pillows into the back to make it a bit more cozy. I hoisted the bluetooth speaker up in the back seat, and positioned it so it could play through the back window. I asked for the food and laid it out for her, then returned to the passenger side to help her out of the truck.

"My dear," I said, extending my hand in her direction.

"Thank you, Charlie."

I helped her up into the bed of the pickup truck, and she found her way to the back near the food. We blessed the food before digging in. I served her a plate and she served me one as well. I think the change of scenery was good for us. She began to open up about work and life. I just listened and nodded, smiled and laughed. It was good to see her light up again. It was long overdue.

"Have you had enough to eat?" I asked her.

"Yes, I'll pack up the leftovers and the trash."

"You will not!" I said, racing her to pack up as much as I could before she could lift a finger. "This is supposed to be me, taking you out on a date."

"Well, date nights for married couples look a little different than date nights for dating couples."

"Well, we're not married yet, ma'am. Put the bag down," I said through a chuckle as Dr. Chris handed the bag over to me. "Just let me love you, woman!"

"Anytime, Charlie. Anywhere."

I kissed her temple and hopped out of the bed of the truck to place the other food in the backseat, away from nature. She hopped out to throw away the trash before I could get back to it myself. I shook my head in her direction and she hustled back to the bed of the truck, hopping up on the tailgate and turning around on her rear to face the lake. I loved this woman more and more with each passing minute.

I returned to the side of the truck and peeked in the bed, placing both hands on my cheeks and looking confused. "Oh my goodness. Where on earth did all of our trash go?"

"I think it's over here, Charlie!" she called.

I walked to the tailgate and stopped in front of her. "I don't see any trash over here ma'am. Nothing but beauty." Her smile, was back again and I couldn't help but lean in to kiss her. There we were in nature, reconnecting like we had before Father's Day. The last few weeks, her kisses were present and sweet. She was there, but there wasn't a longing for more. On that day though, her kisses were hungry and so were mine. I hadn't mentally prepared myself for this space and I was afraid we were going to break the promise we'd made to each other. I tried to stay in the moment, but that particular moment was about to buckle my knees.

Her legs wrapped around mine and reeled me in as close as I could get without us merging into one body. Her arms draped lightly across my shoulders and her hands - one of them ran along the nape of my neck. The other, well let's just say the second that hand moved from behind my head and gently caressed my ear, I was prepared to ask the Lord for forgiveness for what was about to go down. It was at that very moment that a car drove along the road near the truck. I could hear a child asking their parents to honk the horn, and the driver obliged. I opened my eyes to see Joel, my former student, waving to Dr. Chris and I from the back of their family car. I waved back and encouraged her to wave at Joel as well.

"Mmmm...Charlie." She waved without looking in their direction and exhaled deeply. Her shoulders heaved with euphoria.

"Woooo!! Saved by Joel," I said as I took a step back

to look her in the peepers. They begged me to come closer and dared my soul to tango with hers again. I held her fingertips in mine and got lost in her eyes. She was about to draw me in, but I broke away to go turn on the music.

"Charlie, it's a bluetooth speaker. You can connect to it using your phone." I think she was trying to lure me back.

"I need to see if it's on first," I told her as I slowly walked towards the back door of Chief, saying a quick prayer along the way.

"Is it on?" she asked, looking over her shoulder towards the truck cab.

Oh it's on, I thought to myself. "I just turned it on, Sugarplum," I said aloud. I hopped over the side of the pickup bed instead of walking back around to where she was sitting. She slid back into the truck and leaned up against me as the two of us watched the sun begin to set in the night's sky. We sat in silence, listening to the smooth jazz that was serenading us as dusk eventually gave way to the darkness and the stars began to light the way home.

"Dance with me?" I asked Dr. Chris.

"Always, Charlie," she replied.

We danced together in the pale moonlight and I had a burning desire to live like forever while we were together. If there was one thing I learned from Marlo's death, it's that we don't know the hour or the day that our number will be called. I leaned harder into life because of it.

Dr. Chris:

Charlie was the reason that we hadn't broken our promise at the lake that night. For whatever reason, my heart was full of love and I felt a need to show him instead of telling him. He kissed me, true, but I was the insatiable one that day. Had it not been for a well timed visit from my little pal, Joel, the two of us might have taken things a little bit further than we'd intended to when Option 3 was presented. I loved his heart and soul, even more deeply because of his commitment to us. I was ready to throw caution to the wind and let life lead.

That day was good for me in more ways than one. I felt alive again. I had been existing, and just trying to survive from one day to the next. Charlie offered something different, but was open to whatever I was feeling up to in the moment. For whatever reason, this excursion helped me to feel renewed, to reconnect with who I knew myself to be. It also illuminated my expanding love for Charlie on a spiritual level. There was already an abundance of love between us, but the divine energy that drew us together felt like it was deepening by the moment and I had an urge to show my gratitude.

Our attraction was magnetic that day. Charlie doesn't know it, but I was prepared to beg for forgiveness after all was said and done. I've heard people talk about throwing caution to the wind, but that was the first time in my life that I truly felt the desire to do it myself. Life was there, in front of us. We were living it each and every day, and I wanted to live fully.

The two of us sat in the back of his truck watching the sun set, and I wanted to say something about it. I just wasn't sure how to bring it up. Instead, I absorbed every second of his love and radiated as much of mine towards him as I could. I did the same thing when we danced. Not a word was spoken between us, but so much was said as we gazed into each other's eyes.

We danced until the speaker ran out of battery power, then packed up the blanket and pillows, hopped in the truck, and drove home. In silence. The entire way. Not uncomfortable silence, but contented silence.

Charlie helped me out of the truck once we got home, and I used my key to open the door while he gathered the food, and big speaker. It was Friday night. I told him we could get the blanket and pillows the next morning. While I was upstairs washing off the outside in the shower, I heard the bathroom door open.

"Just changing out your towel. I'll be out of here in a second."

"Okay," I called back to him, secretly wishing he would ask to join me in the shower.

That wasn't the first time he'd been in the bathroom while I was showering. At some point, the day after Marlo's funeral, Charlie had to physically help me into the shower at the condo. I was sobbing on the floor of the bathroom and he called to me through the door. I didn't answer. I couldn't answer. I wanted to tell him that I was okay, but the truth was that I wasn't okay in that moment. He calmly told me that he was coming in. He opened the door slowly, draped a towel over my body and helped me up off the floor. Without saying a single word he opened the shower curtain, held out a hand for me to hold as I stepped inside, then left me to stand underneath the water for as long as I needed. I wept because I grieved the loss of my friend. I also cried because of how Charlie loved me. I could not have been in a more vulnerable position than that one, and there he was holding my heart, even though it felt like it was in a million pieces in the moment.

"Hey Chris," he called.

"Yes, Sweetheart?" I replied.

"Meet me in the living room when you're finished showering?"

"What's in the living room?"

"Just come, find out, okay?"

"Okay, Charlie."

As soon as I turned off the water, I remembered that I left my pjs in the bedroom. I stepped out and grabbed the fresh towel that Charlie had left for me when I saw them sitting on the bathroom counter. New pajamas. Actual pajamas, not Charlie's old shorts and t-shirt. Love in action. Grinning from ear to ear, I slipped into my new pjs and headed down to the living room instead of off to bed. Charlie was nowhere to be found, but he left a note for me.

"I'll be down to join you in a minute. Relax here and ask the home assistant to play the Snow playlist."

I heard the shower down the hallway turn on as soon as I finished reading the note. He must have been in there waiting for me to get out of the shower in the master bathroom. I was a bit curious why I was playing the Snow playlist in the summertime, but I trusted Charlie, so I asked my good friend to play it and chuckled as songs by Snoh Aalegra began playing. Charlie literally took a 5 minute shower and came bounding down the stairs to join me in some new pjs himself. Real pajamas, not old shorts and a t-shirt.

I was laying on the wool blanket from my car that he had spread out on the floor. Charlie was smiling as he raised our pillows up in the air for me to see.

"You're spoiling me, sir!"

"Great! That means you're letting me love you," he said as he tossed a pillow in my direction.

"Thank you for today, Charlie," I said as he stretched out on the blanket beside me.

"Thank YOU, for today, Dr. Chris," he said as his

eyebrows raised like the golden arches while he snickered.

"Are you thinking about the kiss?"

"What kiss?" He winked.

"So it never happened, huh?"

"I didn't say any of that."

"Fair enough." I paused to take a moment, reliving the kiss in my mind. "So about that kiss..."

He shook his head at me and motioned for me to rest on his chest like I had grown accustomed to doing. I shook my head no, taking the time to clarify why. "I think we need to talk about it, Charlie."

"Then let's talk about it, Dr. Chris."

"Okay."

"I almost lost myself in that kiss."

"What?"

"Your lips were telling me to let go and live."

"Yours were telling mine that, sir."

"Honestly," he said, motioning for me to rest on his chest since we were talking about the kiss. I rested my head in the nook that seemed to be made just for me as he continued, "I was so temped to let whatever was going to happen, just happen, then ask for forgiveness afterwards."

I laughed. "Charlie, I was ready to do the same."

"Oh word?"

"Yeah, it was almost a problem before Joel showed up."

Nervous laughter escaped from his mouth before a bout of silence filled the air."So, are you ready for that, Chris?"

"When the time is right, we'll know it, Charlie."

"Are you telling me that the time wasn't right this evening, ma'am?" He laughed again.

"If the time was right, we wouldn't have seen Joel

and his family."

"That's definitely the truth. I could've lost my job out there," he joked.

"Yeah, me too," I said as Charlie let his fingers trace the swoop of my pinned up hair. So soothing. I had a feeling I was about to drift off to sleep. "Are we sleeping down here tonight, Charlie?"

He chuckled again, "Yeah, if you're okay with that. I wasn't sure the bed was such a good idea tonight."

I tilted my head back to kiss him goodnight and our bodies took over from there.

Charlie:

I had tried to be more pragmatic with our sleeping arrangements when we got back to the house, but apparently it didn't matter. Life and love were coursing their way through us that night.

Chapter 5
Independence Day

Charlie:

Summertime with Chris was proving to be one of my favorite parts of the year. Because I wasn't teaching, I was more free to visit her at the hospital. I also wasn't exhausted from so many of the other responsibilities that I shouldered during an academic year. Dr. Chris and I scheduled one lunch each week that was dedicated to discussing wedding details. That freed up the rest of our time to be present with each other. It was a great shift for the two of us as we recommitted to the list we created at the beginning of this year, our New Year Promise. We had already gone zip lining together in June, before things got too hot in Kansas City and there was a ropes course that we had our eye on.

I was soaking up the extra daylight hours and the energy the sun was providing me. I hadn't felt renewed in the summers before this one, but there was something about our synergy that made this year feel different. Every day since that night, she and I had spent the evening hours, gliding away in the dark of night, watching the stars hold their position in the sky.

Sometime's she'd stretch out across the glider and rest her head in my lap until she fell asleep. I'd just let her lay there and watch her sleep until she'd wake herself up, typically through some sort of dream that would leave her squirming.

"Which one got you?" I'd often ask her. Sometimes it was a dream about Marlo. Other times it was the dream about the highway accident. The latter of those had me nervous. She had a recurring dream that she was driving at highway speeds and her brakes wouldn't work. She told me that she'd always wake up just before slamming into the back of a semi-truck. It sounded terrifying and that one typically left her trembling when she awoke.

Without the dreams, that was the best part of my day; rocking the night away with my love. So peaceful. So much unspoken love and trust. Well, even with the dreams I still enjoyed it. I just didn't love the impact they had on Dr. Chris.

As June rolled into July, Kansas Citians got excited about the 4th of July. Or maybe moreover they were excited about the fireworks that they decided to shoot off. Either way, the stars were increasingly being drowned out by sulfur the closer we got to the 4th. I was prepared to put our evening gliding sessions on hold until around the 6th or 7th of July, but Dr. Chris wasn't having any of that. She grabbed me by the hand after dinner on the 1st and led me outside after I'd spent the last 5 minutes coming up with a million reasons why we shouldn't go outside. She just listened, didn't say one word to rebut what I was saying. I didn't know where she was leading me when she grabbed my hand, but when the sliding door opened, I knew she didn't care about the sulfur shielding the stars or any of the other 999,999 reasons I had come up with. It was then that I realized how much these evening sessions meant to her as well.

Dr. Chris:

Charlie was going to skip out on the glider that night because of the fireworks. That was my favorite part of the day, just relaxing with him to wind down before we went to bed and started the hustle and bustle of another day. I thought about so much when we were sitting on that glider; work and life. Plus I'd just enjoy the feeling of having his arm around me. Resting on the glider gave me the opportunity to be more present. He and I were looking outward in the same direction. We were building a life together. The wedding was the official union and celebration of it, but we had already declared our intent to grow with each other, in whatever direction that meant. The glider had been gifted to us with the intention of us enjoying it together, regardless of what was going on in the atmosphere.

One night we'd been sitting on it together when a summer storm popped up on us. We looked at each other and smiled, then continued to glide on through the rainstorm. I loved this time of day. I wasn't going to let a little smoke deter us. Plus, I was hopeful that we might see a few fireworks while we were out there. So once he was finished giving me all of the reasons that we should stay inside, I stood up from the table, held his hand, and quietly walked the two of us towards the back door and out onto the patio. I glanced back at Charlie's face and noticed a crooked smile finding its way to the surface. That was usually his tell before he asked where I came from.

Not even 30 seconds later, it escaped from his mouth, "Where did you come from, woman?" All I could do was giggle like a child. In spite of the internal battle I was facing as I grieved the loss of Marlo, Charlie still helped me to feel optimistic about the beauty of what life could become. Our lives were unfolding right in front of us, and I didn't want him to get in the habit of retreating. Both of us made a choice to lean into life with each other. And, when one of us felt the nudge to retreat, it was the other's responsibility to push back. We talked about it that night - after we had watched the sun and danced under the moon. That was the real promise we'd made to each other at the turn of the new year, and with our engagement. He and I were committed to helping each other grow - however that looked.

Typically I was the one who stretched out on the glider, but on that day I sat down in the space where Charlie typically sits. He mockingly stretched out across the glider in much the same manner as I do, and I massaged his scalp as his head rested in my lap. He looked so content, his eyes closed, arms cradling my left hand to his heart.

"Hmmm." He sighed.

"You okay, Sweetheart?"

He nodded slowly. "Yep! Is this what it feels like to lay down in my lap?"

"I don't know. How does it feel to you?"

He began to gently wipe a tear from his left eye, "I don't know how to describe it."

"Loved?"

"Mmm hmm. Adored."

"That sounds about right."

He sniffled, "I love being the giver in this situation, but I think we're gonna have to start alternating ma'am."

I hadn't expected such an emotional response, but I wanted him to know that he could have whatever he wanted. "Every other day, Charlie?"

He laughed through his sniffles, "I was thinking more like once a week." I chuckled along with him. "Is that okay with you?"

"That works, or we can do every other day, twice a week, whatever you want."

"Okay," he paused. "Keep stroking my head, please."

I paused and curiously tilted my head to the side.

Charlie opened his eyes and smiled. "I didn't mean it like that." I continued running my fingers across his scalp and snickered. "So relaxing."

"And now you see why I always fall asleep when you do this to me."

He nodded, and wriggled around in my lap like he was trying to soak up the comfort. "I love you so much, Chris."

"I love you deeply, Charlie."

"I feel it."

"Mission accomplished."

Charlie:

I thought I knew what it felt like to be loved by Dr. Chris until the night we lay underneath the firework-laden sky. It moved me to tears thinking about how I would get to spend every day loving and being loved by her. We had been sheltering in place for two weeks, but with Independence Day falling on a Saturday this year, I thought it might be a good opportunity for us to host some friends and family.

I was still laying in her lap, getting a scalp massage when I asked her, "What do you think about inviting your sister & family, Steve & Sabrina, and Mom and Dad over to celebrate the 4th this weekend?"

My eyes were closed so I couldn't see her face, but her reaction sounded pretty excited. "Yeah! I think that's a great idea, Charlie."

"We can hang out here and just chill. I can grill up some food."

"Let's see if they're open. I'll text Vonne and Mom right now." She tapped me on the top of my head so I could sit up. She needed to go grab her phone, a rarity in the evenings. I sent Steve and Sabrina a group text while she was in the house.

"Chris and I are inviting family over for the 4th. We'd love it if the 3 of you would join us."

Steve replied first, "We're in! Aren't we Sabrina? lol"

Sabrina replied after him, "Guess so. lol What time should we be there, Charlie?"

"How about 4ish?"

Sabrina replied, "Have you asked Chris yet? No, I know the answer to that. Go ask Chris, Charlie. LOL "

Steve replied to Sabrina, "He's still learning. Go ask your wife bro."

Dr. Chris came back in with her phone in hand. "What time are we thinking, Charlie?"

Perfect timing. "Oh, I dunno. I was thinking around 3:45 or 4:00ish."

"4:00 sounds great! I'll text that to Vonne and Mom."

I lucked out. "Cool. I'll see if Steve and Sabrina are available around that time."

I sent a reply to Steve and Sabrina, "I told her 4:00."

Sabrina replied, "You did not. lol You gave her two options and she just happened to choose 4:00."

"You're right. lol" I replied. "See y'all on Saturday."

I watched Dr. Chris, tapping away on her phone. "Vonne and family are in. Mom's checking with Dad."

"Dope. Sabrina, Steve and Jax will be here on

Saturday."

Her phone buzzed, "Looks like Mom and Dad will be here as well."

I patted my lap. "Looks like we're about to check another item off the list," I said to her as she lay her head down for me to massage her scalp.

"What do we need to get for Saturday, Charlie?"

"I have no idea," I chuckled. "I guess we should figure that out and get moving huh?"

"Probably," she replied, looking at her phone. "Wait, Mom and Dad said they'll bring the drinks."

"Well, okay."

"Vonne just said she'll bring plates, utensils, cups and ice."

"Oh, hey," I said, looking at my phone. "Looks like Steve and Sabrina are bringing some potato salad and a dessert."

"So we're left with the meat and other sides?" she asked.

"Looks like it," I told her just before she started to drift off to sleep. I watched her sleeping again. This time it looked more restful than not. The sound of the fireworks didn't seem to matter. So I stayed put, continuing to rock on the glider and caress her scalp with my fingertips until I drifted off to sleep myself. I woke up to the sound of her voice, calling to me.

"Charlie, Sweetheart, wake up so we can go to bed."

I had no clue what time it was, so I asked.

"It's 1:30."

"In the morning?"

She snickered through her reply, "Yes, Charlie. Come on." She extended a hand to help me up off the glider.

"Which one did you have?" I asked wrapping my arm around her waist.

"The semi-truck again."

I kissed her temple. "I'm sorry, Sugarplum. What do you think it means?"

"Probably that I'm overwhelmed and in need of a vacation."

"And here I am asking that we throw a party for people."

"I think the people can help, Charlie," she told me as I locked the door behind us.

"Okay, but we're going on vacation before July is done."

"I'd have to submit a request by the first Friday of the month," she said as we began to mount the stairs.

"Great, you still have time to do it."

"I guess you're right. We'd better decide what day we're going. When do you report back to work?"

"What days, plural, we're going. I have to report back to work on the 27th."

"What if I request the week before that?"

"Works for me."

"Okay, I'll submit my request tomorrow morning."

The two of us were so sleepy we barely made it to the top of the stairs safely. I'm not sure if she was holding me up, if I was holding her up, or if we were holding up each other just enough to make it into the bedroom to change clothes and brush our teeth before bed. I only remember collapsing onto the bed after turning out the lights. Dr. Chris was already in bed by that point. She must have pulled the covers over me because I surely didn't do it myself.

She called from work the next day, "Apparently they've been waiting for me to request some time off.

It's already approved."

"How much time did you request?"

"The whole week, Charlie."

"July 20th - 24th?"

"Yes, and they gave me the weekends before and after off as well."

"Wow! So where do you want to go?"

"It doesn't matter to me, Charlie. I just want to get out of Kansas City for a bit."

"Can I call you back with some options this afternoon?"

"Sure!"

I called her back that afternoon to let her know that I'd picked up the things we needed to host the 4th of July.

"Thank you, Charlie. I assumed we'd take care of it this evening. Now we can just veg out."

"I got you."

"I see."

"So, Victoria Falls or..."

"Like, in Zimbabwe?"

"Yeah, or Steamboat Springs, Colorado?"

"Charlie, really? Africa or Colorado?"

I couldn't help but laugh. It did sound a bit ridiculous when she posed it that way. "I mean, we're only talking about a week."

"Can we go to Victoria Falls on our honeymoon and Steamboat Springs for vacation?"

"Whatever you want, Sugarplum."

"I just want to be near you, honestly. So we could go to Topeka and I'd be happy."

"Topeka it is!"

"I lied. That wasn't the truth at all. We can drive through Topeka on the way to Steamboat Springs though."

"Whatever you want, Chris. I just want you to take a break for a bit."

"Thank you, Charlie. Do you want to talk details tonight?"

"Nope. I'll take care of everything."

"Okey dokey."

Dr. Chris:

The 4th of July arrived and Charlie and I were working like a well oiled machine, tag-teaming on the prep of the sides and warming up the grill, while simultaneously doing a deep scrub of the bathrooms. His place was always clean, so there wasn't much to do. But we wanted to ensure things were tidy anyway because company was coming.

My parents showed up early according to my Dad because, "Your mother wanted to see if you needed any help." The two of us were getting the cushions all set on the patio when they came around to the backyard.

"Charlie, it sure smells good back here," my mom offered.

He gave her a side hug, not wanting the smell of the smoke from the grill to permeate her clothes. "It's good to see you, Mom!"

"You too, son. How are your parents?"

"They're well. When we told them you were coming, they told me to wish you a Happy 4th of July."

"Good, good. Well, send our well wishes their way the next time you talk to them."

"Will do."

The 4 of us hung out on the patio until Steve, Sabrina and Jax arrived. Vonne and the kids joined the fun soon after. The twins and Jax seemed to connect instantly. They were off doing their own thing while Steve and Sabrina met my sister. It was fun watching Charlie and Steve recount the olden days, while my family and I listened.

The richness of their friendship reminded me of Marlo and I got to feeling a bit nostalgic.

"Are you okay, Chris?" Vonne asked.

I nodded slowly.

Sabrina moved closer and rested one hand on my shoulder. "Watching the two of them is making you think of Marlo, isn't it?"

"It is. Friendship is a beautiful thing."

The two of them pulled me near and I welcomed the closeness.

"I'm so grateful to have the two of you standing beside me on New Year's Eve."

"I wouldn't miss it for the world, Chris," Vonne said through tears.

"I'm deeply appreciative of our connection, Chris," Sabrina said. "You saved, Charlie. Have I told you that before?"

"What? No."

"He was becoming a bit of a grinch. Then all of the sudden he was lighter. Steve said it was some mystery woman. I didn't know you were the mystery woman until later."

"I had no idea. I told her." I had a hard time imagining Charlie as a grinch. I'd seen him melancholy and in a bad mood before. I've seen him frustrated and downright angry with the world, but I couldn't imagine him as a grinch.

"Would you look at those three over there, Charlie?" Steve said loud enough to ensure that we knew he was talking about us.

"I'm only looking at one of them, Steve," Charlie said through a flirty wink.

Sabrina shook her head, "I've never seen him so smitten, Chris. What did you do to him?"

I only let out a slight laugh. But apparently it said too much.

"Let's go grab some of those sides from the kitchen," Vonne said, grabbing my arm and Sabrina's.

"Do you need any help?" Mom innocently asked.

"No ma'am. With 6 hands, I think we got it!" Vonne emphatically responded.

We retreated to the kitchen and Sabrina was hesitant to ask any questions. My sister on the other hand was all up in my business.

"So what happened Chris?"

"Who said anything happened?"

"Your laugh said you were fondly remembering something that you did to Charlie, or that he did to you."

"We are not having this conversation, Vonne."

"You don't have to tell us anything, Chris," Sabrina urged, sensing my irritation with Vonne's insistent behavior. "You don't owe us any details."

Vonne sucked her teeth. "She's right, you don't owe us any details." I waited for the rest of her statement. "But I'd love to know."

"I bet you would."

"You're happy when you're with him. I can see it in your smile. I can see it in the ease between the two of you," Sabrina said, causing yet another smile to grace my face.

"I don't know what to say." I paused thinking about Charlie and the dawn of Summer. Another grin spread from ear to ear. "I thought I knew love before, but this is just different."

Sabrina grinned back at me, "The two of you have a dynamic energy together. I bet people probably thought you were together before you were officially together."

"Oh my. Yes! On our first date, people kept assuming we were already a couple. We were just trying to get to know each other and one person even went so far as to tell us to never stop loving each other."

"Oh wow!" Sabrina said.

"Chris, I love it," Vonne giggled.

"I can definitely see how people might think that. You have such a natural connection with him," Sabrina said.

"He feels like home. Always has. I've never known that feeling before. I sure didn't see myself as the type of person who would accept a proposal that took place in front of a million people. But when he dropped to one knee, I didn't see anyone else except for Charlie. We were the only two people present. Vonne was all but sitting right beside me and she was gone. It was just me and Charlie in that moment. I could feel him before I saw him. You know how you can sense that someone is near you? I could sense that Charlie was near me. When he reached out and grabbed my hand, I almost cried. There was an overwhelming sense of returning home. It was like the first time I went back home after leaving for college. It was familiar. It was relaxed. Love was present without pretense or conditions. I love that man."

"I love you too, Sugarplum," Charlie chuckled.

"Charlie, how long have you been standing there?" Vonne asked.

"My guess is about 2 minutes," I told her.

Charlie swooped in beside me and kissed my

temple. "That would be correct."

"How did you know, Chris?" Sabrina asked me.

"I could feel him when he entered the room. There's a warm energy that comes with him. I can feel it in my belly."

"I didn't feel any warm energy, Chris!" Vonne exclaimed.

"Of course not, Vonne. That's between Charlie and I," I told her.

"It's always been there too. I felt it right before she bumped into me, and again when I caught her from hitting the ground. She's like a magnet," Charlie asserted. "Don't mind me, I was sent in here by your mother to spy and grab some ice," he laughed as he kissed my temple again and left the kitchen.

"Oh I love that man," I said shaking off my sudden urge to sneak off somewhere private with Charlie.

"Chris, you look like you want to..." Vonne stopped as Dad walked into the kitchen.

"Like she wants to what?" he asked, Vonne.

"Get through all of the details of this wedding planning," Sabrina piped up.

"Yeah, we were trying to figure out a time for her to try on wedding gowns," Vonne said lying through her teeth to our father, who knew better.

"Next time, you shouldn't add so many details, Vonne," he said through squinted eyes. "That was always your tell when you were little." He laughed.

"Dad!"

"He's right," I told her. "I could always tell when you were lying to me. I just never told you that I knew."

Turning towards Sabrina, Vonne replied, "Sometimes it be your own family!"

"Mr. James, is there something we can help you with?" Sabrina asked my Dad.

"Charlie sent me in here to see if you were still talking about him, and to tell you that the food was ready to be blessed."

"We're on our way out," I said. Vonne and Dad walked out ahead of us, while Sabrina placed one hand on my forearm, stopping me in my tracks. She and I stayed behind for a heartbeat.

"Charlie has a tell when he's been intimate with someone. His overly flirty wink was a dead giveaway to anyone who knows him."

I stood in stunned silence and shielded my face from Sabrina. "He's never done that to me before today!"

"I'm guessing that Steve and I are the only two who know it, but don't feel like you have to tell anyone any of your business. How the two of you show each other your love is just for the two of you to know. If your sister tries to get up in your business again, I got you."

Sabrina and I joined the rest of the family on the patio where Dad was waiting to bless the food. I stood between the twins for the prayer, and Charlie, who was standing beside my Dad and Jax, winked at me from across the way. I heard Sabrina chuckle and I tried my best not to let one out myself. Then I heard Steve, who was attempting to be quiet, ask his wife, "Did this dude just wink at Chris?" I had to purse my lips together to keep the laughter from escaping. I made a mental note to talk to Charlie about it later. As soon as the prayer was finished I watched as Steve made a beeline towards his friend.

He cocked his head to the side without breaking eye contact with him and without saying a word. Charlie rubbed the back of his head and smiled. Steve's head dropped back behind his shoulders, his eyebrows raised high. Charlie stretched his neck and closed his eyes through a deep breath. Steve, man-hugged him and turned towards his son, asking Jax what he wanted on his plate.

We ate. The kids played. We talked about the wedding and work and life. When it got dark, Charlie and I moved towards the glider and watched as the kids and their parents played with the sparklers. I had a fleeting thought about our children doing that some day, right there in that yard. Before it passed, I squeezed Charlie's thigh. He kissed my temple and asked if I could see our future family. I nodded as the two of us didn't miss a beat on the squeaky glider.

Before the night was over, the neighbors had put on quite a show with their fireworks displays and all of us cheered before hugging each other goodnight and parting ways. I enjoyed having our friends and family over, but I was ready to spend some solo time with my partner.

When the coast was clear, Charlie cupped my face in his hands and kissed me with a sense of appreciation that felt new.

"Today was perfect," he told me.

"Today was pretty perfect," I agreed.

"It felt like we were already married and I wasn't sure how that was possible, but I enjoyed myself. You and Sabrina looked like you had an inside joke or two."

I giggled again, "We did. She told me you have a tell when you've been intimate with someone."

"I what?" His mouth agape and eyes wide open, he looked like a child who'd be caught with his hand in the cookie jar.

"You winked at me today. It was really flirty."

"Is that why Steve -" he paused, looking like he was going back through a rolodex of the times that's happened.

"Is that why Steve what?"

"That's why he looked at me like that. Is that how he's known all these years?" He laughed so hard that he held his side like it was beginning to cramp. "All this time I just assumed he was psychic or something."

"No, Sweetheart," I said through laughter of my own. "He's not psychic."

"Well, that's good to know," he said, winking at me again.

"I love you deeply, Charlie."

"I love you so much, Dr. Chris."

The two of us locked up the house and climbed the stairs towards the bedroom. He swept me off my feet before we could cross the threshold of the bedroom door, and I rested my head on his chest, listening to his heart rate pulse furiously.

"Am I heavy, Charlie?" I joked.

He laughed. "Are you listening to my heart?"

"I am. It's pumping pretty hard in there."

"Just feeling alive and full of life tonight. That's all."

Charlie:

The 4th of July couldn't have been more perfect. I couldn't have asked for a better celebration. Our friends and family enjoyed each other's presence and Dr. Chris and I were in sync. She was happy, so I was as well. As it turns out, chasing the sunset was the start of a few really great weeks for us. And, about a month after the start of Summer, Dr. Chris and I were heading to our first official vacation together.

Steamboat Springs was calling our name. We packed up Chief and headed on a road trip across

Kansas and more than half of Colorado. We were closer to Wyoming than we were to Denver. The town itself was beautifully nestled in the mountains. It looked like something out of one of those cheesy and predictable made for tv movies. Quaint and picturesque.

We were open to whatever the town had to offer, and it turns out, we had the chance to do a little bit of everything. They had mountain biking, some hot springs to relax in, a botanical garden, a bit of rafting, an art gallery, fishing, horseback riding, golf and mini-golf, and a place to get in some shopping. We did a little bit of everything.

More than anything, I was just excited to see Dr. Chris relax. The only thing I asked to do was get in a round of golf. Everything else we did together, was at her discretion. She smoked me on the course, by the way. Outside of the trip home to Arkansas at Christmas, this was probably the most relaxed I'd ever seen her. I mean, she would relax with me every evening on the glider, but her guard wasn't completely down like this. Vacation Chris was silly and playful, adventurous and high spirited. Vacation Chris was a site to behold and I just watched and admired her as much as I could, taking it all in.

Dr. Chris:

There was something about the air in Colorado that was light and inspiring. I felt like a different person there. I felt like I was able to let down the guard that typically protects me from the outside world. I did that at home with Charlie, but generally speaking, there was a threshold that I kept when I was in Kansas City.

Charlie was grinning from ear to ear on the drive to and from Steamboat Springs. It was about a 12 hour trip each way, but he loved to drive anyway. He told me that he and Chief had already had some experience driving in the mountains of Colorado, so I made the assumption that he was just down to drive the entire way. About 6 hours into the trip I asked if he needed a break.

"I got us, Sugarplum. You just relax, okay?"

I loved the way this man loved me. Since the moment I followed his mom's advice and told him what I wanted, what I needed, things were different. Things shifted from a sense of drifting apart, to the two of us being more intentional about how we spent our time together. We had the chance to do a lot of talking on that road trip, and I learned a lot about his time as an only child and what he envisioned for his future family; karaoke and game nights, a dedicated puzzle table that we'd work on solving as a family, service Saturdays helping to strengthen our community, family road trips around the country, athletics and/or the arts or supporting whatever dreams his children had, building a wealth of memories and creating traditions that his children, our children, could pass on to their children.

"We don't have to build a family like that Dr. Chris. We can build the type of future we envision together."

"I like your vision, Charlie. It aligns closely with mine."

His broad smile was too much for my heart to handle. Every time I saw it, my body filled with so much joy and energy that I could feel it traveling up my spine and exiting through the top of my head. It was a quick surge, but I'd never experienced anything like it. That vacation was full of surges. Charlie's inner child was oozing from his pores and I felt like I had a chance to see who he truly was at his core. That version of Charlie encouraged me to tap into my own inner child and in some regard, save for the time we were relaxing in the hot springs, I felt like we were two teenage friends who were dancing around their attraction to each other, minus all the insecurities. I loved Vacation Charlie. He encouraged me to let my guard down and enjoy the moment for what it was. Vacation Charlie was playful and that encouraged me to be more joyous.

Because I was in such a joyous mood, I decided to reach out to Marlo's fiancée, Janae. She made a quick visit to hang with Charlie and I for a day. It was on that day that we found and purchased our wedding invitations, and matching earrings for the bridal party while we browsing through the shopping district. When Charlie left Janae and I on our own, we found my wedding gown. She had caught me gazing into the window of the shop as we walked by and asked if I'd found my dress yet. When I told her that I hadn't, she turned me around and led me into the store "just to look." The first dress I selected and tried on was the one I fell in love with. I know my blood relatives wanted to be there for that moment, but family was still present. I could feel in my gut that it was the right choice for me. When I stepped out of the dressing room to look in the mirrors, she teared up. My heart sank as my empath vibes kicked into high gear. I could feel the sorrow in my bones and hugged her with all the love in my body. Hers was the first wedding invitation that was delivered, as I presented her with that and a pair of earrings similar to those I'd picked up for Sabrina and Vonne. I couldn't thank her enough for standing in the gap in spite of the circumstances. I hoped that she'd join us but I understood it if she couldn't.

That vacation had provided just the break I needed. It couldn't have come at a better time given all that was looming on the horizon.

Chapter 6
School's In

July turned out to be a good month all around. Charlie and I grew to understand each other more, and in doing so, we grew stronger in love. He was one of my favorite human beings and I was hoping to bring part of our vacation personas into the Academic Year that was gearing up. We had an idea, but didn't fully realize that our 4th of July gathering and the vacation we took were going to be considered a luxury in just a few short weeks. It seemed, the mystery virus that attacked Marlo's system had started to spread, and life as we knew it would pivot drastically in just a matter of a few days.

That year would prove to be different in so many ways. In person classes weren't going to be a thing because of the virus they were hoping to contain. While that was good for everyone's health, it meant a lot of strain on families and educators alike. There was no perfect option and I knew that it was going to be especially tough on someone with such a big heart for educating children. Charlie was stressed at the thought of what they were expected to do, and they hadn't even started the academic year yet.

I called him on my way home from work one evening, "I'm looking forward to seeing your face, Sweetheart."

He was half invested in the conversation, "Uh huh." I knew something was up.

"Charlie, what's going on?"

"They want me to lead the team for the virtual learning plan."

"That's great right? I mean, you would've been my choice too."

"Yes, but that makes me the fall guy for whatever doesn't work - and I have a feeling there's going to be a lot of things that don't work.

"I understand, Charlie. What's the cap on what you can do?"

"I mean, I can't manage people's reactions to this, huh?"

"Nope. So, just put your best plan forward and let the chips fall where they may."

"You're right, Sugarplum. Where are you now? I can't wait to hold you in my arms after the day I just had."

"I'm in the driveway, Charlie."

I saw him open the front door, his eyes bright. He placed the phone over his heart and exhaled deeply. That joyous smile returning to his face, he bounded down the driveway to my car door. Pure sunshine. He was nothing but warmth and light. He opened my door and helped me out of the car and into his arms. There was no place I'd rather be in that moment. A faint whimper escaped his mouth so I cradled the back of his head with my hand.

"Hey, you okay?"

He nodded. "Yep. Just missed you today. There were so many moments when I wanted to hear your voice telling me that it'd be okay."

"I'm here now, Charlie."

"I know. I feel your love," he whispered. I didn't know what to do with this man. I only hoped that I could love him the way he deserved. "Chris," he started, still holding me in his arms.

"Yes, Charlie?"

"Your tender touch - " he paused. "You feel like sunshine."

It was yet another example of him understanding me, or me understanding what he needs. He sent me into orbit. We were swirling around the love that we generated together like satellites. I didn't know how else to describe it. But it was overwhelmingly terrifying once I identified it. Satellites stayed in orbit by balancing their speed with the gravitational pull from the Earth. If that was the case, then Charlie and I would be in orbit only as long as we could balance the speed in which we circled our own love and the gravitational pull of our love on each of us individually. Without the gravity of our love, one or both of us would end up drifting off into space. We'd already experienced a little bit of that on Easter.

Did that mean that I had to either feel the pull of our love or randomly float away without it? It brought me right back to the thought I'd had when we were graveside. I couldn't imagine burying Charlie and I couldn't imagine the pain that would accompany it. And now that I had experienced it, I couldn't imagine what my life would look like without our love in it. I most definitely would be floating around all willy nilly with the rest of the space junk. Without our love, I'd become space junk. My rational mind knew that I had to be overreacting to this, but I couldn't stop myself from ruminating.

"Hey, where'd you go?" Charlie called out to me, squeezing me twice with his arms.

"I'm right here, Charlie."

He leaned back and looked me in the eyes, "You okay?"

I nodded, uncertain of what other words I could offer in the moment to accurately depict just how wild my imagination was and how big of a role it had played on my current psyche.

I almost lost my mind in that moment, but our love pulled me back into orbit. Crazy how that worked.

I didn't realize just how much Marlo's death would impact me, but I guess it had only been a couple of months since his passing. I know for a fact that I was still grieving. I was just waiting for someone to tell me that it was all a dream, but that hadn't happened yet, nor would it. It's funny how things can change so easily and no matter how much we'd like to, we can't go back to where we used to be. If I could have yesterday back, I'd change it so that Marlo was still here. He was supposed to be my forever friend. I wished that I could hug him once more or pick up the phone and hear his voice. When I closed my eyes, I could see his face, but that feeling wasn't a comforting one. Instead it was heart wrenching. I wished that I could explain it all to Charlie, but my words were escaping me in the moment. Instead, I just randomly wept in his arms.

"I got you, Sugarplum," he told me. "I'm right here. Give me your sadness." Oh, I wished it were that easy. Instead, I sat and wondered of a life that was, but had somehow gone away. *What happened to those days?*

I wondered how long I'd feel like this. I know there was no time limit on grief, but I found myself wondering when it was going to get easier. I was so grateful that Charlie was in orbit with me, because I couldn't imagine going through this without him.

Funny how things can change so easily. I thought about Marlo when we were on vacation in Colorado, but I didn't sit with it for too long. I was good at avoiding things when they were uncomfortable, but not as good at facing them head on. In this instance though, I had a feeling that until I faced it, I'd probably end up swirling around through the same grief cycle.

I hadn't realized that I was still standing in the driveway, car door open, sobbing into Charlie's arms until I heard him. "Let's go inside, Chris," he said as he leaned down, grabbed my bag from the car and locked my car door. "I'll get you some water."

I sat on the couch in a daze, wondering what was about to happen during the rest of the year. I had already found love, lost love, gained it back, then lost it elsewhere. When we share our world with someone else, we offer them a piece of who we are. I wondered if there would always be a piece of me that was missing - a piece that I couldn't get back.

I regularly helped families grieve their loved ones at work, either the loss of their loved one or the loss of a certain way of living. I've grieved the loss of grandparents, but nothing prepared me for that journey.

Charlie returned to the living room with some water, handing it to me as he sat beside me on the couch. "What happened, Chris?"

I had to make a split second decision to tell him the truth or simply part of it. I opted for the complete truth, and I'm sure it threw Charlie for a loop because of his facial expression. "I started thinking about how much I loved you and how we were like two satellites in orbit around the love that we were building."

"That's a dope way to explain it."

"Yeah?" I asked him.

"Oh yeah," he replied.

I chuckled at his enthusiasm. "So I was thinking about that," I sniffled, "and then I started thinking about what I had imagined as we were at Marlo's funeral and it sent me off into deep rumination."

"A spiral of grief?" Charlie asked gingerly.

"Of sorts, yes," I replied.

"I'm glad that you're getting all of that out. I know that it doesn't feel very good when it surfaces, but you have to get it out."

His answer brought a sense of calm that restored my soul.

"Thank you, Charlie."

He kissed my temple and told me that dinner was almost ready. "Are you hungry at all?"

I had a feeling that a warm dinner was just what I needed in the moment. "I am." I knew that Charlie had a rough day himself, so for him to then come home and begin to fix dinner, I was a bit outdone and I started to tear up again.

"He's always with you, Sugarplum. You know that."

"Oh Charlie," I paused between sniffles. "These tears are for you."

"Did you not want me to cook today?"

I giggled, "No, that's not it at all. I just love you deeply and appreciate who you are. That's all."

His grin resurfaced and the sunshine returned to my heart almost instantaneously.

As school officially got underway and teachers were working with students virtually, Charlie's nerves about his additional duties as requested started to drop. His planning gave teachers an opportunity to learn the technology in advance, and his communication plan with parents and guardians gave them practical knowledge to help their students learn. In a land where all things were equal, it would have been the perfect plan. However, we all know there are far too many challenges that some students and families have to face without help to navigate through them. And well, when the stuff hits the fan, there's not much else you can do except try to provide support where and when you can. Sometimes you can't forecast the challenges that end up knocking on the door.

Nobody understood that more than me. Working in healthcare during that year just solidified it. It was already true in years when we weren't facing a pandemic. But holy crap - if that year didn't encase that notion in a glass vault, I don't know what would. When Marlo contracted the virus and succumbed to its side effects, there was still so much we didn't know. He worked in a hospital for goodness sake. You would think this would be the one advantage of being a healthcare worker. But not that year. Not the way our culture prioritizes community vs. self. As I learned more about it myself, my anger in how this was handled grew exponentially. There were things we could have asked people to do that would have prevented the casualties that eventually ensued. But the alleged leader of the free world, decided to use it as a political ploy. People's actual lives were at stake, and he didn't care one ounce about the ripple effect of his actions. Businesses went under, their doors shuttered. People lost jobs and with it, access to the basic resources that we should all be afforded. People lost their lives and families were left in the wake of such a sudden chasm in their hearts. I wished there were something I could do to bring back my friend and the countless others who had lost their lives to the virus. But I knew that ultimately, I couldn't undo what had already been done. The best I could do was help to educate others on the importance of taking the recommended precautions seriously.

The parents of the patients I served understood the importance of that. Our hospital did a phenomenal job of protecting as many of our people as we could. I couldn't imagine working in a space that was overwhelmed with more patients than their staff could handle effectively. My hope was that people began to take things seriously and that we could nip this thing in the bud within the next 30 - 45 days. To do that though, would take a few modern miracles and human beings willing to see each other as people instead of competition.

The country went into lock down mode. People were asked to stay home unless there was an absolute necessity that they leave. Businesses asked their staff to begin working from home. Schools shifted into online learning, which prompted the stress for Charlie, and a lot of other parents and educators alike. The entire country, I would imagine, was under some sort of stress from all of the unknown. Charlie and I began to have daily conversations about expectations vs. reality, which helped the two of us stay rooted in the present, me in particular.

By mid-and especially, late-August those daily conversations became a necessity for maintaining my sanity amid all of the external chaos. I'd had a particularly tough day at Hope Gardens. The powers that be were attempting to shuttle in some patients from hospitals that were at capacity, which was going to put our particularly vulnerable wing in jeopardy. I'd been on the phone and video conferences the majority of the day trying to explain the impact that it would have on our patients improving. They were hoping to transport patients who had tested positive for the virus, and our team was fighting hard for them to transport other patients who were in need of different medical support and virus free. We went around and around about it before I couldn't take anymore of the bureaucracy.

"They're children for Christ's sake!!" I shouted from within my office at the top of my lungs. "Children! You want to expose a hospital full of children, who we've kept virus free up to this point, to a virus that disproportionally impacts those who are already immunocompromised?! What kind of monsters would do that to those who can't care for themselves, to the future of our country?"

I had just called the Board, monsters. I was unraveling at the seams at the thought that this would be the decision they deemed appropriate. I just knew when I left for the day that I was going to wake to find some sort of reprimand. It weighed heavy on my mind on the drive home. When I called Charlie as usual, he had something to offer.

"Hey, Sweetheart, I'm on my way home," I said, my voice heavy with melancholy.

"Okay, Dr. Chris. What happened?"

"Charlie, I don't want to wear my Doctor coat right now. Can you just call me Chris?"

"Sure. What happened, Dear?" he asked, his voice laced with concern.

"I snapped," I said as matter of fact as I could muster.

"Where? Who? What happened?"

"At work on a video conference. I snapped at the board. What they were asking was ridiculous and made zero sense given the population we serve and I lost it."

"What did losing it look like?" he asked with his calm and cool demeanor on display.

I felt shame creep up into my body, "Me yelling at the top of my lungs. Shouting how idiotic and irresponsible their demands were."

"Did you use the word idiotic, Chris?"

"Not directly, Charlie, but I hinted at it. You know I can't share what they were asking us to do, but it was stupid."

"Did you tell them the unvarnished truth?"

"I did."

"Did you say it in a way that they could understand it?"

"I mean, maybe, but I'm pretty sure I made an insinuation about people who would make a request like theirs. So by association, I kind of called them monsters."

Charlie laughed heartily, "I mean, I'm sure it stung, but what you said - was it something that would protect your patients?"

"It was."

"Then I don't see what the big deal is."

"I felt like I had become unhinged, Charlie."

"Chris, did you try to push back on them in a professional manner first?"

"Of course."

"Were they listening?"

"No."

"Which is why you snapped."

"Yes."

"Sometimes, people don't pay attention until you say it with passion."

I paused. I didn't know what else to say. Charlie had seen things differently than I had because he wasn't directly involved. I sure hoped that he was right.

"Chris, you were assertive in challenging their recommendation, and any doctor who cares about their patients would have done the same thing as you. What was your expectation in that moment?"

"That they hear how ridiculous it was the first time I said it."

"Would they have the inside knowledge that you have?"

"I hoped that they would."

"But did they?"

"It appeared not."

"What was the reality of the situation?"

"I had to help them see how their decision would impact everyone else, including those who were already here."

"...and were you convincing in doing so?"

"We shall see, I suppose."

"I know how convincing you can be when I don't think through some of my decisions before I act on them," he chuckled. "I'm sure you were convincing."

"Ummmm, thanks? I think." I said beginning to feel a bit better about snapping on the people who held my medical future in their hands. "I'm around the corner from the house now, Charlie."

"I'll meet you out back on the glider, Sugarplum."

"Yes!!"

"Love you."

"Love you, deeply."

I let myself into the house once I got home, dropped my bag on the floor near the foyer, and headed straight for the back door. I could hear her before I got out there - Ella Fitzgerald, asking what I was doing on New Year's Eve. It was August, but Charlie was smiling away on the glider as he rocked to the rhythm of the song that chased us around as we were first getting to know each other. I maneuvered the sliding glass door open, and

Charlie stood to his feet, his hands open and waiting to greet me. I leaned in for a hug and received his now-trademark kiss to the temple.

"Dance with me?"

"Always, Charlie."

He waited for me to place a hand in his before twirling me around the patio, pulling me near, and singing softly in my ear. Funny how something so simple could transform my mood. I don't know if it was the dancing, or Charlie, or dancing with Charlie that did it. My guess though, is that it was a combination of all of these things working in concert that helped.

The song was on repeat and we danced like we had on the streetcar. Hand in hand. Eye to eye. Our souls connecting with each other and envisioning how New Year's Eve would look this year. I hoped that everyone would stay put so we could celebrate with our friends and family. As it stood in that moment, we'd have to either push the date or keep things simple and intimate. I was okay with the latter. In fact, Charlie didn't know this, but the two of us could get married in his backyard and I would've been just fine with that. We didn't need the venue that we secured. We had the rest of our lives to figure out. One day wouldn't deter that. One day wouldn't disrupt the rest of that. One day was not going to impact our forever. I wasn't willing to let it.

So, I let go of those worries and we danced and danced until one of us was hungry. It was me. I was the hungry someone. My stomach howled like a wolf and Charlie placed a hand over my belly like there was a child inside or something, raising an eyebrow of suspicion in my direction.

"Yes, I'm hungry, Charlie."

He chuckled, "I know you are. I could feel it grumbling down there before it decided to holler at us." I shook my head at the thought that Charlie was dancing close enough to feel my hunger pangs. How did we end up here, and so quickly?

Still holding my hand, he danced over near his portable speaker and picked it up, dancing with me back into the house, towards the kitchen for dinner, which he had waiting for us.

"Charlie, I don't know if I do a good job letting you know just how much I appreciate you."

"I can feel it."

"But I want to say it more often," I told him, leaning back so he could see my face. He leaned in, turning his head in my direction to demonstrate that he was listening to me. I couldn't do anything else but laugh, which prompted him to place a hand near his ear, cupping it like he couldn't hear me.

"I appreciate and love you like no one else, Charlie."

He placed both hands over his heart, pretending like he was taken aback by my words. "I know your stomach is Growly McGrowlerton down there, but do you think it can wait about 5-10 minutes while I warm the bread?"

"I'm sure it can. In fact, I'll distract it by changing clothes and washing my hands before we eat." I hustled out of the kitchen hoping to change faster than it took for the bread to warm up.

The two of us ate that evening and discussed Charlie's day. I'm not sure if there was a full moon on that day or what, but as it turns out, I wasn't the only one who had an outburst that day.

"I needed this more than you know, Chris."

"What do you mean Charlie?"

"Well, today was a troubleshooting nightmare. Our educators are tech savvy, but they're not an IT department."

"What happened?"

"Every technological glitch you could imagine. You know we have students without reliable internet already. So they're in and out of the virtual classrooms, but then our teachers were having issues with the district's laptops, so they were having to modify their lessons on the fly, which they do in person already. But the level of ingenuity it takes to modify a virtual lesson for students when you're working on unstable tech, is ridiculous. We had a district employee in our virtual staff meeting at the end of the day and he was complaining about how he logged into multiple classrooms and the teachers weren't present."

"Oh no."

"Yeah, so I listened to him go on and on and on about how it was unprofessional and the teachers were unreliable, mind you, these are the teachers who also have children whose virtual lessons they're also monitoring, so they're both educator and parent in the same window of time - anyway, this guy is yammering on about how they have no business in the classroom if they can't be present."

"What did you do, Charlie?"

"I asked him if the students were working while he was in the rooms."

"What did he say?"

"He insinuated that they were doing the assignments in spite of the teacher's absence."

"Oh my."

"Yeah, talk about obtuse!"

"Uh oh."

"I tried to wait it out, but when he asked who was in charge of the virtual learning at our school, I let him have it."

"He wasn't ready."

"He wasn't. I stuck up for our educators and told him about the things he wasn't able to see from just sitting in a seat and looking at a computer screen. I told him about all of the things they have to manage and shift on a regular basis, and this joker was unimpressed."

"What did you do?"

"I offered him an opportunity to watch video of a complete session where a teacher's laptop froze and they still found a way to log in without video and keep the students on track, because of the rapport they had built with the students prior to these tech issues with the crappy supplies they were given."

"Was he willing to watch it?"

"I dropped the link in the comments of the video conference so everyone, including our principal, had access to it."

"And what happened?"

"He acted as though he was going to need to run it up a chain of command. But the building principal shut that down real quick."

"I'm so glad you have support like that, and that you're willing to step in and support others as well. They'll remember that, Charlie."

"I don't care if they do or don't. It was the right thing to do."

We had long before finished eating. "Should we go back out to the glider for a while?"

A broad smile graced his face. "That's my favorite part of the day."

"Mine too, Charlie."

We rocked to the sounds of Ella, until the day turned into night and I was too tired to keep my eyes open. I stretched out on the glider and rested my head in

Charlie's lap as he ran his fingers down the length of my hair. This had become our safe space, our refuge from the outside world. Before I drifted off to sleep, I made a mental note to send a thank you to his parents for the gift of peace, something we needed that day, that month, and that year more than ever.

Something heavy seemed to be brewing. I could feel it in the air, but had no idea the magnitude of its impact.

Chapter 7
Labor Day

Charlie:

School was only in session for a few weeks before the mandates rolled in for the community to pause in an attempt to get this thing under control. Once we made it through the initial 30 day stay at home orders, people were itching to see their friends and family. The city's hope was that the spread of the virus would have been minimized with people acting like responsible human beings during that month at home. Restaurants and businesses were starting to ease back into the practice of serving people with mask restrictions in place. Small gatherings of 10 people or less were recommended to take place outside. I needed some time with my brother, so I asked Steve if we could catch up with them over the Labor Day weekend. We found a time that weekend that worked for Dr. Chris, since she still had to work on that Monday. But the four of us and Jax caught up on how we'd spent our time in quarantine. Their backyard was the perfect place to relax, add a bit of distance between us, and still feel connected to them.

Jax, we found out, much like other students his age

was struggling through his online learning sessions.

"I'm bored," he told me when I asked him about what was going on with his classes.

"What would make it better?" I asked him.

"If we could play games to learn it would be better."

My educator mind was working overtime and Dr. Chris could see it.

"Charlie, I'm sure you can find some things that work later. Just hang out with your godson, Sweetheart."

She was right. I was in full troubleshoot mode and even though I was geeking out about the possibility of creating some change that would help students learn, I was about to make this Labor Day reconnection a pretty boring day for everyone else.

Jax asked his Dad and I if we'd toss around the football with him. That left Sabrina and Dr. Chris to their own womanly devises, which I loved for her. Marlo's passing left a gaping hole in the friendship department for Chris, but Sabrina stepped up to support her in a way I've never seen before. She never attempted to fill the void, but rather she was there to hold her up and straighten her crown. It was much the same way that she supported Steve, but he was her partner and I'd grown to expect that between the two of them. I guess I hadn't paid attention to the number of times she had straightened my own crown before, but thinking about it, that's just who Sabrina was at her core. She was a walking, talking, support for all of us, which made me wonder - who helped to straighten her crown when she needed support. I loved my friend, but I could see him missing the signs that she was in need. Maybe she just told him. I made a note to keep my eyes open to see if there was something I could learn about the way that she loved on her people. I was always looking for ways to love harder and deeper, especially in connecting with the people I cared about. If there was something I could pick up and practice now that would help Dr. Chris and I grow stronger in the long run, I was here for it. I wasn't willing to run the risk of leaving something on the table so to speak. What she and I were building both required and deserved my whole heart.

As Steve and I took turns tossing the football to Jax, we took a moment to catch up on everything that we'd missed since Independence Day. The Shutdown had impacted his business and he had to let people go so they could request unemployment pay from the state.

"It was one of the hardest decisions of my life. I never thought I'd have to make a choice to voluntarily let people go."

"I understand man," I told him, looking at the anguish smeared across his face. How have they all fared during the shutdown?"

"From what I know, they're all okay. I tried to find a balance between staying in contact and letting them know I wanted to rehire them when the world opened back up, and giving them space to navigate through this crap however they needed to."

"I don't know how you do it. So many lives in your hands."

"Yeah, it wasn't easy, that's for sure. So how about you? You're teaching on a computer now?"

"It's pretty much the most challenging way to reach young students. Attention spans in the classroom are short-lived, but in front of a screen they're pretty much non-existent. We're constantly shifting from one activity to the next. Complete worst case scenario for everyone; parents, teachers, administrators, everybody."

Steve whistled. "It's all stupid, man. They should've just waited a year. I feel so frustrated watching Jax try to navigate through this." He passed the football to Jax and asked him to share what the teacher caught him doing on Friday.

"Dad! Noooo!"

"Wait until you hear what your Godson did," he said chuckling heartily.

"Dad. I can't! And don't tell him!" Jax urged as he charged after his father.

"Show him then!" Steve said exuberantly while swatting away his son as his laugh continued to swell in volume.

Jax froze in place mid-lunge. Steve, still laughing, pointed at his son, "Do you see this mess?"

I started to laugh at the pose that Jax was making then lost it immediately as Steve told me that he was doing this during his virtual classes.

"What? Jax! You aren't doing that, are you?" I said, trying to understand, and not to laugh as hard as I had initially. Jax unfroze and grabbed the football from his Dad.

"I did it," he said, his eyes lowered to the ground.

"We get a message from his teacher that she's caught him doing this twice now. She called on him and he pretended to be frozen, then she told him that she could see him moving and he unmuted himself and answered the question. The last time she said she noticed him practicing his frozen state."

"Jax, why do you freeze like that?" I asked him, trying not to laugh.

"Well, earlier in class, I was moving around in my chair and she saw me and told me not to move. So I froze," Jax said very matter of fact.

I nodded, then looked away so as not to laugh directly in his face.

"Why were you moving around in the chair, Jax?" Steve asked him.

"It was fun, Dad! Those classes are booooring!"

"They are?" I asked him?

"Yeah. I wish we played more games!" Jax replied.

"I hear you buddy," I told him.

"So what's good with you and the Good Doctor, Charlie?" Steve asked, shifting the subject to more personal matters.

"Man, just pushing through the shutdown together. Helping each other navigate through this stress. Loving and supporting each other through something I don't think either of us expected to have to deal with."

"It's wild right?"

"Yeah, man."

"Sabrina's been a straight up rock."

"That's what she does. Have you asked what she needs?"

"She usually just tells me what to do when she needs something."

I laughed. Dr. Chris was the same way, but I wasn't talking about chores so I redirected my question, "Yeah, Chris does that too. It's great that I don't have to guess about that kind of stuff, but sometimes she needs emotional support and I don't notice it until she's already bursting with tears."

"That's hard."

"Yeah it is."

"Sabrina usually tugs on my shirt sleeve."

"What does that do?"

"That's her sign that she's about to boil over, so I wrap her up with my arms and cover her from the world for as long as she needs."

"That's dope."

"That's when I feel the most like a protector. She doesn't know it, but I live for it."

"Did she ask for you to do that, or how- "

"Nah, one day in college, I was on the video games and she had been calling my name. I kept telling her 'one minute, one minute,' like a young idiot. It went on and on, and finally she came and tugged on the sleeve of my hoodie. I took a quick glance at her face and she already had tears welling up in her eyes. I paused the game and just held her. I asked what was wrong, but she wouldn't speak. So I told her to tug before she got to tears the next time. She's been doing it ever since."

"Man."

Steve shrugged, "I know, it's cheesy."

"Nah, I'm trying to figure out what I can do with Dr. Chris. She's still navigating heavily through her grief right now."

"I thought about what it would be like for you to suddenly be gone. Can't imagine it. Shit hurt, bro."

"Same man. And they'd known each other longer than we have. Just as close too. I just wish I could help her."

"I know you. Just keep doing what you're already doing. You're probably helping more than you know."

"I hope so," I said as Steve's words echoed around in my head. Maybe I was trying to hold onto as much hope as possible. Sometimes it felt like I was spinning my wheels trying to figure out how to help, and when I asked, she didn't have the words to tell me herself because she was grieving. I figured it was something I should probably talk to Dr. Chris about in a time when her grief wasn't visibly present.

Dr. Chris:

The guys went to toss the football around and Sabrina and I had the chance to chat with each other without the presence of my sister or parents. And with the guys in front of us, Charlie couldn't sneak up on our conversation like he had on Independence Day. I didn't realize how much I missed having a friend to confide in until she and I had the chance to chat briefly that afternoon. I didn't know her well at the time, but I got the vibe that she was truly interested in helping people shine.

"So, Sabrina, thank you for supporting me on the 4th. My sister can be a handful at times, but I truly appreciated having you there to run interference."

"You're welcome, Chris. If Charlie loves you, I love you by default, but I also know you're a pretty great human without him too." I smiled as she continued, "not that I'm suggesting you leave him. I'm not suggesting that at all."

"I didn't think you were."

"Okay, good. It just struck me all of a sudden how crazy that could have sounded."

"Not crazy at all."

The two of us relaxed into our seats on the patio as we watched the three of them throwing the football around to each other. They were in a full conversation, but I had no idea what they were talking about. There was laughter, which was exactly what I was hoping Charlie would get the chance to do today. He was stressed at work and so focused on helping me through my crap, that I wanted him to have at least one day where he didn't have to navigate through a mine field of stress. His heart was so big that I couldn't imagine him not trying to help if I needed it, but I knew that too much stress would crack even the strongest and most sturdy beam.

"Chris, how are things going for you?" Sabrina asked as she watched me, admiring my fiancé from afar.

"They're okay. Lately, it seems like I have days that

are stressful, and days that are really stressful. But Charlie helps me to deal."

"Do you ever tell him what you need help with?"

"Not really, not emotionally anyway."

"You know they don't think like we do, right?" Sabrina said through a snicker.

"I definitely know that!"

"Charlie can't read your mind anymore than Steve can read mine."

I nodded. "How do you tell Steve what you need?"

"I don't. But I tug on his sleeve when I need to be wrapped up and cocoon away from the world for a minute."

"And he does it every time?"

"Every single time without fail."

"How does he know to do that?"

"It started in college. He was playing some video game for hours, and so I was studying while he was playing."

"Uh huh"

"He played for so long that I ran out of stuff to study."

"Oh no."

"Yeah. I was only studying to distract me from the fact that I was feeling overwhelmed with school and missing my home and family."

"So what happened?" I asked her.

"I didn't know what else to do. I kept waiting for him to take a break, but he just kept playing. Eventually I was on the brink of tears and I just kept trying to hold them in, and hold them in, and I couldn't hold on any longer. So I tugged on the sleeve of his sweatshirt and he looked at me for a split second, then back at the game."

"Steve!"

"Yeah, I almost left the room, but before I could

pivot, he paused the game, dropped the controller and just held me in his arms."

"Aww,"

"Mmm hmm," she was getting choked up speaking about it. "He asked me what was wrong, but I didn't have the energy to use any words at that point. I was just completely and totally overwhelmed. Then his arms whisked me away to safety."

"Wow."

"Yep. He told me to tug before I get to tears the next time. So I did."

"That's pretty awesome."

"It is. Low-key though, I think he loves it just as much as I do. He just snuggles in after a while. It's one of the cutest and most endearing things ever."

I could tell how much those snuggles meant to her by the starry-eyed glow that had draped her face. I imagine that's probably how my face would look if I told someone about our evening glider time.

As Sabrina and I were chatting away, I caught Charlie sneaking a peek in our direction. So did she.

"He loves you so much Chris."

I chuckled.

"Just look at how he's looking at you on the sly," she chuckled.

"It drives me crazy in the best way possible. He was so unexpected."

"If you could go back in time before you met him, what would you tell your past self?" she asked. It was a deep question. One I wasn't sure I had the answer to, so I paused in serious reflection before answering.

"Wow. I'm not sure. I wouldn't want to change anything about the way we met, or how we learned to trust and love each other." That was the honest truth. Charlie and I had some bumps, but those ultimately helped each of us grow stronger. Is it worth it to possibly risk your own growth and development for the sake of potentially making something easier to navigate? Who's to say we'd have the same outcome? Who's to say we'd be together, eyeing each other from across the backyard at that very moment? "I guess I might encourage myself to trust myself and listen more," I told her with sincerity.

"Yeah, that's probably the only thing that I'd encourage myself to do too. Sometimes I find myself listening with an attitude, which - let's be honest, absolutely alters the way I hear what Steve has to say," she said with a smile as she waved her fingers in Steve's direction. I nodded, understanding what she was hinting at.

Charlie:

"See Charlie, they're over there looking at us right now," Steve told me as he seductively waved to his wife. He and Sabrina had been flirting with each other like that since college. It used to make me roll my eyes, but today I got it.

There she was, standing across the yard gazing into my eyes like I was standing right in front of her. I know I was smiling before I realized it was happening. I just don't know how long it took for me to recognize that my body's natural reaction to her attention was fully evident on my face. Her face held the same expression that it did that night we met - one part excited to see you, one part is this really happening, two parts magnetic attraction. All I wanted to do in that moment was hold her tight, but Steve was still speaking.

"I know they're talking about us," he said as he glanced in my direction - catching me in the middle of my love-struck stupor. "You good bro?" he laughed.

I placed my hand over my heart, still looking at Dr.

Chris, who signaled with her head for me to come see her. "I'm good," I told Steve as I started walking towards my love. He asked Jax to grab the ball and followed me to the patio. I greeted her with a kiss on the temple and her warm smile was a gift I didn't know I needed. I instinctively wrapped her up in a big bear hug and rested my cheek on the top of her head. I could feel her weight shift into me and I closed my eyes in contentment. She held onto me a bit longer than I expected. Given all that was going on in the world at large and in her world personally, that set off an internal alarm and I shifted into protector mode.

"Are you okay, Sugarplum?" I whispered into her ear.

"I am," she whispered in return.

"You sure?" I asked a bit more audibly, but still in hushed tones.

She nodded into my chest, "Mm hmm, just absorbing your love, Charlie."

I was ready to leave in that moment. Alone time. We needed alone time. "How long are we staying here?" I laughed into her ear.

"You tell me, Charlie! I'm here with you," she giggled - knowing exactly what I was asking without me needing to be direct about it.

I kissed her on the temple again and released my embrace to find Steve and Sabrina lovingly looking in our direction.

"What?" I asked them.

"Charlie, you love her without reservation," Sabrina told me.

"Huh?"

"You didn't care who was nearby. I mean, your boy for how many decades now - you just left him while he was talking to you to come stand with your lady."

I squeezed Dr. Chris around the waist as Sabrina continued, "You didn't even know what she wanted, if she wanted anything at all."

"I didn't. She gave me a look."

"That's exactly what I'm saying. Your heart is wide open to her," Sabrina finished as Dr. Chris began to rub the small of my back. I got what she was not so subtly hinting at.

Even Oakley, the woman I had intended to propose to, wasn't able to draw me out of my comfort zone like Dr. Chris could.

"Does she do that to you, Steve?" Dr. Chris asked.

"Since day one." He laughed.

"Really?" she followed again.

"Oh yeah," that was Steve's simple way of saying, without a shadow of a doubt that he had been open since before they officially met.

"Should we eat something?" Sabrina asked before the conversation got awkward.

"I can help you grab the food from the kitchen so they don't have to mask up, Sabrina," Steve offered. "Jax, come help us grab the food so we can eat out here."

Wingman 101. Give your boy a chance to step up to the plate. Steve was a pro. He stayed advancing around the bases so I could have an at bat. As they left, Sabrina cut me a look that said, "we're coming right back y'all."

Dr. Chris moved to help me arrange the chairs so there was still a bit of distance between them. I tried to sneak a kiss between furniture moving. She offered me her cheek, each time. And each time, it only further fueled the fire that was burning within me. Move a chair. Kiss her cheek. Slide the tables together. Kiss the other cheek. It was a tango that had me hooked. She only need look at me the wrong way and I was on my way to getting kicked out of Steve and Sabrina's house for eternity.

"Do you know how much I love you?" I asked Dr. Chris, right as someone stepped back outside carrying some of the food.

"No, how much, Charlie?" Steve asked, catching me off guard.

Dr. Chris, moved to the chair beside me. "Tell me later?"

"Certainly," I told her.

"How much?" Steve continued to joke as Sabrina and Jax came outside with the rest of the food.

I extended my arms wide towards Steve, and chuckled, "THIS MUCH, FRIEND!" prompting Jax to jump up for a hug. I had grown accustomed to not hugging kids, especially during a pandemic, but Jax didn't give me an opportunity to stop him, to turn away, or to tell him that I couldn't hug him because I didn't want to pass anything along to him. Instead, I just cherished the one hug that I'd received from someone other than Dr. Chris in the last month or so. Funny how things can change so easily. I didn't consider myself a hugger until they were no longer on the table - no longer safe.

As we tended to do, the four of us chatted away the daylight hours and lingered outside through the still of night. Dr. Chris and Steve traded barbs in much the same way as he did with everyone else that he cared about. She was officially part of the family. It wasn't that they didn't get along before, because they did. In fact, Steve was the one who facilitated our second meeting. But he didn't trade one two punches with just anyone. He and Oakley had a different type of edge in their interactions. Initially I thought it was part of his typical friendly jabs. Looking back on it now, neither of them were very friendly with each other. I had the chance to ask him about it that night and I found out that he never trusted Oakley.

"Why didn't you tell me that before I went and bought a ring?" I asked him as the two of us were washing dishes in the kitchen while the ladies relaxed outside.

"I figured she'd show herself at some point."

"She definitely did that."

"Plus, I figured maybe you saw something that I couldn't see."

"She was who you saw. Let me ask you about Dr. Chris though, since we're talking about people you didn't trust," I said, hoping he would understand where I was leaning.

"What about her?" Steve asked, unwilling to make an assumption about the question that was on my mind.

"Do you think..."

"Don't overthink it, Charlie."

"Overthink what?"

"This is her. I knew it when I met her, and you knew it when you met her too."

I nodded. Receiving just the confirmation that I needed to hear and understanding that she and I were connecting the way I thought we were. I'm not sure why I had questioned it. I could feel it in my gut. I knew it. It was just so unexpected. I hadn't known her for a full year yet, but my life had changed so much that I was almost unrecognizable. I had so much more joy and gratitude in my heart than I had before. I didn't want to miss something before we officially joined our lives together. I wanted to love her forever.

Dr. Chris:

Sabrina and I were treated to a dish free evening

to relax on the patio as the fellas took care of business in the kitchen. Charlie had been eyeing me all evening long. I couldn't tell if he was checking to see if I was okay, or if there was something else on his mind. I hoped that he wasn't having second thoughts. I wanted to love him forever. I had been trading jabs with Steve all evening, and I wondered if that had changed the way he saw me.

"I know Steve was peppering you with his replies and questions tonight. I hope it didn't bother you."

"Oh, I was okay with it. That's how my family rolls, so I was more than used to holding my own."

Sabrina laughed. "I think you did just fine."

"Do you think Charlie was okay with it?"

"Charlie, was admiring the way you held your own. The last one,"

"Oakley?"

"Yeah, she and Steve bumped heads on the regular. In fact, you're the only one that Steve has really approved of for Charlie, not that it matters. But, you know what I mean."

"I got you."

"So how are things with the wedding planning?"

"They're going. In fact, I think just about every decision has been made. We had anticipated Charlie's free time being cut in half, so we took care of the bulk decisions before he returned to the classroom. Thank goodness we did. Even the virtual classroom has been taxing on him - time and emotionally speaking."

"I wondered about that."

"He has a hard time turning it off. There's no separation anymore. Before, he used to drive to school and could leave it behind on his way home from work. Now, he closes his laptop, but he's still in the same space where he educates his students."

"Oh no."

"Yep. I thought we needed a vacation before. Turns out, we need a may need a mini-vacation every weekend. But where are we gonna go during a pandemic?"

"To the backyard," Sabrina laughed.

"That's about the only place we can go. I mean, it's been nice here, but there's always that lingering thought about whether or not I'm putting someone else at risk with my actions."

"I get it. I feel the same way, and we have Jax to think about too. We had to determine what his school option would look like for this year, and now that we're in it, it's really hard on him, all of us really. Steve is pitching in and helping out quite a bit, but we're not teachers. I want to keep him safe, but I also don't want him to fall behind because the two of us are not in a position to help support him the way he needs it."

"I understand the dilemma. It's such a hard spot to be in as a parent. Every decision you make is done with Jax in mind; his health, his future, his emotional and physical well-being. The right answer is the one you make, even if you second guess yourself."

"I just don't want to be the parent who screws up their kid."

"Trust me when I tell you that I've seen those parents come into work. You are not that parent."

Sabrina, started to shed a tear. It was the first time I'd seen her cry. It was the first time I'd seen her be vulnerable and emotional. It was the first time I'd seen her be anything other than superhuman. I wanted to hug her and let her know that I was with her, but the pandemic wouldn't let me be myself. So instead I reached out for her hand and squeezed it tight. Offering her love in the best way I knew how at the moment.

Steve and Charlie had finished washing the dishes

and joined us back out on the patio. Charlie, joked about us touching during a pandemic before he saw Sabrina's face. Steve sat down beside her, clueless as to what was going on with his wife. She tugged on his sleeve and he gazed upon her face.

"Oh, sorry, Sabrina!" he hurried through his lips, rushing to stand to his feet and lifting her from her seat as he rose. He wrapped her in his arms and held her softly. Her face buried in his chest, Sabrina gave Steve all of her body weight. Charlie held my hand and rubbed his thumb across the tops of my knuckles as the two of us gave them a bit of space to just be.

2020 was a rough year on all of us, and there was a silent acknowledgement that each of us was facing our own internal battles that others likely didn't know we were carrying. That was rough. It was exponentially hard on everyone, but love carried us through it all. Love from friends. Love from family. Love from ourselves. Without it, that would've been an unbearable year for us all. We all needed to lean on each other the way Sabrina leaned on Steve. I looked Charlie in his eyes, and nodded without any other words. He nodded in return. Ours was a look of acknowledgement, a look of affection, a look of love, and a look that said it was time to give them some space.

Charlie patted Steve on the back without speaking a single word and I did the same to Sabrina. Before they could move, the two of us slid out of the backyard through the gate, hopped in Chief, and headed home for the night. Neither of us said a word. Things had been heavy all day. The weather was unseasonably humid, and it seemed to mimic the political climate as well. Heavy pressure on all fronts. As if it were cued by God himself, the skies opened up on our drive home. A drenching rain poured from a seemingly cloud-free sky, like they were meant only to wash away the pain of the world. It rained the rest of the drive home and only got heavier as Charlie put his truck in park in the driveway. We continued to sit in silence, neither of us watching the rain, both of us watching each other. The water streaming over Chief sounded like a room full of students drumming their fingers on their desks. It was a relaxing sound and I started to lean my seat back and directed my gaze through the sunroof, towards the sky.

"Chris," Charlie began. I knew it must have been serious. He only dropped the Dr. from my name when he wanted me to know something significant.

I continued to point my gaze towards the sky, "Mm hmm?"

He spoke softly. "Tonight was interesting. It awakened something within me."

Interesting? I tried to turn towards Charlie as calmly as possible. "How so? What did it awaken?"

His face shifted from serious to adoration. "Chris," he paused, taking a minute to place his left hand over his heart. "I don't know if you know just how much I appreciate you."

"What do you mean, Charlie? You tell me - you show me every day."

"Every day?"

"Every day," I repeated.

"Watching you give Sabrina a space to be Sabrina instead of Super Sabrina, watching you hold your own with Steve, watching you with Jax, watching you not worry about where I was and whether or not you needed to be right by my side the whole time, I loved all of that. You just were. You've always felt like my family, but today more than ever, it felt like you've been in my life forever."

"Charlie."

"Every time I looked at you tonight, I wanted to tell you."

"I wondered if I'd done something wrong. Your face showed pensive but I couldn't tell if it was good or bad."

"Steve said the same thing when we were in the kitchen. He asked me if I was alright, then told me that he and Sabrina had been struggling being in the same space together without a break."

"I kind of sensed that. Sabrina didn't say anything about it, but she seemed more relaxed when it was just the two of us."

"I offered to watch Jax for a weekend so they could get some type of break. I know I should've spoken with you about it first, but-"

"No. I was thinking the same thing while we were there, but I just hadn't found an opportunity to talk to you about it."

The rain beat down on the roof of the truck, washing the leaves from the winshield as the skies continued to release their weight on the rest of us. Charlie leaned across the truck to kiss me, but his seatbelt caught him before he could make it to my face. He hustled through his struggle to unbuckle the belt and I opened the truck door, ready to hop out in the rain.

"Where are you going? Let me get the door!" he bounded out of his truck and hustled through the rain to my side of Chief, extending a hand to help me down. I waited for him, even though I didn't want to. I understood it was his way of demonstrating his love.

So I craned my neck for a kiss to thank him. Charlie obliged. There we stood, in the driveway, getting soaked from the rain that was sent to wash our troubles away. The droplets rolled down the curves of my face and cooled my skin. The shirt I was wearing began to cling to my back. He held my hand and led me to the backyard where our engagement gift awaited us. There we sat, already drenched, allowing the rain to cleanse our souls as we glided the night away.

The more time marched on and the closer we inched to the wedding date, the more Charlie and I leaned into strengthening our connection with each other. The more we leaned, my anxiety about messing up our relationship started to drift further and further away from my mind. I was so glad that I had him there with me to weather the storms of life. And, after our time with Williamsons that night, I was really looking forward to building our own family. I could finally envision them again, our kids. Two boys. One girl. I had stopped dreaming in June as the nightmares took over, but all of that was getting released.

That was thanks in part to the solo trip to the lake Charlie had encouraged me to take. It was a much needed break from all of the stress. I closed my eyes and drifted back to that day, the leaves applauding in the breeze as the winds picked up. Water broke along the rocks that littered the lake's shoreline as I sat, wrapped under a blanket, my knees tucked to my chest, shoes beside me, pondering about life; what is and what could be. My thoughts drifted back to him, always back to him. I envisioned his touch, his arms wrapped around me, providing shelter and warmth, and placed one hand on my heart as I tried to still my heartbeat. I could feel its echo pulsating through my back.

I'd come so far in such a reatively short period of time. That thought floored me as I nestled my head into the nook of Charlie's arm and tears began to mix in with the rain that streaked down my cheeks. An ominous clap of thunder rumbled in the distance as this natural affinity grew deep and cavernous for the man whose arms had become my refuge. I'd come so far.

Chapter 8
Autumn's Dawn

Charlie:

The beginning of September brought great challenges with it. Not just for Dr. Chris and I, but for our friends and family as well. We'd found ourselves as the spare wheel in an intimate moment for Steve and Sabrina and quietly excused ourselves so they could be with each other. The rain hit us hard, and I wondered how we were going to get home safely. Then I had a fleeting thought about how we were going to get into the house safely. More than anything though, there was an unspoken bond between the two of us as we sat still in the truck. I wondered what she was thinking about as she gazed across the cab at me. I loved her tremendously, but I wasn't sure she knew how much. Before I could stop it, my mouth just opened up and I started blabbing away all of my thoughts, including how I had offered the house as a space for Jax to hang for a weekend without talking to her about it first. I was anticipating a bit of friction, but instead I received more confirmation that she was my person.

As we kissed in the rain beside the truck, I could

feel my worries washing away. I laced my fingers between hers and led her to the backyard so we could continue the tradition of our nightly gilder time. This woman was the center of my world and I wanted her to know it, to never question it. So we sat together on the glider my parents gifted us and allowed the rain to continue to wash over us. There was something almost therapeutic about it. I held her in my arms and we snuggled together in the rain. I didn't know who I was anymore. I was myself, but I felt like a better version of me. Charlie 2.0 maybe? All I knew was that I was enjoying every day that I got with her. She was such a free spirit once she granted herself the grace to trust herself, but I don't know how many people would be able to guess that about her. I got to see all versions of Dr. Chris, and for that I felt lucky.

As Summer drew to a close and Autumn came in with her chilly days and longer nights, Sabrina and Steve asked to cash in on that child free weekend I had offered. Dr. Chris had spent a few nights that week, getting the guest bedroom ready for Jax. I thought it was already prepared for a guest, but by the time she was done adding her touches, I wanted to stay in it myself. My house was starting to feel more and more like home, little by little. She was adding her little touches here and there, and I loved discovering them. Her blender, tucked away in the corner of my kitchen. Her stand mixer, hidden in a previously empty cabinet that she had converted to hold this pneumatic stand mixer lift. *When did she have time to install that?* Her towels and mine co-mingled with each other in the towel closet. Her side of the closet began to fill out even more. Her hair products in the bathroom cabinet - so many hair products. Some of her books on the shelves beside my books. I even started taking my shoes off at the door when I came in, the way we used to do at the condo. Our lives had become enmeshed and I welcomed every new discovery I stumbled across, even the loose strands of hair that seemed to be sprinkled around the house. With so many of her things here, I wondered what could've possibly been left at the condo.

"Do you think Jax would like -" Pick a noun, any noun and insert it at the end of that sentence. She was nervous about Jax joining us for the weekend, and she wanted so much to make him comfortable. I reminded her that her niece and nephew had stayed with her before. "I was nervous then too. But these are my sister's kids. I had a bit more wiggle room with them. I don't know Jax, yet."

"You have a lifetime to get to know him, Dr. Chris. Just be yourself. He already loves you."

"How do you know that Charlie?" she asked, her voice and eyebrows full of concern.

I held her arms and looked her directly in the eyes, "Because you took care of him when he broke his arm. If you were a mean doctor, you'd know it already." She nodded.

I'm not sure when it happened, but it felt like the two of us had switched roles. I used to be the over-thinker and I learned to let go by watching her navigate through life. Now, here she was, stressing over every small detail to compensate for her nerves as she became the resident over-thinker.

"What would help you feel more comfortable?"

"I think I'll probably be like this until he gets here," she snickered, acknowledging her own over-stimulation. I kissed her on the temple and asked her to let me know if she came up with something I could do to help.

The weekend came for Jax to join us. In a normal year, I would've just taken him home with me from school. But Steve dropped him off, looking mighty dapper.

"He has everything he could possibly need in his bag. I tried to get him to pack less, but he's convinced he's going to be bored here."

"Dad!" Jax barked embarrassed to have been told on.

"What's my phone number Jax?" Steve asked, then listened as Jax repeated it back to him. "And your mother's?" Again he listened as Jax began to recite his mother's phone number. "How about your Godfather?"

"Why do I need to call him? I'll be with him all weekend?"

"What if you get lost?"

"I'll call you and mom!"

"No buddy, not this weekend. You'll call Mr. Charlie."

Jax recited my phone number with a spiteful look adorning his little face, as if to prove to his father that he knew it.

"I knew you had it. We'll see you on Sunday. Okay bud?"

Jax had already plopped down on the sofa, "Okay Dad!"

"Well, I think that's the best I'm gonna get today," Steve joked.

"You're looking mighty spiffy, sir."

"Yep. We have a whole thing planned."

"Yeah?"

"Mm hmm," he said, adjusting his bow tie and raising his eyebrows.

"Alright," I said dapping him up.

"See you Sunday, bro."

"Sunday."

As soon as I closed the front door, I was met with an invasive question from my Godson.

"Mr. Charlie, where's Dr. Chris?

"She's at work, Jax. She'll give me a call when she's on -" My phone buzzed. It was her.

"Hey Sugarplum!"

"Hey Charlie, I'm on my way home."

"Okay, well, Jax and I will be right here waiting for you when you arrive."

"He's there already?"

"He is."

"I was going to-"

"IS THAT DR. CHRIS?" Jax shouted as I was on the phone.

"It is, buddy."

"Can I talk to her?"

"Sure, hold on," I said to Jax before turning my attention to Dr. Chris. "I'm gonna put you on speakerphone okay, Sugarplum?"

"Okay," she nervously replied.

"Hi Sugarplum!" Jax shouted towards the phone.

"Jax, you can't call her that. Only I can call her that."

"Okay Mr. Charlie. Hi, Dr. Chris!"

"Hi Jax! Is Charlie taking good care of you?"

"I don't know yet. I just got here."

"Oh okay."

"Are you on your way home?"

"I am, buddy. I'll be there soon."

"Okay."

"Do you need anything?"

"Ummm. Chicken nuggets?"

"I think we have some there."

"We do."

"With fries?"

"Sure do!" Dr. Chris replied.

"Okay, that's all I need. I'll see you soon."
"Okay, Jax."
"Be careful!"
"Will do, buddy."
"Okay, Sugarplum!"
"Jax," I firmly replied.
"Sorry. Okay, Dr. Chris."
"I'll see you soon, Dr. Chris," I told her.
"Okay, Sweetheart."

She must have only been a few minutes away from the house when she called, because she was at the house in no time. Jax, who had been keeping an eye on the driveway from the front window, met her at the door. Not knowing what kind of day she'd had, I wouldn't let him go outside to greet her, so he was bouncing behind the storm door, waving in her direction. I watched from the front window as she got out of the car with her bag and waved at Jax. He met her with a big hug as she stepped inside the foyer.

"Hi Dr. Chris!"

She stooped down to his level to give him a hug and looked at me incredulously. I couldn't explain it if I tried. My own Godson, who brushed right on by me, was hugging my fiancée like SHE was his godparent.

Dr. Chris:

I didn't know how to explain it. Work had been rough, and Jax was already at the house. I drove home that evening, wondering if I'd have time to destress so I wouldn't give my frustration to anyone else. But before I could fully step into the house, Jax was there, hugging my stress away. It was the strangest thing. I looked up at Charlie, who was wearing a sappy smile on his face, which instantaneously put me in a good mood. My two guys for the weekend, had greeted me at the door and I wondered if this is what it felt like to be married with kids.

I stood up to greet Charlie with a hug, and he kissed me on my temple.

"How was your day, Sugarplum?"

"It was rough but it's much better now," I said rubbing Jax's head as he watched the two of us love on each other.

He laughed, "You guys kiss each other a lot."

"She's my bride, so I get to do that."

"When I find a bride, can I do that?" Jax asked Charlie.

"As long as you're old enough to find a bride," he replied.

"How old is old enough?" Jax asked excitedly.

"What's with all the questions about finding a bride?" Charlie asked his Godson, who simply shrugged his shoulders.

"Jax," I began. "Do you have a girlfriend?"

"Dr. Chris!" Jax shouted.

"So, is that a yes?" I asked him.

"It must be," Charlie said. "He just got so quiet."

"I see," I said.

"Well, Jax," Charlie continued. "Let's go to the kitchen to make some dinner. I'll show you how to take care of your bride."

"Okay," Jax said as he trailed closely behind Charlie.

I headed upstairs to the master bedroom to get changed for the evening before being called downstairs for dinner. Charlie had asked Jax to set the table and gave him the freedom to use whatever he wanted for serve ware. We had multiple forks, mixed plates and cups, and paper towels draped across the plates. It was the cutest thing I'd seen in a while. I heard Charlie whisper something to Jax before he came running out of the kitchen.

"Dinner is served madam!"

"Oh, great!"

"I'm going to get your chair," he told me before he pulled it away from the table.

I sat down and held my breath as Jax pushed the chair up to meet the table, while I was still sitting in it. As he ran back into the kitchen to grab some food, I quietly and quickly separated my abs from the table edge before he could return. He and Charlie returned with the food and the three of us ate chicken nuggets, fries, and carrot sticks for dinner. We washed the dishes together and then plopped down on the couch for a quick movie with Jax, before it was time for him to head to bed. He lay down on the bed in the guest room and asked that we cracked the door so we could hear him if he needed something.

I got all the way to the base of the steps when I heard him call for me. I tilted my head towards the room, "Yes, Jax?"

"Could you read to me?"

"Certainly. Do you have a book?"

"There's one in my bag. I'll grab it."

I ascended the stairs, uncertain what book I was about to read, but ready to help Jax get comfortable for sleep. We read it together three times. The first time, I read it to him. The second time, he read it to me. The last time, we read it to each other. By the time we got to the last line, he yawned through it. By the time I turned off the lights, he was out.

I closed the door, leaving it slightly cracked and turned to find Charlie sitting at the top of the stairs, gazing in my direction.

"What?" I asked him.

"Nothing," he said.

"What?" I asked again.

"You're so patient with him," he smiled. "I almost fell asleep listening to your reading voice."

"Yeah, right!" I joked with him.

"Are you ready to get in some glider time?" he whispered.

"We can't leave the house, with him in here."

Charlie held up a white object, "I put a baby monitor in there. We can take this outside with us and hear if he needs something."

The thought of Charlie protecting both our tradition and Jax, set off a switch inside me. I looked at him lovingly and helped him up off the steps.

"Let's go outside to the glider, Sweetheart," I whispered in his ear.

"You don't have to tell me twice, lady," he said, quietly kissing me on the temple.

We inched down the steps, taking care to avoid the creaky 3rd step, then eased out of the house to the backyard to get in our time on the glider for the evening. We talked about work and the challenges and wins for our respective days, but most of our time was spent chatting about Jax and how comfortable he was around us. It eased my nerves to see him open up to me so much this evening.

"When he was ready for his bedtime story, he asked for you," Charlie reminded me. "Not his Godfather, who's been in his life since the day he was born. He asked for you, Chris."

"You jealous, Charlie?"

"Only of Jax. You don't read any bedtime stories to me!"

"I'll read you a bedtime story if you want, Sweetheart."

"Read me one tonight?" he playfully whimpered. I nodded in his direction.

"You got it."

Charlie:

Friday night was great. Dr. Chris was amazing with Jax. No shocker there. Her heart was so big that there wasn't a doubt in my mind that she'd be great with him. I sat outside the guest room and listened as she encouraged Jax to read to her, helping him sound out the words that challenged him, affirming him when he sounded them out on his own and got them right. As I sat outside the room, I envisioned her doing the same with our children. I was looking forward to that chapter of our lives, whenever it came, but I was fully enjoying this moment in front of us.

We kept our evening tradition alive and wound down from the day's events with a few stolen moments together, underneath a blanket, on the glider. Before turning in for bed, I cajoled Dr. Chris into reading me a bedtime story. She pulled up a story on her phone and read it the same way to me that she had to Jax. I snuggled in beside her and fell asleep as her soft voice soothed my heart. I'm not sure how Jax made it through three readings. He must have been fighting sleep. I on the other hand, gave her my complete attention and enjoyed the moment of comfort that came right before slumber.

Saturday morning came and Jax woke up before me. He knocked on the bedroom door and called for me.

I opened the door and stepped into the hallway.

"Good morning, buddy."

"Good morning, Mr. Charlie," Jax grumbled.

"Did you sleep okay?"

"Yes I did." He nodded.

"Are you hungry?"

"Yes, sir."

"Should we fix some pancakes for breakfast?"

"I like pancakes!"

"Pancakes it is. Why don't you head to the bathroom and I'll meet you downstairs in the kitchen. Go quietly, buddy. Let's see if we can surprise Dr. Chris with breakfast in bed."

"Okay," he whispered as he shuffled down the hallway toward the bathroom.

I peeked in the bedroom to give Dr. Chris a heads up that we'd be back with breakfast so she could make sure she was decent.

"Okay, Charlie," she said, drifting back to sleep before I could fully close the door. I hoped she would remember this conversation when I opened the door again for breakfast.

I put Jax on the pancake mix while I lay strips of bacon across the griddle.

"How are those measurements coming along, buddy?"

"Okay I think."

"You think? This is our breakfast we're talking about here, Jax," I told my Godson as he giggled behind me.

"Yes, I think."

"Okay," I said turning around, "let's check out those ingredients."

He and I ran through each ingredient on the recipe, checking off the ones that he had already added to the mix.

"What's buttermilk?" Jax asked, his little face all scrunched up in the center.

"We don't have any buttermilk, but we can sub in

some milk with lemon juice."

"EWW GROSS!"

"Let's call it our secret ingredient, okay?"

Jax stuck his tongue out and shook his head from side to side, like that was the most grotesque thing he'd ever heard. "I'm not telling Dr. Chris that there's lemon juice in her pancakes. She'll never eat them!"

"That's why it's called a SECRET ingredient, pal."

"Got it."

I put the pancakes on the griddle after the bacon was finished cooking and asked Jax if he'd pour some of Dr. Chris' juice from the fridge into 3 juice glasses.

"What kind of juice is this, Mr. Charlie?"

I eyed it, then sniffed it, and came up with nothing. "I'm not sure Jax."

Jax looked at it, then sniffed it and poured it into our glasses. "It just smells like juice to me," he said, shrugging his shoulders after putting down the larger carafe. The two of us continued prepping breakfast and I pulled a tray down from the top of the refrigerator. We loaded it with her plates of food and the juice and Jax followed me upstairs to knock on the bedroom door for me.

"Dr. Chris?" he paused, waiting for an answer before knocking again. "Dr. Chris, we fixed you breakfast!" Jax exuberantly announced through the door. Still no reply. He knocked again. "Sugarplum," Jax said, pretending to lower his voice to be me. "I have some pancakes for you." He snickered as Dr. Chris asked us to come in.

She was still in bed, the covers pulled up to her chest, pajamas still present, wiping sleep from her eyes.

"I'm so grateful for the two of you," she said as I waltzed into the room behind Jax. "Thank you for this. Where's your food?"

"Well, us guys are going to eat in the kitchen this morning," I told her as I sat the tray on her lap and placed a kiss on her temple before unleashing my resonantly whispered, "Good morning, Sugarplum" in her ear.

"Good morning, Charlie," she smiled back at me.

"There's lemon juice in your pancakes!" Jax shouted like the words had been burning his throat.

"Mmmm. Sounds delicious, Jax!" she joked.

"You'll have to let us know when you finish eating," I told her. She nodded in reply before asking if we could bless the food together.

"Jax, will you do the honor?" she asked him.

He hit us with the God is Great, classic and we both said Amen.

Dr. Chris:

They brought me Charlie's famous fluffy pancakes, bacon, some fresh fruit and juice. Breakfast in bed. I was about to get up and meet them downstairs before I remembered Charlie peeking in earlier to let me know that they were going to bring me breakfast in bed. I initially thought it might have been a dream, but I heard the excitement in Jax's voice as he continued to exclaim just how much he thought I was going to love getting breakfast in bed, so I stayed put.

Just as I had finished eating, I heard another knock on the bedroom door. It was Charlie, coming to retrieve the tray. He and I had a stolen moment before I went to get cleaned up for the day. Jax had requested a board game filled day and the three of us had plenty of time to get the competition rolling.

Charlie wasn't very competitive, but I'll admit that I had a bit of an edge when it came to competitions. Good thing Jax was a child or he would've seen a different side of the doctor. We started with the longest game in the history of board games. I've never seen anyone actually finish a game in its entirety. Usually someone turns over their properties and quits, or things erupt in anger. Jax was just as serious and patient as could be. I had long sold all of my assets to him, but Charlie was hanging in there. By the time they finished the game it was time for lunch. Hours had passed. Hours playing one board game that I vowed to retire from this household after Jax won. Charlie and Jax headed to the backyard after lunch and played outside as I got our roast chicken dinner started in the slow cooker. I watched the two of them playing outside in the backyard and envisioned Charlie out there with our children someday. He caught a glimpse of me in the window and flashed his charming smile in my direction. Now that had seen it, I couldn't unsee it. Now that I had felt the anticipation aligned with our future, I didn't want anything else - no matter how terrifying the unknown felt.

One of the things this pandemic exposed was our frailty and vulnerability as human beings. No matter how much we plan to create the perfect foundation to build upon, it only takes one thing to shatter the base and cause everything to come crumbling down. I had watched the story of a young mother trying to cope with the loss of her spouse after they had succumbed to the impact of the virus. She was abruptly left to raise 3 children with the help of her friends and family. Nobody planned for any of this, but life sometimes hands you a 1-2 punch. The thought of something like that happening to us, caused me some pause. But I leaned into the feelings that could have easily dissuaded me from the possibility of something so great.

Charlie and I had chosen each other from the end of our first date. It was a choice to explore what was brewing underneath the surface and give it space to see if it was worth tending to. We actively chose each other every day, even when it was hard because of life's surprises. But choosing to love him was an easy decision to make, even when he was being stubborn. The two of us made a conscious choice to stay open and trust each other, to extend unconditional love and forgiveness - and man did I need my fair share of that. We chose every day to make an effort to keep things light and flirty, while building an intimate connection with each other. We stumbled into this connection, but we chose to stand with each other every day. It was greater than any love I had experienced before. I didn't know what to do with it except continue to invite it into my life, and to do that, I had to get out of my own way.

So I smiled back at Charlie as he returned to playing catch with Jax, and eventually, I joined the two of them outside - bringing water with me, because that's how I watched my mom love on my dad, Vonne and I. My heart was full.

"Water break!" I announced as I stepped out on the patio. Jax hustled to the table to grab a glass, thanking me between hearty gulps. Charlie moseyed over to the table and did the same, eyeing me as if he were frustrated that I was lifting a finger. It was a rare opportunity for me to demonstrate my love in action at Charlie's house. So I stuck out my tongue in his direction and watched him roll his eyes at me in reply.

"Dr. Chris, do you play catch too?" Jax asked.

"I haven't played in a long time, buddy. But yes, I can throw and catch, if that's what you're asking."

"You should challenge her to see who's better, Mr. Charlie."

"I don't think that's such a good idea, Jax," I said.

"Why not? Do you think you're going to lose?"

"Not at all. I just haven't thrown anything in a very long time, Jax."

"I can show you how to throw again if you want?"

"Okay, Jax. Let's go."

We spent the next 30 minutes throwing the ball back and forth, Jax in teacher mode and me, pretending like I was learning from him. Charlie sat on the glider and watched it all go down. Before too long, Jax had declared that I was officially ready for the challenge. "C'mon Mr. Charlie!"

Charlie stood to his feet and listened as Jax laid down the ground rules. "No cheating!" Jax said as he looked in Charlie's direction. The two of us eyed each other and my competitive side began to creep out. Jax gave us 2 minutes to throw as many perfect passes as we could complete. He asked Charlie to go first, which was fine by me, as that gave me the chance to know what I needed to beat instead of setting the bar for Charlie. He was calm, cool, and accurate. Leaving me with 2 minutes to hit a goal of 10 to tie and 11 to win. Before he started the clock, Jax moved the target closer to me, prompting an outcry from Charlie.

"So this is how we're playing, Jax?"

"What? She just learned how to throw again!"

"You can move it back, Jax. We don't want him to think we're cheaters," I confidently said.

"Okay, I'll move it back, Dr. Chris."

Jax moved the target and set the timer. "Go!" I watched the look on Charlie's face after I nailed the target with my first throw. After two in a row he began to nod. By the time I hit 5 in a row, he knew he was in trouble.

"How much time is left?" I asked Jax as I nailed my 6th attempt as well.

"It's only been 30 seconds!" Jax shouted as he

jumped up and down. I slowed my pace but still hit the 10th target just after a minute had passed. Charlie inched closer to me to watch my next attempt. I missed then glanced in his direction. Jax ran to Charlie's side, attempting to push him out of the way so I had a bit more space to work.

"It's okay, Jax. Let him stand where he wants to stand," I assured him. Jax nodded and backed up.

"You have 30 seconds left!"

Charlie stood directly behind me, not touching me, but still close enough to do so. He whispered three words in my ear, attempting to distract me. I studied the target, raised my arm, and with 10 seconds to spare, turned to face Charlie. "You promise?"

He nodded. I let it fly and nailed my last throw.

"Let me know when you want to cash in on that."

"Sunday evening," I said checking out the look on his face. He nodded, looking a bit sheepish.

"Sunday evening it is, my Dear."

"You won!!" Jax shouted as he came running over to congratulate me before turning his attention to Charlie and challenging him to the same competition.

Saturday night after dinner, movies, his shower and bedtime stories, Jax hugged the two of us and asked when he could come visit again.

"Anytime buddy," Charlie told him. I nodded. I welcomed his spirit in the house. He brought a layer of levity and light to our world. It was a much needed break and a welcome addition to the energy between Charlie and I. We had a chance to work together to take care of someone other than ourselves and I was surprised at just how strong our communication was. As we sat on the glider that night, Charlie mentioned the same sentiment to me.

"I wasn't expecting to feel this deeper connection with you today," I told him.

"Me either, but I like it," he began as we continued to glide away in my favorite place. "Every day. Deeper still and I'm loving every surprising second of it." He gazed deeply into my eyes and shook his head at me. It was the return of his 'how did she get here,' look.

"What, Charlie?" I asked, hoping he would explain what he was thinking.

His smile widened as he ran his fingers through my hair, "I don't know how to say it."

"Say what?" I asked, hoping to be let in on his grand secret.

He shrugged, "Just loving life. That's all." I nodded in return, accepting his answer and not pushing for more. But rather, sitting in contentment, basking in the love that he and I shared and were building upon day by day. If we could have run off and eloped at that moment, I would have gladly welcomed the opportunity to do so.

"I love you deeply, Charlie," I told him as I stretched out on the glider to enjoy the quiet of that chilly autumn night. I wondered what, if anything, could change that.

Chapter 9

Halloween

Charlie:

Dr. Chris had been such a trooper, hanging in there with me during my struggles with online learning and helping to keep Jax occupied when I ran out of things for us to do on his weekend visits throughout the month of October. Seeing her with him just solidified my desire to spend the rest of my life working to make her smile and craft our slice of the world together.

I tried everything in my power to be that person for her. I truly did. But sometimes the best intentions lead to unforeseen circumstances. We had a rule about who took care of the other depending on whose space we were in. Since we had been spending the bulk of our time at the house instead of her condo, it meant that I was shouldering the majority of the work - willingly I might add, but still taking care of it and her nonetheless. I hadn't realized what kind of impact that would have.

There were moments when she would sneak to wash the dishes and I'd get on her about our "rule." There were times when she would start to prepare dinner and I'd be frustrated about it. Again, it was only because I wanted to take care of her. But I soon found out just how much damage I had done.

We were on the glider one evening and she was relaxing in my arms, cozy and snuggled up under the wool blanket we had migrated from her condo closet.

"Charlie, can I ask you a question?" Her tone was serious and I instantly had a knot in my stomach.

"You can ask me anything, Sugarplum," I replied.

"Anything?"

"You're my bride. You can ask me anything." She cracked a smile, but was still serious nonetheless. I hoped it wasn't as serious as her face hinted at, but I braced for the worst.

"Can we talk about the rule?"

"What rule?" it truly had slipped my mind.

"Whomever's place we're at...that rule."

Still unsure of where this was going, I hesitated, "Sure."

She was quiet - unusually so.

"I sometimes don't feel like I have a place here. Like I'm a guest."

That's certainly not what I was expecting to hear.

"But your stuff is almost all over here."

"I know it is, but I've found myself thinking about taking some of it back little by little."

My body was rigid. Stiff as a board. I was paralyzed with fear. "Why would you do that?"

"I just feel like I don't belong here, Charlie. I love this, our evening glides. I love spending time with you. I love you. I love us." I was listening to her words and having trouble comprehending how she could feel like she didn't belong. "I want nothing more than to start our lives together, but-"

But?

"-I don't feel like I'm given the space to demonstrate my love to you the way I want to when I'm here."

I hadn't seen that coming either. I nearly whispered to her, "What do you mean?"

"I love that you want to take care of me because we're in your space, Charlie. But at some point, as we were moving my stuff in, little by little, I had hoped that it would become our space and by default, that rule that we have would go out the window."

"Chris, I love you. I just wanted to show you that. I wanted you to know it. I didn't want you to have any questions."

"Charlie, I want to do the same. But every time you stop me from taking care of something, you rob me of the opportunity to do the same thing that you wish to do for me. You stop me from doing things I naturally do to demonstrate my love. Then it feels like I'm not able to be a true partner in this relationship."

"I didn't think about it like that. That's not what I want. We're in this together."

"Sometimes it feels like you're in this to demonstrate that you're a good guy. I don't know if that's what you're doing, but that's how it feels. But at what point do I get to feel like I'm your partner in this?"

"I'm sorry, Chris. How do we find a balance here? I don't want to stop taking care of you."

"Don't chastise me for trying to take care of things around the house. Allow me to demonstrate my love for you to you - directly."

"I guess I can-"

"Charlie."

"Okay. I can do my best to-"

"Charlie."

"I'll catch myself." I paused, reflecting on her words. "Why didn't you say anything to me about this before?"

"I tried to. You were too caught up in your own chivalry to hear me."

How did I miss it? She tried to tell me. I was stuck in my own head.

"Are we okay, Charlie?"

"Yeah, of course, Sugarplum."

"You sure?"

"I'm just going back over every time I've stopped you from taking care of me."

"Don't focus on -"

"It was a lot, wasn't it?"

"Can we move forward from this point and not look back? We can't change any of that."

"Yeah." I said I could, but I found myself steeping in that moment. Lost in my thoughts, I gazed at the same spot on the patio long and hard enough to bore a hole in it, and I didn't know how to stop.

We rocked on the glider for another 10 minutes or so before she asked if I was ready for bed. She looked at me with concern. I didn't know how to move forward. I didn't want to say or do something wrong and I was hyper focused on messing up, which typically meant that I would eventually mess something up.

Dr. Chris:

It took a lot for me to tell him how I felt, but I knew I needed to say it. His mom's powerful message had stuck with me. It owed it to myself to honor how I was feeling, and I owed it to Charlie to be honest with him. I knew he was an over-thinker, so I tried to be very specific in the words that I chose, but somehow it still felt like I hadn't communicated well enough. The two of us sat in uncomfortable silence on the glider for at least 20 minutes. I'd asked if we could move forward together and not look back and he agreed to it. I couldn't help but feel the tension that gathered in the crisp fall air that evening. I peered up at him to see if he was okay and his worry lines were dancing across his forehead. Hoping to break his concentration, I asked if he was ready for bed. He looked like he was afraid to move so I lifted the wool blanket that had been providing a cozy shelter and stood to my feet, draping it around my shoulders like a cape. I stretched out a hand for Charlie to take so the two of us could go inside and get ready to call it a night.

We helped each other into the house, locking the doors behind us and turning down the house for the night. Shades drawn. Lights off. Upstairs to the bedroom to retire for the evening. He was stoic, standing strong and fierce, but I guessed that there was turmoil brewing inside. I rubbed his back as we brushed our teeth together in the bathroom. He nodded to acknowledge my presence then rinsed his mouth like everything was normal. I did the same and changed into my pajamas in the bedroom. Charlie leaned on the bathroom doorframe, peering into the bedroom after he had finished brushing his teeth. I smiled at him as I climbed into bed.

"I'm sorry, Chris."

"For what, Charlie?"

"Everything."

"What is everything?"

"Well, not accepting your love, getting silent."

I nodded towards him and patted the side of the bed where I was laying. Charlie stood upright and gingerly walked towards the bed, his eyebrows raised as though he were asking for forgiveness. I patted the mattress again and asked him to sit down. He obliged and I reached for his closest hand, intertwining our fingers together. I didn't say a single word, just gazed into his eyes and allowed them to communicate how I was feeling. I loved, Charlie with my entire heart and just thinking about it brought a grin to my face. I nodded reassuringly.

He cleared his throat and then spoke in a near whisper. "We were supposed to talk about Hope Garden's costume thing tonight, Chris."

"You're right. We were," I affirmed, still gazing at him lovingly.

"Do you want to talk about it before we go to sleep?" he asked attentively.

"We don't have to," I offered, still fondly checking out his orbs.

His stare was passionate and intense. It penetrated every crevice within my heart and soul. "I don't want us to forget to come back to it."

I fought to catch my breath as his round-eyed gaze shook my steadiness. I was glad I was already laying down. "We won't do that, I promise."

"Okay," he said with hesitation.

"Kiss me goodnight?" I asked, to let him know that I was ready to turn in for the night. He eased in slowly, pausing to rest his forehead on mine. It was endearing and loving, and I was content allowing that to be our goodnight kiss for the evening. It was far more intimate than some of our quick pecks goodnight.

He whispered softly, "I love you, Sugarplum."

"I love you deeply, Charlie." I could barely get the words out before he cupped my face and kissed me gently. In that moment I felt seen and safe. I thought I was sleepy, but my mind had been changed.

Charlie:

I was so anxious about whether or not I'd been giving her the opportunity to love me that I was ready for the day to be over. I was seriously looking forward to the new sunrise, then she extended some grace, so much grace. I didn't know how else to thank her, so I kissed her in much the same way she had kissed me at the lake.

When I opened my eyes the next morning I felt like the luckiest man alive. I lay beside her, watching her unknowingly bathing in the last bits of moonlight that were peeking into our bedroom window. I was grateful that it was October, that meant that The Fresh Grind was selling cider again. I know we were trying to spend as much time at home as possible, but I placed an order for pickup on the app and took the short drive downtown for a curbside pickup - still in my pajamas.

By the time I returned, it was just about time for her alarm to sound. So I was trying to be as quiet as I could, in case she was catching those last few winks of sleep. I closed the front door and removed my boots and coat, then slowly snuck up the stairs, being careful to avoid the squeaky spots. I cracked the bedroom door open just as her alarm began to sound. She stretched her body into strange contortions as she began the process of waking herself up.

"Good morning, Sugarplum," I said with a perma-grin.

She yawned and cooed, "Good morning, Sweetheart. You're already up?" she asked as she reached for her glasses, placing them on her face and warming up her eyes through rapid blinks.

"I am," I said simply.

She patted the bed. "Come lay here in love with me for a few more minutes?"

I nodded, the piping hot order from The Fresh Grind, still tucked behind my back. The closer I got to the bed, the more suspicious she became.

"Why are your hands behind your back?"

I shrugged.

"Charlie, are you okay?"

I nodded.

"What are you doing?"

"It's October and we haven't had any of this yet," I said, raising two hot apple ciders each with a spoonful of sugarplums.

"Charlie, where did you get those from?"

"The Fresh Grind. I placed a curbside order."

A smile began to grace her face as I handed her one of the to-go cups.

"Thank you, sir."

I nodded and kissed her on the cheek, sitting beside her on the bed before taking a sip of my cider.

She shook her head at me and took a sip of her cider.

"What?" I asked her.

She continued to shake her head no.

"There's something."

She shrugged. "Just waking up like this - Charlie, I appreciate you so much."

I nodded. "Likewise, my Dear." I loved watching her face light up. "So let's talk about this Hope Gardens thing."

"So early in the morning?"

"Yes ma'am."

"I guess we can talk about it now," she said sipping more of her cider. "The hospital," she yawned, "is trying to find ways to celebrate Halloween with the children without bringing too many people into the actual walls of Hope Gardens. Still trying to minimize exposure and risk for everyone, you know?"

"Mm hmm. What did y'all come up with?"

"I'd love to see a virtual costume party or something similar to that."

"I think that's a great idea."

"You do?"

"Yeah, is there a way to stream it into everyone's rooms?"

"Probably. I haven't gotten that far yet."

"What else would people do there?"

"I'm thinking they could trick-or-treat from breakout room to breakout room or something like that."

"You're giving me ideas for what we could do with the kids at school. Thanks!"

"What?"

"Yeah, I was already going to be dressed up for the day's lessons, but this could give us a 'party' option."

"When you figure out the details, would you mind sharing them with me?" she laughed.

"I'd be happy to help once you and your team figure out the details."

"I'll probably be taking you up on that, Charlie. I'll even pay you for it," she winked.

"You're a mess, woman," I chuckled as I rose from the bed. I leaned my cup towards her for a celebratory "clink," even offering a "Cheers to a great day." as our ciders connected. "I'm gonna go get ready."

She giggled. "Okay, Charlie. While you're doing that, I'm going to enjoy the warmth of the bed for a few more minutes."

"Okay. Don't go back to sleep. I'm not coming back in here to wake you up again like I did yesterday or last week, or the week before that."

With her eyes closed and her cup of cider resting against her sternum, she laughed, "Okay Charles Lane."

"Oop, did she just use my government name? I know, she didn't just call me that," I pretended to be aghast. "Go ahead and test your luck madam," I laughed.

Starting the morning with a cider with sugarplums brought out a different side of Dr. Chris. I liked it. I made a mental note to plan for this more regularly - at least once per month if I could swing it.

In the meantime, Dr. Chris and I had the chance to do some deep planning for both her costume party and the one for the elementary school. She asked if I would be willing to "attend" their virtual party with her, and I told her that I'd be wherever she needed me to be. We only had to figure out what our costumes would be. I loved that she trusted me enough to go along with my wild ideas.

Dr. Chris:

I loved that he trusted me enough to let go. His eyes were softer than I'd ever seen them. It was rare for him to willingly give up control. I guessed that he must have taken my words to heart. Watching Charlie encourage me to lead was something else. I told him what I needed help with and he stepped up to offer support where he could. I also offered the wildest suggestions for Halloween costumes that I could think of.

"Care Bears?"

"Hmm...there's a thought."

"Adam and Eve?"

"Now those would be some interesting costumes. Not much to wear I wouldn't think."

"Riiiight. How about a matador and a bull?"

"I see where you're going with that one."

"Frankenstein and the Bride of Frankenstein?"

"Getting warmer. How would the children respond to me dressed as Frankenstein?"

"Might be a bit scary."

"Mmm hmm."

"How about if I dress as a pilot and you dress as a flight attendant?"

"That could work."

"Mary Poppins and Burt?"

Charlie's gaze shifted. There was possibility written on his face, but no words escaped his mouth.

"Woody and Jessie?"

"There's a snake in my..."

"Charlie!"

He laughed with a rascally expression, "Boot...in my boot. What were you thinking ma'am?"

"Milk and Cookies?"

"I think I like where you're going here."

"Salt and Pepper?"

"Wait, like the condiments or like the Rap Duo?"

"The former, Charlie," I said matter of factly before turning to the next option. "Peanut Butter and Jelly?"

"It's peanut butter jelly time. Peanut butter jelly time."

I shook my head at the song and dance combination that was taking place in the living room. Charlie is an all or nothing type of man. If he's going to dance, it's all out.

I attempted to change the costume,"Two Cheerleaders?"

"Peanut butter, jel-ay - , peanut butter, jel-ay -" he shouted, still dancing.

"How about if we try a-"

"Peanut butter-jelly-peanut butter-jelly-peanut butter-jelly-with-a-baseball-bat!"

I shook my head again and tried to ignore him, but I think that fueled his passion even more. He leaned in front of me and continued singing.

"Peanut butter-jelly-peanut butter-jelly-peanut butter-jelly-with-a-baseball-bat!"

I tried to fight back my laughter, but there was nothing on earth that made me feel more gleeful than having the man that I love attempting to make me laugh. He would stop at nothing until I cracked a smile and that's just what he got. It started with a sly smile through pursed lips, then it began to break in the corners of my mouth. Before I knew it, I was chortling as he kept his solo dance party going, beckoning me to join him.

"Peanut butter, jel-ay - , peanut butter, jel-ay -"

It was futile for me to pretend I didn't want to join in on the fun. "Peanut butter jelly with a baseball bat!"

The two of us danced around like two carefree souls shouting out the lyrics to that silly song. As Charlie continued to go, I asked him if we had a winner. He nodded, "I think so."

"Now the better question. Who gets to be the peanut butter and who gets to be the jelly?"

"Well," he said, finally slowing down his sweat inducing dance. "You're sweet, so maybe you're the jelly."

"Kinda cheesy sir."

"You liked it. I can see it in your face." He was right, but I feigned shock instead of acknowledging that.

With our costumes decided, I found my way to the kitchen to prepare my lunch for the day. That was mid-October, and we didn't speak about the details again after that day. I only knew that Charlie was going to take care of getting or creating the costumes for us. I had no idea what else would be needed of me.

Charlie:

I had worked through the details of her virtual Halloween party for work, and those for my school's virtual party. They were fairly similar so I mostly needed to focus on one and then duplicate it for the other, adding a few necessary tweaks here and there so it was specific to what each location needed.

I loved creating like this and I loved even more that she gave me the chance to use my passion to help serve the children at Hope Gardens. I had so much to be thankful for and I stopped to acknowledge those things each and every time they crossed my mind. It was a habit that my grandmother had encouraged me to start during a time when I was sitting around counting my losses.

"Focus on the wins, Charlie. Don't you have some of those too?" she asked me.

I did. It was a turning point for how I saw the world. It definitely wasn't an easy shift. There are moments when I still have to stop and refocus to this day. But I always hear her words rolling heavily through my mind.

About a week after I found myself walking through the weeds of planning two parties, it struck me that I had not yet ordered the costumes that we were supposed to wear to Dr. Chris' party. I thought about how she had trusted me with securing two slices of bread for us to wear, then thought about how disappointed she would be that we didn't have them, at least the costumes that looked like the ones she was looking at online when she suggested it. I found myself starting to spiral inside one of those moments where I was sitting around counting my losses before I heard my grandmother's voice.

"Focus on the wins, Charlie." *Focus on the wins.* "Don't you have some of those too?" I do have some wins. I thought to myself. Then just like the snap of a finger, I was counting my blessings again. Those brought perspective and a faster chance at troubleshooting. My brain went into overdrive. I researched online and found a place in the city limits that had the jelly outfit that she wanted, but for whatever reason, the peanut butter on a slice of bread was not available. Were people really dressing up for Halloween as just a slice of bread with peanut butter? I had no idea, but I decided to expand my search and I found one that would be available for pick up on Halloween Saturday. The only catch - it was an hour and a half away from Kansas City. Seemed worth it to me so I reserved it.

Since Halloween was on a Saturday that year, my school's party was held the Friday before. Things were smooth sailing as far as logistics went, which left me with great hope for Dr. Chris' Halloween party.

Saturday arrived and Dr. Chris and I started the day with some cider. The party itself wasn't scheduled to start until 3pm, so I had ample time to drive out west to Manhattan, pick up the costume, and get back to Kansas City with time to spare.

I showed Dr. Chris her costume and I never thought I'd see someone so excited to dress up like a slice of bread. She started singing the same song I was singing to encourage her to choose this as our costume idea. Thinking of the million things that were on my mind to do, I only nodded along with her.

"Are you okay, Charlie? Where's your peanut butter costume? Let's try them on!"

This woman. She was so excited she could barely contain it. I loved her enthusiasm, but it made me even more nervous to tell her that I was about to go run a 3 hour errand.

"Will you make it back in time for the party, Charlie?"

"I should have plenty of time, Chris."

"Okay, be careful as you go."

Well, that wasn't so bad. I had hyped up her response to be something far more dramatic than what I actually received in return. Overthinking things again. I had lots of time to overthink my own overthinking on my trip.

Dr. Chris:

Three hours, he said. Charlie had left to run his errand almost 4 hours ago. The holiday party was about to start and I hadn't heard anything from him. I was nervous about the party, but more than a little concerned about Charlie who was missing in action. I didn't want to hover, but it wasn't like Charlie to say he'd be somewhere and not actually be there, so I sent a quick text.

"Hey Sweetheart. Just checking to make sure you're okay."

I set my phone aside and followed the instructions Charlie left for me and got the virtual Halloween party started. We patched in our DJ and her music, and let her do her thing. I checked my phone for a reply between every song. Nothing. I hoped that meant he was driving and not in a position to check it. Once the children and their parents started "showing up," I had to shift my full attention into hostess mode with the other hospital staff. I was upstairs in the guest bedroom with earbuds in, so I couldn't hear much of anything that wasn't happening in the virtual party.

The costume "parade" was about to start and all of the children and their families were going to have the chance to rotate from room to room to view the hospital staff and their families, rating their costumes in the process. There I was thinking about how silly I was going to look being just a slice of bread with grape jelly covering me. I was working through how I was going to somehow deem myself a slice of toast, when the bedroom door opened. In walked Charlie, my literal other half, with his peanut butter outfit on, shaking his head like he had just had a harrowing experience. He kissed my temple and whispered, "I'm sorry." His head quickly tilted to the right, eyebrows raised high, and pulled a mini baseball bat from behind his back.

"Should we give it a go?" he asked.

I pulled out my phone and connected to the bluetooth speaker that we used to play soothing bedtime sounds for Jax on the weekends that he stayed with us. Just as the first guests visited our room, the music kicked on.

"It's peanut butter jelly time! Peanut butter jelly time! Peanut butter jelly time!"

The two of us morphed into the goofiest dancing sandwich halves my patients had seen. There was a steady stream of visitors to our room. Some of them returned for a second and third time with their friends to laugh with, or maybe at, and dance with us. The two of us were exhausted by the time the costume parade was over. When they closed all of the breakout rooms and sent everyone back to the main room, the DJ was playing Peanut Butter Jelly Time and all of the children were dancing with their families. Charlie and I joined in. It was two and a half minutes of pure joy watching everyone dance in their own unique way.

"See what you inspired, lady?" he whispered in my ear as we were dancing.

"That's all you, Charlie," I replied.

The rest of the party went off without a hitch and the crown for the best staff costume went to the two of us. The DJ, in her infinite wisdom, closed out the Halloween party with the same song that had everybody moving. As we ended the party from the admin side and closed the laptop, I nearly collapsed with exhaustion.

"This was so much fun, Charlie. Thank you for working through the details and logistics of this for me! I couldn't have done it without your help and hard work."

He was unusually hard on himself. "I should have

been here to help you get it setup. I didn't think it would take 4 hours to go get this costume. I thought I would be back in time. I'm sorry, Chris."

"Charlie, you drove for 4 hours to get a costume that you only wore for 30 minutes?" I asked, completely taken aback by what I had heard. He nodded silently.

I kissed him with all the thanks I could muster.

"What was that for?" he asked, completely confused.

"I can't believe you drove 4 hours to complete our costume."

"If I would have ordered them sooner, I-" I placed my finger on his lips, shaking my head from side to side and stopping him from going down that meandering path of pity.

"Focus on the wins, Charlie. You planned a dope party for the patients and staff of Hope Gardens. You left phenomenal instructions that allowed me to set everything up correctly on my own. You got our costumes for us. Those are huge! Focus on the wins."

He looked at me like he'd seen a ghost. I asked him what was wrong.

Charlie:

She had just told me to focus on the wins - the same thing my grandmother used to say to me. I was so taken aback I just stared emptily in her direction. She called my name. I'm not sure how many times, but I snapped to when I realized that I'd heard it twice. Even the way she called my name sounded like my grandmother. It felt like I had seen a ghost in action.

"Yes, Sugarplum? Sorry."

"Where did you go? What happened?" I assumed she was talking about my errand.

"Well, I forgot to reserve our online order, but I found a costume shop here that had the Jelly costume but not the Peanut Butter costume. So I went ahead and got that for you and I went down the rabbit hole of the inter-webs trying to find a matching Peanut Butter costume. I found one, but it was in Manhattan, KS."

"That's about a 2 hour drive from here!"

"Yeah, I thought it was only an hour and a half from Kansas City. Didn't take the location of the house into consideration. Anyway, I reserved it for pickup and thought I could make it there and back in a little over three hours."

"Oh no!"

"Yeah. I didn't account for any traffic because nobody's traveling for football. But because there's nobody traveling for football, the highway was under construction. One lane between Topeka and almost all the way to Manhattan."

"How on earth did you make it back here in time?"

"Well, I got to Manhattan and they had the costume in a child's size, not an adult size."

"How did you?"

"I told them what was going on and how I needed the costume for the children's hospital party and they called a store in Salina, KS."

"Further west of Manhattan?"

"Yeah, should be about 45 minutes west. Someone hustled down the highway to drop it off to the store in Manhattan. It only took them about 35 minutes to get there. They must have been flying."

"Wow."

"Yep. So it took me almost 2 hours to get there because of traffic. Then I waited another 35 minutes for the costume to arrive at the store before I could leave Manhattan. Then it took me another hour and a half to get back here."

"How did you get back here so fast?"

"I refuse to answer that question."

"Charlie, how fast were you driving?"

"I had a highway patrol escort."

"What!?!"

"Yeah, while I was in the store, a highway patrolman overheard me talking about needing to get back to Kansas City in a hurry because of the hospital's Halloween party. He asked if I wanted an escort between Manhattan and Topeka. I told him that he didn't have to, but he wanted to. So he and another officer sandwiched Chief, and we skedaddled down the highway."

"All of this and then you come back in good spirits and dance with me for 40 minutes?" her body softened. Tense muscles relaxed.

"Yeah, of course. What else would I do?"

"Charlie. I can hardly believe you."

"It's true."

"Oh, I believe it's true. I just can hardly believe you would go through all of this for the kids at Hope Gardens."

"I would do it again in a heartbeat, Dr. Chris. I love you just that much." I believed that with my whole heart.

"You are ridiculous!" she squealed as she kissed me on the lips, the front of our costumes connecting, finally forming a peanut butter and jelly sandwich.

"It's peanut butter jelly time," I joked.

"Peanut butter, jel-ay!" she joked in return. "Can you help me out of this thing?"

"You bet," I told her as I asked her to pull her arms inside the slice of bread, lifting it gently over her head. She returned the favor for me. I felt a sense of relief as soon as the bread was lifted off of my body. Relief that those plans were complete. Relief that the work was done. Relief that things had gone relatively smoothly - for the most part. Relief that I had survived that trip to retrieve the costume. Relief that she was so understanding. But more than anything there was a tremendous sense of relief that the best of things had yet to come.

As soon as I saw her face when I entered the guest bedroom - all decked out in my costume, full of hustle and filled nearly to the brim with anxiety that I had arrived too late, I felt an instant wave of calm wash over me. She was my person. She was the one I had waited for.

I stood in front of her, the steam that had been encased in my costume leaving my body at a rapid pace, I graciously acknowledged how grateful I was that she was in my life. I was counting my wins and my literal other half, the jelly to my peanut butter, was a major win. She had said the same exact words that my grandmother had used to encourage me, and I'm not sure she even knew that it had happened. I just took it as yet another sign that I was right where I belonged.

I held her close and kissed her on the temple.

"I'm so grateful for you, Chris," I told her.

"I love you deeply, Charlie," she replied in return.

Dr. Chris:

That moment was peaceful and serene. Just the two of us, holding each other's hearts on Halloween. Our costumes on the floor beside us, displaying the connection we had with each other.

He was everything that I wanted in a partner. He was everything that I needed. And I - I felt like I was everything I wanted to be in that moment. I was enough. He was enough. We were enough, and in just a couple of months we were about to step beyond any place we've ever been before, and then it all changed in the blink of an eye.

Chapter 10

About Last Night

Charlie:

Seeing Dr. Chris with Jax on the weekends he spent with us and watching her bring joy to the children of Hope Gardens offered me some insight on how she would potentially be as the mother of our children. I was continually blown away by her. I knew that she and I would make a great team together. That was pretty evident, but throw a child into the mix and all of a sudden things are different. I knew it would probably be different with our own children too, but I was willing to bend however I needed to bend, and flex however I needed to flex, to ensure that she and I would continue to solidify and grow our relationship so we could be of service to those around us.

From the moment I saw her I knew that I loved her heart and I wanted dearly to cherish this woman for as long as I could. Time though had a way of increasing its speed exponentially the older I got. And this year was no exception. I was quickly approaching my 40th birthday and I had the chance to reflect on all of the things I said I wanted to do vs. all of the things I had actually done. Sure the pandemic brought with it some restrictions, but there were things I should have been able to do in spite of that. Every year I created a list for myself of the things I wanted to accomplish by my next birthday. It was my birthday promise to myself, a way to continually live life. I had spent the first few years after graduation in Corporate America just watching the time fly by. It was time I could have spent actually enjoying life or contributing to society in a much greater way. I promised myself that I wouldn't allow life to slip through my fingers. I didn't want to wake up one day and realize that five years had passed me by without so much as an inkling of growth.

This year's birthday promise was shorter than normal. "In my 39th year of life I want to spend more time in nature, set aside one hour per day to focus on building my dream, acknowledge the little things, and love more deeply."

I hadn't done too bad at that. I certainly had the chance to love more deeply thanks to Dr. Chris. I also spent more time in nature and began to acknowledge the little things more often than not. Generally speaking, three out of four ain't bad. But when the fourth thing is a personal dream, it might tip the scales in the other direction. I knew that I could potentially have spent more time working on it, which is probably what caused more frustration than not. But ultimately it was my choice to let that slide into the background. Here I was regardless, just a handful of days away from a big birthday, sitting still to listen to what this year's list could include.

I didn't know how the next year would look as I eventually became someone's husband, so I told myself that I wouldn't set any birthday promise for this go round. Maybe it was practical. Maybe it was pitiful. Whatever you call it, I had talked myself out of setting an intention for the year.

Dr. Chris:

Charlie was about to reach his 40th birthday, a milestone year. I remember it well. I was almost two years removed from that one, but the amount of reflecting that I did was ridiculous. So many thoughts of "I should be here already," "I should know this already," "I should have a family already," wore me out before I could even turn 40. Then I realized when I woke up on my 40th birthday, just how young it actually felt. When I was 29, about to turn 30, I felt like I was going to wake up with creaky knees and a bad back. Let's be honest, my knees did pop a little louder on that morning, but I certainly didn't feel however I had worked up in my mind that a 30 year old would feel. So I set out to live in the moment instead of worrying so much about what wasn't yet. Don't get me wrong. I still worried. I still do, as a matter of fact. It's just much less than what it was in my 39th year of life.

So I recognized what Charlie was experiencing in the days leading up to his birthday. On the evening of Halloween, he and I had talked about the plans to celebrate alternatively as November 11th would be upon us before we knew it. He decided that he didn't want to do much of anything. I decided that would be a travesty. I called his mom and got her thoughts on things. She encouraged me to follow my gut when it came to Charlie. She told me that our souls knew each others already and that whatever decision I made would be the right one. So, I asked if she and Mr. Hughes could be available for a surprise video call for Charlie. I wanted to get as many people on the call at the same time as possible. Jax, Steve and Sabrina, Charlie's grandparents, my family. They were all scheduled for the same time, I just had to get Charlie on board some kind of way.

The week before his birthday, Charlie had asked if we could recommit to our list. He wanted to be intentional about working our way through this year's promise. So we did. We found our way back to the shelter to serve. We went horseback riding on an unseasonably warm afternoon. We made plans to tackle some of the other items after his birthday. But for his special day, I wanted it to be exactly as he wanted. Charlie requested nothing special. He only wanted apple cider with sugarplums. So I made a special birthday batch for him here at the house.

He specifically asked for "nothing major," so I gifted him a monthly subscription to a box service that provides a smattering of food options for the modern man's pantry. Cooking is such an experience for him. I had hoped that new food options might spark a new interest or something.

Charlie was so willing to love on others, but much like me, was uncomfortable with the idea of others celebrating their love of him. It was such an odd dichotomy, but there we were nonetheless. It was an interesting mix of feelings, that's for sure. So we set out to celebrate his birthday as quietly as possible.

The morning his birthday arrived, I rose before him, definitely a rarity. I snuck down to the kitchen to warm up some cider and place it in the big mug I had bought just for this day. I cooked a few slices of bacon and was in the middle of whipping up some french toast for him when I heard the bedroom door crack open. I froze in place, listening to ensure that was actually what I'd heard before I spoke. I heard the creak of the 2nd stair tread from the top and I knew for certain that he was up.

"Back to bed, mister! I'll be up in a minute!" I lovingly shouted in his direction. I heard the faint sounds of his feet pacing back upstairs and down the hallway and then his childlike chuckle before hearing the bedroom door close. A deep exhale escaped my mouth. Apparently I was more anxious about all of this than I had realized. I hurried, knowing that even though it was his birthday, it was the middle of the week and both of us still had to work to do. Onto the same tray that Charlie had used to serve me breakfast in bed on the morning before my birthday went the french toast, bacon, and his new mug, along with the latest mason jar of freshly crafted sugarplums that I had made while he was running his errand on Halloween. I had to hide them in the back of the fridge. It was like he could sniff them out as soon as I made them. They were almost always gone in the blink of an eye. The only exception was when I hid them.

I slowly carried everything up the steps towards the Master Bedroom and softly knocked twice. There was no response. I knocked again. Nothing. I shifted the balance of the tray to one hand and opened the door of the Master Bedroom, anticipating that I'd see a sleeping Charlie, laying in bed. Instead I saw a bed, neatly made and empty. I glanced around the room, the tray full of breakfast food in my hands. No Charlie in sight. I softly called his name, "Charlie?"

He replied immediately, "Yes, Sugarplum?" My head turned sharply in the direction of his voice, but I still didn't see him.

"Charlie, where are you Sweetheart?" I asked him.

"I'm on the floor."

I walked around to the other side of the bed, tray still in hand, and saw Charlie curled into Child's Pose, on his knees and shins, his legs tucked beneath him, body draped forward, head burrowed into the carpet and arms stretched out in front of him. My head tilted sideways in curiosity. "Are you okay?"

He mumbled, his face still planted in the carpet. "Mmm hmm. Something smells good!"

"I fixed your birthday breakfast."

"Oh okay. Thank you," still immobile.

"Do you want me to leave it on the bed for you?"

He finally sat up so I could see his face. I could tell that he had been crying.

"Oh Charlie, what's going on?" I asked, setting the tray of food on the corner of the bed.

He took a deep breath in and let it out slowly. "Just grateful, that's all, Chris."

I nodded, getting down on my knees to meet him where he was. I extended a hand towards him, which he took in his as he smiled. There we were, the two of us, beside the bed on our knees, hand in hand, gazing into each others eyes and not saying a word. At least two minutes had elapsed before I softly squeaked out the words, "Happy Birthday, Charlie."

"Thank you," he whispered in return, placing his right hand over his heart and smiling in my direction. He fiddled with the ring he had placed on my left hand, spinning it in circles around my ring finger.

"The planet seems a little loose today," I chuckled.

He looked down at the ring, then up at my face. "Do they still call it that at Hope Gardens?"

"They do," I shrugged.

He shook his head and apologized.

"What are you apologizing for, Charlie?" I asked him with sincerity.

"I know you don't like a lot of attention like that. I wasn't trying to add that to your life."

"It's fine, Charlie. You know we can't control other people's reactions or responses. I happen to love my ring in spite of what other people have to say about it."

"What else do they say about it?" he asked, suddenly worrisome about other people's thoughts and actions.

"Nothing worth worrying about, Charlie. Are you ready to eat? Your birthday breakfast is probably getting cold."

He looked over at the tray of food sitting on the bed then back at me. "Is this why you got up early this morning?"

"It is."

He laughed. "I was coming to find you when you shouted at me to go back to bed."

"I was in the middle of fixing your french toast."

"Are you going to eat with me?" he asked lovingly. Without warning the sound of the smoke alarms on the first floor pierced the air with their sharp warnings.

"Oh shoot! My food is still on the griddle!!" I could suddenly smell the smoke wafting up to the second floor so I could only imagine what the kitchen and first floor must have looked like. I sprang to my feet in a split second, but Charlie somehow beat me both out the door of the bedroom, down the stairs and into the kitchen.

The entire first floor was full of thick dark smoke that seemed to billow from the kitchen. I couldn't tell if something was on fire or if my french toast had just been overcooked to a crisp. Charlie couldn't either.

"Grab the fire extinguisher for me!" he shouted back for me as I trailed behind him.

I stopped at the pantry and grabbed the extinguisher while still keeping an eye on Charlie, who was waving a towel around trying to clear the air in the kitchen. As soon as he slid the griddle from the burners, the flames licked the side of the pan, prompting me to panic and expel the extinguisher's contents in Charlie's direction. In my defense, I couldn't see him turning off the flames of his gas stovetop through the dense smoke. The only thing on my mind was that he was about to catch fire himself, so I acted as anyone would if they thought their loved one was about to do so.

Charlie didn't move. I don't know if it was shock, confusion, frustration, or a combination of those things. I only knew that he was deathly still.

Charlie:

There was love. There was still. There was smoke. There was panic. There was one flame. Then there was whatever the hell comes out of a fire extinguisher. It was everywhere. Cooktop. Countertop. My pajamas. I closed my eyes in the knick of time, but my mouth was another story entirely. I stood still for a few moments trying to make sense of what had just happened before the effects of the fire extinguisher hit me.

I gagged and coughed. My lungs burned. My nose itched. I had doubled over as my body worked to expel whatever toxins were just unleashed in my direction. I was about to wipe my face clean but Dr. Chris urged me not to touch anything. She spun me around to the sink, leaning me over the cast iron trough to keep the water from hitting the floor.

"Oh, Charlie. I'm so sorry. We have to rinse this off before it does any damage."

Damage? What the heck? I listened as intently as I could. I'm pretty sure that stuff had found its way to my ears as well.

"Just lean forward and let me wash your face." She was gentle, but she worked diligently to ensure that she had thoroughly rinsed the toxins from my body. I suddenly had a taste of what she must have been like at work. Up until this moment, I had only seen her interacting with her patients in a more celebratory capacity. Here though, she was in full doctor mode. "Let me see your hands," she gently demanded as I placed them into the sink as well. "Good, I'm going to turn your head to the side to rinse out your ears, but I'll place a paper towel into the ear canal first to keep it from flooding you out. Turn to the right for me." I turned to the right and felt surprisingly relaxed as the water ran over my ears and Dr. Chris' hand followed behind it to make sure there were no lingering spaces that she had missed. "Okay, I'm going to do the same on the other ear. Turn to the left for me Charlie." I turned in the opposite direction, my stress level continuing to decrease the longer I stayed under the care of Dr. Chris.

She had such a soothing touch. *This woman.*

"Dr. Chris, the back of my neck is itching a little." She gently guided my face back over the sink, nose down, and inspected the back of my neck.

"There's a little residue back here too, Charlie. I'm going to need to rinse your neck and probably your hair too, okay?"

I felt like a helpless little child, "Okay."

Then her fingers took over, washing away the residue and massaging my scalp. I shifted right back to that relaxed state before the coughing returned.

"Do you know if you inhaled any, Charlie?"

"I mean, probably so. I gasped right before you sprayed it," I chuckled through my coughing fit.

"I'm so sorry, Sweetheart. I thought you were going to catch fire!"

"It's okay," I squeezed out through the coughing which continued to get worse.

"You're going to need to breathe in some steam," she handed me a towel to wipe my face, neck and hands.

"I'm so sorry, Charlie." I looked up at her after wiping my eyes and saw tears beginning to well in hers.

"Hey, hey," I could see she was starting to get upset, "It's," cough-cough-cough, "okay, Chris." She switched the water from warm to hot so the steam would start to rise. I leaned over the sink, the same towel draped over my head to catch some of the steam for my impromptu breathing treatment. It cut out my cough almost instantaneously. As I leaned over the sink, I felt her hand caressing my back, rubbing from one side to the other. It almost felt as if she were soothing my lungs from the outside in. I shifted my weight from one foot to the other as I hovered in the steam.

"Charlie, I bet a steam shower would work as well, so you don't have to stand in this awkward position."

I nodded.

"Do you want me to get the water started for you?"

"Suuuuure. That would be good."

"I'm so sorry, Charlie. I'll run and do that and get a bag for your pajamas. I'll put those in the wash as soon as you're out of the shower. And while you're in there, I'll clean things up down here," she said as she let out an exasperated sigh. I felt bad for her. I know she must have felt terrible about it, but the whole scene was kind of funny as it replayed back in my mind. I started to chuckle underneath the towel, my shoulders and my head shaking with the laughter that became harder and harder for me to control. I could barely hear her steps as she returned to the kitchen.

"Oh, Charlie, are you okay?" She sounded distressed.

"I'm fine, why?" I asked, lifting my head from the sink and removing the towel to look her in the face.

"I thought you were crying!"

"Oh, no. I was laughing. I just envisioned the entire scene as it played out again. I can only imagine what my face must have looked like as that stuff was flying in my direction."

She began to smile a little but held herself back.

"Is the shower running?"

"It is."

"Thanks for getting it started. Are you coming with me?" I asked, my face full of hope.

"I have to clean up this mess so it's not waiting for us at the end of the work day."

"What if I said it's my birthday wish?" I'm sure I probably looked like a rascally child. I definitely felt like one in the moment.

"Charlie," she was still feeling sorry for herself. I could see it all over her face and in the way her shoulders slumped towards the floor.

"Focus on the wins, Chris. There's breakfast in bed that we can split. We'll be able to clean this up. This is definitely one for the memory books." She nodded. "Are you coming with me?" She turned off the water, slid her hand into mine and followed me out of the messy kitchen.

Dr. Chris:

Charlie was so forgiving. That kitchen was wrecked. I was emotionally so. I was upstairs turning on the shower and starting to think that I had ruined the day. When I came back down to the kitchen all I saw was his shoulders bouncing up and down. I couldn't hear him over the sound of the hot water that was running in the sink. So I assumed that he was upset. Turns out he was laughing at the whole scene. He invited me back upstairs to split the breakfast that was untainted, and start the day again. We got cleaned up for the day and I hustled off to work, whistling a different tune.

He was in good spirits when I left him and I'd

hoped that the day would encourage more of the same. Around 11 that morning, I sent him a text from work. "Hey Sweetheart, hope your birthday is fantastic. I left some lunch for you in the fridge - BEFORE the fire and the, you know. You were there."

"I found it a few minutes ago. I was just about to send you a thank you text. Are you doing okay?"

"I am doing just fine over here."

"Slippery when wet."

"You're terrible."

"You love it."

"I'll see you this evening. Call before I leave."

"Love you."

"Love you, deeply."

I should have known that he'd joke about my slip that morning. For whatever reason I was clumsier than usual on that day. Maybe I was stressed about that evening. Maybe it was overwhelming me. I knew that I had a chance to really surprise him if I could pull it off. Maybe it was more a case of distraction instead of me being cloddish.

Either way, I was definitely off my game so I spent the better part of my lunch break focusing on the plan and following up with our families. I navigated through my co-workers and their nosey comments and questions about Charlie's birthday and The Planet and what they thought I should do for him that night. Just nosey for no good reason. That was the reason I hadn't brought anyone to the hospital before. They didn't know how to act. I was pulling out of the parking garage when Jake asked me if I had big plans for Charlie's birthday. Now who in the heck told him?

I needed to know the answer, but not enough to stay and ask. Instead I smiled and nodded and drove out of the garage. I called Charlie on my way home. He didn't answer so I left a message for him.

"Hey birthday man, I'm on my way home to finish the celebration. I hope the rest of your day went well. I'll see you in a few minutes. You better not be in the kitchen cleaning up."

I hung up the phone and continued my drive towards his home. Our home. I wondered aloud how in the world I ended up with Charlie. It still hadn't been a full year since the two of us had met, but it felt like we had spent at least three years together. Maybe I was just feeling three distinct phases of our relationship. I wanted so badly to pick up the phone and call Marlo in that moment. He would have had so much to say about it. He would have wanted to join in on the fun. He would have found a way to encourage us all to enjoy each and every moment of life and to celebrate big on those special occasions like birthdays. I wondered if he would have been able to convince Charlie to celebrate out loud. Knowing Marlo, he absolutely would have. I had gone through a cycle of emotions since his death; denial, anger, bargaining, losing the core of myself in a slight depression before finally accepting that he was gone. It didn't make it any easier accepting it, but at least it helped me to remember him fondly.

I thought about what Marlo would have done to celebrate Charlie on his big day and I made a pit stop on my way home to pick up the biggest balloons I could find. When I pulled into the driveway, Charlie met me outside. I waved to him from the car, but I wasn't sure if he could see me.

He came bounding down the steps and opened my car door like the gentleman that he was. I held his hand as I stepped out and motioned for him to meet me at the trunk.

"Meet you at the trunk? What kind of business is

this?" he asked.

"Just open it," I urged him. Charlie lifted the lid of the trunk and the balloons, which had been weighted with an anchor, popped out like the surprise that they were - even to me.

"Oh snap!" he shouted. "I love them. Thank you so much!" Inside my head, I thanked Marlo for the nudge. Charlie carried my bag and the balloons into the house and I walked in with the plan for the even bigger surprise that was on its way. Before I could get to it though, I noticed that the house smelled particularly clean. I looked back at Charlie, who smiled at me and shrugged his shoulders high towards his ears.

"Did you clean the kitchen?"

"May-haps I did," he chuckled. "May-haps I didn't."

"Charlie, I was supposed to take care of that when I got home."

"I thought you sent the people here."

"What people?"

"The cleaning crew that showed up to clean the kitchen and wipe down the walls."

"What cleaning crew, Charlie?"

"I didn't clean anything, Chris. I promise. I thought about it, but I remembered you telling me that I didn't give you the chance to demonstrate your love. So I didn't clean anything, even though it took every ounce of restraint I had. Swear it."

"What cleaning crew, Charlie?" I asked again.

"There was a van of people who showed up in masks and hazmat suits. They said they were a birthday surprise and they went into the kitchen to take care of the mess. I tried to tip them but they said there was no charge to me."

"What on earth?"

"You didn't send them?"

"I barely had time to eat lunch today. I didn't have the time to even think about researching a company who could do something like that, let alone calling or contacting them!"

"Well that's weird."

"You're telling me!"

I had no earthly idea where the cleaning crew had come from and I wasn't going to try to figure out it either. All I know is that it was as pleasant a surprise for me as it was for Charlie. It gave me the chance to settle in and get things set up before dinner instead of rushing around and cleaning in a maniacal manner. Charlie sat at the kitchen table and told me about his day while I prepared his favorite meal; his mom's homemade lasagna. She gave me the recipe a week or so ago, and I reviewed it to ensure that I had everything at the house ready to go for tonight.

Charlie had no idea what I was preparing for dinner, other than that it was a special birthday meal. He tried to watch me as I was preparing things. He even asked if he could help, which I quickly rebutted with the notion that this was his "birthday dinner." His mom sent me a text, checking in to see where I was in the process of baking the lasagna. "Just put it in the oven," I replied as quickly as I could before Charlie could catch a glimpse of who I was texting or what we were texting about.

"You look like you're up to something, my bride." That was a first. I'm not sure if it was the fact that he knew I was up to something or the fact that he called me his bride that made my head turn on a swivel. I blinked rapidly, sifting through half truths to get me through to a place where I could serve up his birthday feast.

"I do?" I asked, stalling a bit longer.

He nodded slowly, "You do. What are you working on?"

"Who said I was working on something Charlie?"

"I can see it in your face. Your lips just disappeared as you sent that reply to whomever."

"My lips just what?"

"Disappeared, Sugarplum. You tucked your lips into your mouth."

"What makes you think this is something that means I'm up to something?"

"Purely observation, my dear."

"Oh okay, Charlie." I hadn't addressed his statement, yet. I had hoped to stall a bit longer, then his mom replied to my response and I tried my hardest to not flinch.

"Are you going to check that?" he chuckled.

"I'm fixing your birthday dinner, Charlie. I'll get it later."

Charlie:

All of the signs were there. She was trying to ignore her phone in much the same manner as I had when I tried to surprise her on the day before her birthday. Her breathing was more shallow than usual. Her lips were pursed tightly as though she were trying to hold in a secret. She tried hard to keep me involved without shutting me out of all the details. But she was definitely holding onto the details that would spoil the surprise. I was getting a kick out of watching her navigate through this while trying her hardest not to lie to me. It was cute, but I wanted to see what would happen if I called her out.

"You look like you're up to something, my bride," I offered fairly nonchalantly.

Her face danced the tango. She blinked like an eyelash had taken a dive onto her eyeball. I was hoping she would just tell me because I was anxious like a child the night before Christmas. I just wanted in on the secret. It looked like it was a good one.

"I do?" she asked me - her face still doing a jig. She was so cute. I tried my hardest not to laugh in the moment, but it was so hard. I nodded as slowly as I could, hiding my smile before reiterating that she definitely looked like she was hiding something. I asked what she was working on to see if I could get even a small hint about what was going on, or rather what was coming.

She wouldn't bite. In fact, she wouldn't even answer the statement that I had initially made. Eventually she asked me to set the table. I think she was just trying to get me out of the kitchen, honestly. The ornery side of me wanted to stay and prod a bit more. The respectful partner in me surrendered, gave in and set the table. I stayed in the dining room as she finished prepping. She joined me in the dining room while the food was in the oven.

"So I know you know that I'm up to something, Charlie." *Oh, here we go!* I thought she was just going to completely ignore or dance around it. Instead, she came in tap dancing directly on it.

"I do," I nodded and smiled. I was glad that she wanted to address the pink polka-dot elephant in the room.

"Well, you're right," she started. I smiled as she continued, "Soon you'll know what it is because you'll be able to smell it."

I took a deep whiff of the air in the dining room. I didn't smell any dinner yet, though I could smell the heat of the oven. I started trying to guess what she might have been preparing for dinner. The truth is I already knew. I saw her put the lasagna noodles away in a hurry when she came back from the grocery store. She didn't know that I saw, and I didn't want to ruin the surprise.

Her beautiful smile was lighting up the room even though her head was dipped in embarrassment. I smiled in her direction. "I really wanted to surprise you, Charlie."

"You did, surprise me, Dr. Chris! You got up early and cooked breakfast this morning. You came home from work and almost immediately started cooking my mom's lasagna while listening to me carry on about my day."

"You knew?"

"I knew it when you came home from the grocery store."

"I really tried not to spill the beans."

"I know, I know. I just happened to see you put the lasagna noodles away and we never have any of those here."

"Good point."

She shook her head at me and sat in silence. I looked intently at her face. I studied her body language. I was locking this moment into my memory banks as the time that she tried to pull off a surprise and I called her out on it. I loved the thought of getting to do this with her every day. Surprising each other, demonstrating our love in action. I was glad that she called me out on my crap even if it caused a bit of paralysis in the moment. She made it feel okay to celebrate myself. I leaned in for a kiss but the oven timer sounded, causing Dr. Chris to jump up from her seat.

"Oh, that's the timer. I thought it was the smoke alarm again," she said as she sauntered into the kitchen. I chuckled, remembering what that morning was like for both of us, but especially what it was like for me. I still had a bit of a nagging irritation in my throat, but it wasn't anything worth getting uptight about.

"You sure it's the timer?!" I joked with her.

"Yes, Charlie," she chided from the kitchen, before returning with the salad and baking dish of lasagna. It smelled just like my mom's lasagna. "I need to grab something from my bag, I'll be right back," she said as she disappeared from the dining room, leaving me in there with the mouth watering smell of the lasagna that she had prepared for my birthday dinner.

"This smells amazing, Sugarplum. Just like mom's lasagna! I've had some lasagna that was close before. I even made some by taking my best guess at what her recipe was since she wouldn't share it with me. How did you get something so spot on?"

She shouted from the other room, "How did I get what so spot on, Charlie?" but her voice got louder the closer she got to the dining room. So I knew she was on the way back in, which meant we could bless the food and eat. I was anxious to see if it also tasted like my Mom's lasagna.

"The lasagna! How did you get it to smell just like hers?" I restated.

"Well, why don't you ask your Momma how I got it to smell like hers."

The sass! Did she just sling a momma joke my way? "Did you just-" I rotated sharply in her direction and jumped in my seat when I turned. There was a laptop in my face and a video conference full of the people I loved, all sitting around their tables, waiting to eat the same lasagna and salad that was in front of me.

"Happy Birthday, Charlie!!" they all shouted in unison. Dr. Chris set the laptop on a stack of books in front of us and kissed me on my temple.

"Wow! Are you kidding me?" My heart was pumping. I thought I had foiled the surprise. The lasagna confession was a distraction. She was good!

My grandfather asked everyone to bow their heads so he could bless the food.

"Lord, we thank you for bringing us all together to celebrate the anniversary of Charlie's birth. He's truly one of a kind and we appreciate the opportunity to share part of our lives with him as much as we are grateful that he willingly shares part of his life with us as well. Lord, we thank you too for his bride, Chris, for bringing us all together to celebrate in a way that allows us to be together even though we are physically apart. We thank you for safe keeping and for allowing us another momentous opportunity to celebrate together. We look forward to the nuptials and celebrating with the bride and groom. We ask that you continue to keep us all in good health until a time that is safe for us all to be together in person again. We ask this in Your name. Amen."

Grandpa's prayers were always an adventure, but this particular one touched a soft spot on my heart. I glanced at my bride, whose hand I had the opportunity to hold on this day and the days to come and I squeezed a bit harder than normal after the prayer. She mouthed the words, "Are you okay?" and I nodded, knowing if I tried to speak that I'd have tears flowing down my face. "I love you deeply, Charlie," she mouthed towards me.

"I love you, Sugarplum," I mouthed in return.

"What are you two lovebirds gushing about over there?" Steve asked loudly, prompting laughter from everyone.

"So mom, did you give Dr. Chris your lasagna recipe?" I asked, slightly changing the subject.

"May haps I did. May haps I didn't," she laughed.

"Did the cleaning people show up on time today?"

"Oh, it was you!" Dr. Chris and I laughed together.

Mom nodded. "When Chris texted me this afternoon and let me know what happened this morning, I knew she would be pressed for time to clean all of that up and still make dinner, so I sent in a little help."

"Thank you so much," Dr. Chris gushed. "I thought Charlie cleaned it up, but he promised that he didn't do it. He thought I sent the cleaning crew to the house to take care of it. We knew we'd figure out who sent them eventually."

"Mom, you're too much, really."

"What happened this morning?" Dr. Chris' Dad asked. Her Mom leaned in to catch him up on the story.

The dinner was phenomenal. The company was unexpectedly awesome, and the two of us even had the chance to get bundled up and glide outside in our favorite spot for a few minutes.

"Thank you for creating such a memorable birthday," I smiled down in her direction as she sat beside me, her head cradled in the nook of my arm that seemed to have been created just for her.

She looked up into my soul. Her eyes both dreamy and hungry. "Charlie, thank you for extending so much grace today. I'm grateful for so much. I certainly wasn't aiming for a smoke-filled birthday morning."

I attempted to supress the unyielding passion that was starting to rise in my chest. "That was one tiny blip on the radar compared to the rest of the day. Plus, I got a scalp massage that I wasn't expecting," I said, prompting laughter from my bride.

"I wasn't expecting to have to hose you down, that's

for sure," she said shaking her head.

The mischievous side of me came out before I could stop it. Words spilling from my mouth like a swollen river. "Plus there was the..."

"Are we certain that they're not still listening to us?" she jokingly interrupted, her eyes still steadfast and penetrating, speaking far louder than any words that escaped her mouth.

I kissed her on the temple and absorbed her relaxed energy. The feel of her cold cheek against my chin caused me to raise the blanket and cover us a little more diligently. She leaned into my chest, her eyes, glitteringly frolicsome. I could read her like a book, but I wanted *her* to tell me what thoughts were scrolling through her mind.

"What's up? What you thinking right now?" I asked her, a lively smile tipping off my excitement. She moved swiftly, raising the blanket just high enough to stradle me on the glider before slowly lowering her thighs down to my lap. No words. I couldn't form them. I could barely breathe. All of the sudden I was roasting. I'm sure I was sweating. There had to be steam rising from underneath that blanket.

This woman.

She leaned towards me and nuzzled her cold nose into my neck, just behind my beard. The feel of her warm breath tickled and I giggled like a child. I couldn't help it.

"Hmmmm. I love it when you giggle, Charlie," she said, allowing her lips to lightly and innocently nip at my skin.

I was thrown off balance. Flustered. My insides were turning lustful flips. I whispered, not in an act of seduction, but because I didn't have much air to spare to push out any sound. "You wanna be starting something, ma'am?"

Her voice, hypnotic. "I gotta be starting something, sir."

It was undeniably intense. She had my full attention and focus. Somebody could've been rummaging through the inside of our house at that very moment and I wouldn't have cared. "Out here, Chris?"

She feigned innocence, "I'm just trying to keep us warm, Charlie. That's all." Her hands. One caressed the nape of my neck. The other lightly traced its way across my eyebrows, then down the center of my face, pausing to playfully rest on my lips.

I didn't have any words, just primal noises the likes of which I hadn't even heard myself make before.

She shushed me and continued to tickle my neck with featherweight kisses. It had to be 98 degrees underneath that wool blanket, but I didn't dare move it on the off chance that one of the neighbors was outside. I withstood about all I could take, before I allowed my hands to wander. She was already my safe space. She was already home. Then the warm and sensual resonance of her voice egged me on.

I leaned into her ear and all but begged, "Let's go inside, Sugarplum."

She pulled back and looked me square in my eyes. Piercing. Scarcely blinking. Passionate. Frank. It was a tranquil yet savagely spiritual connection. "Let's not, Charlie."

I froze.

This woman.

Her tone was calm and unbothered. "We're at home," she urged. "There aren't any windows within eyesight of the glider."

I shook my head in disbelief, maintaining her expectant eye contact and biting my lower lip. Only one word faintly escaped my mouth, "Whaaaaat?"

CHAPTER 11
THANKSGIVING

Dr. Chris:

I was grateful for the chance to shower Charlie with so much love on his birthday. The two weeks that followed were nothing short of chaotic. We were narrowing in on our wedding day. Thanksgiving was a few short days away, and both sets of parents wanted to know where we were going to visit. Charlie and I found ourselves making a lot of decisions remotely, me from work and him from home. The condo still had stuff in it. We hadn't moved too much recently, as there was an overflow of tasks to complete. I knew in order for it to be a priority, that we had to schedule it as such. I relied heavily on Charlie's assistance, not something I was used to doing before this year, but I had done a lot of that recently. He was so steady when it came to supporting me. It was a relief to share the load with someone.

The Monday before Thanksgiving had arrived, our deadline to share with the parents where we would be for the holiday. With Charlie's district on Fall break, it gave us the opportunity to resume our in person lunches. So, as we finalized the reception menu and our in-person weekly wedding meeting drew to a close, Charlie and I had a chat about the holiday season and what that would look like for the two of us. There were lots of options on the table. A visit to his family, a visit to my family, creating Thanksgiving ourselves at home, sharing the holiday with Steve and Sabrina, visiting multiple families in one day. Thank goodness for options. People had taken things seriously this year at the onset of the pandemic, but we were able to decrease the spread and nip it in the bud. With so many options on the table, I offered an alternate option of divide and conquer.

"Charlie, I know we're not married yet, so if we need to split up for the holidays this year then I'm okay with that."

"Where you go, I go," he was adamant. "I'm fine with whatever the decision, and I know your extended family gathers for Thanksgiving so if that's where you're leaning, let's go!" It made me smile to think about him keeping my family and their traditions in mind. I thought back to Christmas Eve, last year and how I asked if I needed to follow him so he could spend more time with his family. His answer was the same then as it was today, "We travel together, Chris."

"What if we stay here for Thanksgiving and spend Christmas in Arkansas again?"

"Sounds good, Sugarplum," his eyes were full of love and I didn't know what to do with what I was feeling. I shook my head from side to side, which confused him. "No? It's not good?"

"No, it's good, Charlie. I was just..." I inhaled sharply, "Stethoscope."

He reached for my hand and held it up to his heart. "Me too, Chris. Me too."

I could only think about the adventures we were

about to embark upon as we went on our journey through life together. I felt like I was about to hitch my cart to a star, like we were going to take off on a rocket. The sky truly was the limit with the two of us partnering together in life and I was beyond excited and so ready for it.

Thanksgiving arrived and the two of us snuggled in bed for as long as we could before stepping outside the door of the bedroom. Charlie offered to fix us some breakfast and I didn't stop him. I was a little hesitant to cook without supervision since the fire incident on his birthday. I know it was an irrational fear, especially considering the reason that things had gotten out of control. I knew I'd work my way up to it eventually, but I was reasonably nervous since a cleaning crew had to be called to the scene because of my lack of oversight.

Charlie was just as patient about it as he could be. He brought his special french toast back upstairs on a platter for the two of us to share as we watched the Thanksgiving Day parade on the small tv that was tucked on top of the chest of drawers. He was so charming and his actions endearing. I felt lucky that he chose me to share the rest of his life with.

Charlie:

She was so captivating and lovable and I felt like I must have been born under a lucky star to end up with Dr. Chris in my life. It was such a simple morning, breakfast in bed, watching the parade on tv and reminiscing about our childhoods spent watching the different cold, snowy, and windy parades that they'd held over the years. We laughed about the time the floats hovered over the crowd like a threat because they had to shorten the ties with such windy conditions. Then there was the time that the float was punctured by a street light and started slowly deflating throughout the course of the rest of the parade. I was enamored by the idea of the two of us sharing a laugh over the same thing, miles and miles apart in location and in heart. But there she was nonetheless, sharing in the little things in life and stretched out across our bed in the most innocent way possible.

"Was the food okay, Sugarplum?" I asked before glancing down at the empty platter and chuckling. "Did you get enough? Can I fix you something else?"

"No, Charlie. I'm okay. I'm not sure why I was so hungry."

I eyed her suspiciously, wondering if our carelessness on my birthday had given us something else to look forward to next year. She caught my stare and I couldn't help but chuckle.

"No sir. Don't put that in the atmosphere yet," she said with a giggle.

"What would we name him?"

"Oh, it's a boy already? What if he's a she?"

"Well then, what will we name the twins?"

"So now there's two babies in there?" She laughed. "Charlie!"

"How about Cleophus?"

"Linzer and Louvennia."

"Well that was very specific. Do you have a connection to those names?"

"They're old family names."

"I feel like there's a story there."

"There is," she said. I waited quietly for her to fill in

the blanks. But there was no filling in to be had. I left it right there and instead opted to gaze deeply through the windows to her soul.

"I love you so much, Sugarplum."

"I love you deeply, Charlie."

"Stethoscope."

"It's in the trunk," she said as she placed the palm of her left hand on the pulse of my heart. "You're checking out just fine to me."

I moved the empty platter to the desk and returned to the bed to snuggle beside her, shoulder to shoulder, our feet hovering above the pillows, as we watched the rest of the parade. I felt like a teenager again, but without all of the angst.

"Twins huh?" she joked to cut the silence that had been hanging out with us.

I chuckled and finished, "Uh huh."

Once the parade was done, I found my way back downstairs to wash the dishes I'd used to make breakfast while she was getting cleaned up. By the time I was finished washing, she was showered and dressed. I'm still not sure how she managed to change so quickly, but that's something I'd grown accustomed to. We swapped jobs as I tossed her the towel on my way to the shower. By the time I got back downstairs she had dried and put them away before pulling out the sweet potatoes she made me watch her make the night before.

I know she was nervous about burning down the kitchen, but I tried to get her to think about how many times she'd cooked in this kitchen without something smoking or catching fire. She didn't need me in there.

Either way, I was hoping to sample some of those sweet potatoes before we took them to her parents' house but I was denied at every attempt and ask.

Instead we packed them up, along with one of the pies she made, and we found our way out to Chief to head out for the afternoon. I opened the door for her, "Are you in?"

"We are," she joked. I shook my head at her, trying to stifle my smile as I closed the door and hustled through the chilly November air to the driver's side door. As I hopped in the truck, I caught a glimpse of Dr. Chris rubbing and looking lovingly at her belly before looking up at me with love in her eyes. "What if, Charlie?" she asked me, her voice full of hope.

The smile widened across my face. I couldn't contain it. I didn't answer. I shifted the truck into reverse and checked for traffic before backing out into the street and heading towards her parents' house. I loved her for wondering what could be and doing so with optimism. Only Kenny Loggins had the answer to my lack of vocabulary in the moment. I opened my mouth and started to sing.

Dr. Chris:

Charlie had been silent the entire ride. We had joked about whether or not I was carrying a child or two, but I was thinking about it all morning long. What if I was? The more I thought about it, the more hopeful I became. I peered over at Charlie who bit his lower lip as he drove. It was a tell that he was deep in thought, typically encouraging thought, but deep down the rabbit hole nonetheless. Seemingly out of nowhere he started belting out the lyrics to "Danny's Song." Yep - Kenny Loggins. I didn't see that coming at all, but I loved his voice. So I absorbed the moment. So calming and stirring, and that song, so full of hope. My grandmother and I used to sing it together at the piano so I joined in. We sang until we hit the driveway for my parents' house.

"None of that baby talk in here, please. Okay?"

"How crazy do you think I am woman?" he chuckled.

We were the first to arrive and I slipped into the kitchen to help mom corral all of the food before we moved it to the table for the family. Charlie helped Dad finish extending the table and moving the extra chairs upstairs into the dining room. I could hear the two of them talking and laughing from the kitchen which made my heart smile. Mom caught my eye and smiled at the look on my face.

"He's a sweetheart, Chris."

"He is Mom."

"Do you need anything for the wedding?"

"I think we pretty much have everything covered. We did the final taste test a couple of days ago. My dress is ready. Charlie has the rings. The venue has our decorations. Sabrina and Vonne have their dresses. Steve and..." I paused, swallowing down the lump that caught in my throat. "Steve has his tuxedo and we're going to light a candle for Marlo." I could feel my eyebrows as they huddled in for comfort in the center of my forehead.

"Oh Chris, I'm so sorry. He'll be there with you on your wedding day. I know he wouldn't miss it."

"I know, Mom. He sends me nudges every now and then to let me know he sees me."

"You two had a special bond. I used to think you'd get married, but he was definitely not your type," she laughed.

"I have a type?" I knew I did. I just wanted to see how much Mom thought she knew, and then she described it down to the minute details.

"...and a little bit adventurous with a soft spot for family."

"Okay. So I have a type. Is Charlie -"

"Charlie is definitely your type," she laughed, right again. "Charlie is THE guy though." Mom put down the gravy ladle and looked me in my eyes. "When you find yourself wondering why you got married to him, just remember the way he looks at you when he doesn't know you can see him."

"Have you ever wondered that with Dad?"

"He's looking at you right now. Use the picture hanging on the wall to check out his reflection." My eyes shifted quickly so that I wouldn't miss it. There he was, moving chairs and gazing lovingly in my direction. I started to fall in love with him all over again. "None of the others ever looked at you like that, Chris. I knew Charlie loved you the moment I saw how he looked at you as you walked towards the house to introduce him to us last year." I nodded. "Your momma knows."

"I know you do, Mom."

The family began to arrive, all of Dad's siblings and their families, plus Vonne and her family. I'd hoped to be by the door to introduce them to Charlie, but I never quite made it there in time. There was a constant refrain that echoed throughout the entryway to the house.

"Soooo...this is ChARlie!" then laughter would ensue, and Charlie would introduce himself while commenting that I was somewhere in the house helping out. Soon thereafter, the family would migrate into the dining room or kitchen to let me know that they'd met, Charlie. "He's quite the looker!" I'd raise my eyebrows and nod at their comments and smile as they told me how much they were looking forward to joining us for the wedding.

Every now and then I'd lock eyes with Charlie as I was checking to ensure he was okay. He'd always flash a smile in my direction and tuck in his lower lip like he was holding in a secret. I wondered how many childhood stories he heard just in the time before we blessed the food to eat. I'm sure there were too many for him to count.

Once the food was all prepared and the table set, Dad called everyone to gather around the table. Families filed in together, all standing so we could bless the food before sitting down to eat. I waited for Charlie so we could sit beside each other, reaching out for his hand and squeezing it so he knew I was glad he was with me.

Charlie:

She squeezed my hand and I was glad to be beside her. I caressed each finger and looked around the table. All eyes were on the two of us. I smiled and nodded towards her dad, recalling what he and I had just talked about as we were setting up the extra chairs in the dining room.

"Are you ready for January 1st, Charlie?" he had asked me.

"Yes, sir. I'm looking forward to each day in front of us."

"There will be more good days than bad in a year. Remember that, Charlie. Lean on that when things are tough."

"I can do that," I told him very matter of factly. "You've been married for almost 50 years. What other advice do you have on building a strong marriage?"

"Treat her like a girlfriend that you'd want to marry you."

"What's that Dad?"

He stood up straight. "Look at her in the kitchen with her mother." I turned in her direction and watched their synchronized dance around the room, lifting and moving dishes, adding serving spoons to the food, working with each other and not against each other, collaborating with the same goal in mind. "They've been preparing Thanksgiving meals together since Chris was little. It didn't always look this in sync. Her mother told her what she needed, and Chris honored her mother by doing it. There were years when teenage angst kicked in and everything was asking for too much in Chris' eyes, just like any teenager. But her mother stayed steady and Chris still helped out in her own way. There were a few years when 'Cille, needed more help than she normally did, and Chris, because she had years of watching her mother, stepped in and picked up the slack without even so much as a word. This dance that they have now is the product of years of them learning how to communicate with each other, extending grace, and anticipating each other's needs. That's marriage."

I nodded, understanding exactly what he was talking about, but still a bit confused about how the girlfriend reference was related.

"The way you're looking at Chris right now, that mix of love and admiration, sneaking a peek at her when she doesn't know you're looking, that's how you treat a girlfriend that you want to marry. It's the same way you keep a wife. She doesn't know it, but I still look at 'Cille like that."

"Grace, communication, patience and learning to anticipate what she needs..."

"...and love, Charlie. Love her with everything in your heart. Let her feel it every time she's near you."

"Even when I'm mad?"

"Especially when you're mad," he chuckled. "Never introduce doubt, even when it starts to creep in. Remember this moment and the years it took for them to get that dance together in there. Then remember why you wanted to marry her in the first place and how you feel right now as you're looking at your future wife."

"Lucky. Incredibly lucky." I glanced to my left and noticed the grin that graced his face as he was sneaking a glimpse of his wife.

"Me too, Son."

It made me think about my own dad and grandfather, and the ways in which they treated their brides. There's a reason Grandpa had called Chris my bride on Christmas morning. The way you view someone has a direct impact on not only how you treat them, but how you interpret their actions as well. So while my bride almost caught the kitchen on fire fixing us breakfast on my birthday, my only goals were to make sure that we were safe, the house was in as decent shape as possible, and that she understood the first two goals in that order.

When she hung back and waited for me to enter the room so we could sit beside each other at dinner, I knew this was my first opportunity to put into practice the advice her dad had just gifted me. She squeezed my hand and instinctively I caressed each finger.

I learned a lot about Chris and Vonne at Thanksgiving dinner. Lots of funny ammunition that I could tease her about later. After dinner, desserts and a few games with the family, I helped her dad put the dining room back in order before setting up a video call with my parents. Chris and I wished them a Happy Thanksgiving before being promptly asked if we could pass the phone to the James family. They chatted with each other non stop, in much the same manner as they had when they first met each other last Christmas. I left my phone and a charging cable with them as we slipped out of the house to go watch them flip the switch on the Plaza Lights.

There we stood, in our winter coats, hats and gloves on, in the chill of the night, waiting for someone to power on the Christmas lights that stretched across the rooflines of this entertainment district. It was well worth the wait as we stood atop the parking garage to see the glow as they lit up the sky. She stood in front of me and rested the back of her head directly on my heart. It reminded me of our first date and spurred me into action. Our one year anniversary would be coming up in less than a month and I knew exactly what I wanted to do to celebrate.

"Are you okay?" I asked her. There was no answer, so I leaned in closer to her ear and asked again, "are you okay?"

She nodded, "I'm so grateful for you, Charlie."

"I appreciate you so much, Sugarplum," I said as I kissed her on the cheek in time with the lighting of the lights. I hadn't planned that type of magic, but I wondered if it was orchestrated by Marlo.

Dr. Chris:

The timing was perfect. We stood and observed the lights for a little bit before returning to Chief to head back to my parents' house. When we arrived, they were still talking to Charlie's parents. Charlie and I looked at each other and shared a smirk. He had just attempted to bet me that they'd still be talking, but me knowing how our parents got along, I didn't take him up on that. I knew they'd still be talking. We had only been gone for about 30 minutes.

What I hadn't anticipated were the jokes from the extended family about where Charlie and I had disappeared to. We told them the truth, but they didn't believe it until they saw the footage of the two of us on the local news. That brought a whole other level of scrutiny that made me giggle. "His kiss turned on the Plaza lights!" "That must have been packed with passion!" "So how do you turn on the lights at home, Charlie?" "Uh oh, the hallway light is out. Somebody find Charlie and Chris!" They were ridiculous really, but I loved them all and as backwards as it may sound, the jokes were a sign that they liked Charlie a lot. He even earned a new nickname that evening when my youngest uncle asked for Sparky. Once the rest of them heard it, they ALL ran with it. Even Corbin and Christina called him Uncle Sparky and Charlie humored them all.

Once Charlie's phone was returned to him, we wished everyone a good night and made our way back to the house. It was still a bit chilly, but Charlie made a beeline to the backyard to turn on the patio heater so we could get in our evening chat on the glider. I ran to the closet to grab the blanket after changing into my fleece lined joggers and the hoodie Charlie had gifted me for Valentine's Day. When I met him outside, his face held the same gaze of admiration as it had when I was standing in the kitchen with Mom earlier that day.

"What?" I asked him, hoping it would give me a glimpse into what he was thinking.

"Just waiting for my bride. That's all," he said as a sly smile perked up his facial expression. He offered me a seat on the glider and sat down in sync with me as I draped the blanket over the two of us before snuggling into my favorite shoulder nook. It was so cozy and warm, and it felt like home. We had already morphed into Hollywood's image of an old married couple and we hadn't even known each other for a complete year yet. I didn't see him coming, but I wouldn't trade this new reality for any amount of money or certainty.

Chapter 12

Happy Anniversary

Charlie:

The weather that December was better than I could have imagined. Temperatures hovered in the 50s and low 60s instead of the 30s and low 40s that we were accustomed to feeling. Not that it mattered too much for me, because I wasn't leaving the house to go to work. But for the wedding forecast and one other very sentimental day this month, I'll admit I was paying close attention. I had big plans in place, to celebrate our one year anniversary. I know it was just a couple of weeks away from our wedding, but the 20th was an important day for me.

Dr. Chris was working nearly non-stop in December so she could be free for our wedding at the end of the year. So, on Sunday, the 13th of December - the anniversary of the day she stumbled into my arms, I sent Dr. Chris a special delivery; hot cider with a spoonful of sugarplums and a note that said, "Thanks for bumping into me. Hope this drink keeps you as warm as you keep me everyday." I received a text from her once she received it.

"I love you, deeply Charlie. Thank you for catching

me, and for the cider."

"Best catch of my life. Love you," I replied in return.

That night, the temperature dropped into the 20s, but after a hot dinner, we danced together in our coats, stocking caps, gloves and scarves, under the stars. I hummed the tune to "What Are You Doing New Year's Eve?" and she led us to the glider to rock for a bit.

One week later, on the 20th of December, I called her phone and left a voicemail for her.

"Hi, Dr. Chris. It's Charlie Hughes. I was just in for a Check-up with my Godson, Jax. It was really good to bump into you again today, and I'm glad I can place a name to the face of the woman who's been running through my brain for the past week. I'd love to meet you for lunch or more cider someday soon. Feel free to give me a call at this phone number or on my landline. 816-555-1234. Yes, I have a landline, which pretty much makes me a dinosaur. Anyway, I look forward to speaking with you soon."

She called me back and I purposely sent the call to voicemail. Her text reminded me why I loved her so.

"Hi Charlie, my shift will be finished soon. Can I call you when I leave?"

"I'll be waiting for your call."

"Okay, talk to you in a few."

It was the same conversation that she and I had on the day of Jax's follow up appointment. I grinned from ear to ear as I answered the phone, attempting to pretend that I was the message asking her to leave a voicemail.

"What are you smiling about mister?" she asked

with a chuckle in her voice.

Dr. Chris:

Charlie had made it a point to recognize both the day that we unofficially met, and the day that we officially met - a week after. After texting him that my shift was almost over, I was left with a memory of the latter that he didn't have any knowledge of. After ending our first call on that Friday, Marlo had waltzed in with an empty cup in hand, letting me know that he had been attempting to listen in on our conversation. It was a bittersweet memory of my dear friend, that made me cry and smile. So when Charlie answered the phone and I heard his smile, it was a welcome calm to the emotional storm that had begun brewing inside of me.

I asked what he had been smiling about and he asked how I could tell that he was smiling. I was impressed that he remembered our first few interactions in such great detail. Our conversation returned to the simple things and we stayed on the phone until I pulled into the driveway. His truck was missing, but I used my key to let myself in. There was a note on the entryway table that he was packing up some of my stuff in the Condo so I wouldn't have to worry about it.

"Charlie, you're at the Condo?" I asked after reading it to myself.

"I am. Do you mind if I stay here tonight?"

"I was hoping to see you this evening sir."

I switched to a video call so I could see his face. He accepted it and showed me the progress he'd made.

"Wow!"

"Mmm hmm. I've been busy while you were working."

"I see!"

"I can't wait to see you tomorrow, Sugarplum."

"I'm glad I was able to get the next two weeks off, Charlie."

"Me too, Chris," he looked a little misty eyed.

"Aww. Are you okay, Sweetheart?"

"Just looking forward to having the chance to celebrate with you, that's all."

"Yeah?"

"Mmm hmm," he attempted to fix his face and I watched as his demeanor began to shift. "So hey,"

"Yeah?"

"When was the last time you went through your mail?"

"Probably late May. I've just been stacking it on the island."

He nodded, looking like he was trying to find the best way possible to say what was on his mind.

"Did I miss a bill or a check or something?"

"No, but I think you have some mail here from Marlo."

"I do?"

He attempted to read my face, "I think so, but I'm not sure."

"I was just thinking about him after I got your voicemail. It probably is from him."

"Funny, that's about the time that I found this," he held up something that looked like a card envelope. It was definitely Marlo's handwriting. A tear jumped from my eye like it was parachuting from a plane.

"I'm sorry, Chris. I didn't mean to-"

"Charlie, it's a happy tear. I don't remember having anything else with his handwriting on it, so I'm overjoyed that you found that. Thank you!" I said as he nodded solemnly. "Will you set that aside from the rest of the mail for me?"

"I'll leave it on the countertop and I'm placing the rest in this box labeled mail."

"Sounds good. I'm so grateful for you."

He perked up a bit. "What?"

"I was thinking I'd have to spend a day or two packing the rest of my stuff during the break."

"Well, I was looking forward to getting everything all boxed up and loading it in the truck to bring home for you."

"How much is left?"

"Just the items in the drawer of your coffee table."

He had been really busy.

"So I was thinking," he started, pausing to look at the screen.

"Yes?"

"About this furniture...we can move my living room furniture into the basement and move yours into the living room. Then I was thinking about the bedroom furniture. Can we merge our dressers into the master? The style is pretty similar."

"That works for me if it works for you, Charlie."

"I want it to be our house. I can already see some of the places where your artwork will liven things up."

"I've always felt welcome in your home Charlie."

"Yeah, but this is going to be our home, Chris. I want people to see us in it, not just me."

"I gotcha. We'll figure it out. We have time, right?"

He nodded.

"So, Charlie."

"Yes, baby."

"If you're almost done packing everything, can you come home tonight?"

"Negative. I have some plans in store for tomorrow."

"Oh yeah?"

"Yes, ma'am. Meet me at the Fresh Pantry tomorrow

morning?"

"11:30?"

"Indeed."

Charlie:

We were on the phone for the majority of the night, just like we were the year before. It felt different flirting with her on the phone instead of in person, but I enjoyed it just the same. She had no idea what was in store for her the next day. The thought of it, made it hard for me to go to sleep, so I stayed on the phone for as long as I could. We brushed our teeth together at the same time and climbed into bed, sweet talking each other for as long as we could. I missed her presence and so looked forward to seeing her tomorrow. Honestly, the thought of it made me a little bit nervous.

I woke up the next day ready to go. I cut some clippings from the winter honeysuckle that had grown wildly since the last time I'd seen it and placed them in the same red vase that I'd given her last year. Truth be told, that was the reason I was in the condo in the first place. I wanted to find the vase and cut some clippings from the bush that had grown from last year's clippings. Then I saw just how much packing needed to be done and I got to work, hoping to alleviate some of the stress of doing it herself.

Stems and vase in hand, I grabbed the red scarf that I borrowed from her a year ago and headed out of the condo towards the elevator and my truck. I drove as quickly as I could to get to The Fresh Pantry before she arrived, so I could ask for some help, just as I had last year. I didn't see her car or her when I stepped foot inside, so I got to work handing out stems and waited in the same booth for her arrival. I saw her quick pace as she hoofed it towards the door of the restaurant. I watched as her face lit up when a young girl asked for her name and handed her a honeysuckle stem. I spied some rosy cheeks as she continued to be showered with stem after stem of blossoms. The host ushered her towards the back and she giggled while guests handed her stems as she passed by. I stood to greet her just as she reached the table and reached out for her hand, kissing the back of it as I gazed into her eyes.

"Oh Charlie," she gushed, looking as if she wanted to hide a little bit.

I offered her a vase for the stems that she cradled in her arms but before she could sit down, I dropped to one knee.

"Charlie what are you doing?" she squealed.

The restaurant got eerily quiet as all eyes appeared to be on us. Then a faint tiny voice from the first child to give her a stem of honeysuckle, "Momma is he gonna ask her to marry him?" Light chuckles filled our hearts - all of us. I steadied myself.

"Dr. Christina James, a year ago today we had our first date. It started much like this and before we knew it, before I knew it, I found myself staring into the eyes of my bride. With so much going on in the world, I feel lucky to have met the way we did and I'm looking forward to exchanging rings with you as we set a promise for our lives together. I love you, Sugarplum."

"Charlie."

"Can I marry you next week?"

She cupped my face and grinned, "Of course, Charlie."

I stood and kissed her like tomorrow wasn't promised and I needed her to know that I loved her today. The restaurant-goers applauded with vigor and we sat down to order our brunch.

"I missed you yesterday, Charlie."

"It wasn't the same sleeping in your bed without you there."

"Same," she replied as I stared into her eyes.

"Does it feel like it's been a year to you?"

"It feels like longer to me, honestly. Like we've fallen into our own life groove." I couldn't find any words. I may have let out a contented sigh, but I'm not sure if I just felt it or if I let it escape my mouth.

The food arrived and we ate from each other's plates, like family. When it was time to go, I carried the honeysuckle stems in my arms and thanked the guests who helped me pull off the surprise. Well, those who were still there. Thankfully it was warmer this year than last, so we didn't have to hustle to her car. Instead, we took our time, strolling hand in hand in silence. I buckled her vase into the back seat and hopped in the passenger side.

"So, we can continue to recreate last year's date or we can-"

"I want to recreate the date, but the blanket is at home, Charlie."

"Is it?" I asked.

"Isn't it?" she asked.

"Pop the trunk," I said, hopping out of the car and heading towards the back end of her car. I reached in and pulled out the wool blanket that we'd been using in the backyard and headed back to the cabin.

"When did? How? Is that the same blanket?"

"It is," I laughed.

"How did that get in there, Charlie?"

"I put it in there before you went to work yesterday."

"I thought you were in bed sleep before I went to

work."

"I was. I put it in there before I went to bed."

"But we went to bed at the same time."

"I'm a genie. What can I say?"

"Charlie," she was still trying to figure out the how when the streetcar rolled by a few streets west of where she was parked.

"Are we waiting for the next street car or do you want the second option?"

She froze, uncertain which answer was the right answer.

"If I choose the street car am I living in the past?"

I shrugged my shoulders and waited patiently for her to choose. She leaned on what was familiar, so we dashed to the streetcar stop and held each other as we waited for its arrival. We rode it to the river market, which was considerably more empty given that our date happened to fall on a Monday instead of Saturday as it had the year prior. Thanks leap year. We walked off what we could from brunch and then headed back to the streetcar, riding it to Union Station. A quick photo with the tree and off to the Christmas Spectacular that was all dazzled up inside, then off to Monarch Square for a little community singers performance and some hot cider. The streetcar was empty again as it was time for us to head back to the cars, but there was no jazz trio riding with us this time. Instead, I hummed the tune in her ear and we danced together on the streetcar. As we debarked the street car the operator asked how long we had been married. I told them that we were getting married in a little more than a week.

"Always keep the romance alive," they told us. "That's how my marriage has thrived after 45 years."

We wished the operator congratulations and hustled off to the car for part three of the day-long date. Our drive to the plaza was uneventful, but our carriage ride started off with a bang.

"Well, look who it is!" the driver chuckled in our direction. He was the same man who had ushered us around last year. "I knew I'd see you two again."

"Out of all the people you served last year, how do you remember us?" Dr. Chris asked him.

"It's the glow around you," he said as he helped her into the princess carriage.

"The glow?" she asked.

I started singing the song from The Last Dragon, "When you got that glow!"

He laughed and offered me a hand into the carriage. "Yes, the glow. The glow. It's almost like you exude love. It's nearly angelic."

She looked at me for confirmation.

I nodded. "I see it every day, Sugarplum."

"What on earth?"

The two of us laughed as she sat with the blanket on her lap, attempting to make sense of what she'd just heard. I lightly kissed her cheek as she started to settle into the nook of my arm, covering our legs with the blanket. He turned the radio on again, and Ella sang her heart out to us.

"Do the two of you have New Year's Eve plans?" the driver asked me.

"We're getting married!" I told him.

"My guy! What a way to start a new year."

"Yessir!"

Almost as if on cue, just as he had finished asking about the child who waved to us last year, a car pulled up beside us and paced the horse. Dr. Chris waved and giggled, tapping me on my arm.

"Charlie, someone wants to say hello!"

I turned my head to find Jax, hanging his head out

of the window. Steve fussed at him to get his head back inside the car and Sabrina wished us a Happy Anniversary.

"Friends of yours?" the driver asked.

"That's my best man, her matron of honor and our godson."

Dr. Chris:

Our godson. That was the first time he had referred to Jax as our godson. My heart. This entire day was a beautiful reminder of what we had been building for the last year. I was absorbing the energy of the moment and was fully present as my emotions began to bubble up to the surface.

Charlie kissed my temple and we rode the rest of the way in silence. I'm talking carriage ride and car ride back to the fresh corner. When I parked beside his truck, he asked if I was okay. I nodded. Still at a loss for words but completely overcome with emotion.

"I'm going to put this in the back okay?" he asked as I nodded in reply. He came back to the driver's side window with the earpieces of the stethoscope already in his ears. I stepped out of the car and leaned back against the door. Charlie placed the chest piece over my heart and listened intently, staring deeply into my eyes the entire time. I stood up straight and returned his gaze. His hands fell to his sides and he opened his palms face up, as if asking for a hug. I nearly leapt into his arms and he squeezed life into me. I closed my eyes to create an imprint of the moment on my memory; his scent, the feel of his arms welcoming me in, the rise and fall of his breath, the feel of the cool air teasing my face, the stethoscope sandwiched between us.

When I opened them again, he was leaning in to place his forehead on mine. This time there was no ringing cell phone to break up the moment and I nearly went weak when he softly kissed me. It was everything I had imagined a year ago, and a bit extra because we'd already began building our life together. I followed him back home, lamenting over just how much I loved my life with Charlie in it. We skipped the glider that night and instead opted to go straight to bed after staying up so late on the phone the night before. Plus, we were getting up early to go get a tree.

The next morning I made a point to rise earlier than Charlie so I could fix breakfast for us while he was still sleep. I was determined to fix a meal in there by myself again, and I did.

When he woke up, there were two trays of food in bed, one that mimicked his meal from last year's pre-tree breakfast, and one that mimicked the turkey breakfast sandwich that I'd had.

"Mmmm. Good morning. Did you order this, Chris?"

"I got up early and fixed it Charlie."

He looked astonished and proud, and excited that I took such a big step towards overcoming my fear of burning down the house. His prayer that morning was that we be covered in protection in everything that we did.

The plan was to cut down a tree, bring it back here to decorate, and then chase the Christmas Star in early evening. It was the Great Conjunction, Jupiter and Saturn were nearly aligned in the sky, creating an image of a star so bright that it would draw wise men towards it. With Christmas falling on Friday, the tree farms had all closed for the season on that Sunday. Chief carted us to hardware stores and empty tree lots, before we found a new Randolph at a big box store.

Charlie's phone buzzed in his pocket as he was working to secure and tie down Randolph. "I'm not sure who's calling me, but they've called three times in a row. I can't even reach in my pocket to check my phone to see who it is. Can you grab it out of my pocket for me, Sugarplum?" he asked sounding concerned.

Just as I was about to reach into his coat pocket to grab his ringing phone, it stopped, but mine began to ring. We looked at each other, immediately aware that something was wrong, but uncertain of who was tied to the trouble. I grabbed my phone. I softly spoke to Charlie, "It's your mother," before I answered the call.

"Hello?"

Charlie:

I didn't know what was wrong, but the look on Chris' face let me know that it was serious.

"Yes ma'am. I'm here with him. He's tying the Christmas tree down to the truck right now. Okay. Okay. Oh gracious. Can I put you on speakerphone so you can tell him? Okay, I will. I love you too, Mom."

By the time she had finished speaking with Mom, I had finished tying down Randolph and was standing immediately beside her, awaiting whatever news she was ready to hand to me. "What is it Chris?"

I could tell she was nervous. She was fidgeting with her coat zipper. I held her hands in mine and asked again, "What is it Chris?"

She looked me in the eyes, inhaled deeply, swallowed hard and exhaled the message from Mom. "Your mom wants you to call her. Your grandfather had an accident and he's in pretty bad shape. They don't know if he's going to make it."

"What kind of accident?"

"I'm not sure, Charlie. I didn't get very much information."

"Let's get Randolph home, Chris."

"Charlie?"

I walked towards her door and opened it, helping her inside and asking if she was in. She nodded, unsure of what to do with my response I'm sure. I closed her door and said a prayer for my grandfather as I walked to the driver's side door. When I opened it, I found Chris' head bowed and eyes closed tightly, silently offering the same thing I had done as I tried to steady my pulse walking around the truck. *This woman.*

I started the ignition and The Little Christmas Tree was on the radio. I tried my hardest to hold back the tears that were quickly rising to the surface of my eyes, but I could only think about how much Grandpa loved to sing this song. I was afraid to call and find out the details and afraid of not calling and missing an opportunity to say goodbye to him. I had my hand on the gearshift, but I couldn't bring myself to shift from Park to Drive. Dr. Chris placed her hand on top of mine and told me it would all be okay. My throat tightened, suffocating any words that I thought I was going to speak. In that moment her presence made it okay for my heart to break, for me to fall apart. The tears rolled uncontrollably down my cheek and she sat gently with me, audibly praying for peace to cover my soul.

"Charlie, Sweetheart, squeeze my hand if it would help for me to drive us home." I squeezed as hard as I could but I felt weak. I wasn't even sure if she could feel it, then she unbuckled her seat belt and hopped out of the truck, walking purposefully to the driver's door and allowing me to step out and collapse into her arms. She held my heart, right there in the parking lot. I didn't know what I needed in that moment, but she seemed to innately understand what to do. I'm not sure how long she shared her energy with me, but eventually we walked to the passenger side of the truck and she asked me if I was in before closing the door. She hopped in the truck and closed the driver's door.

"Call your mother, Charlie," she said as she turned down the volume on the radio. She drove us home and somehow I found the courage to call Mom back. I listened as she told me about what happened. I tried to be brave as she explained that he was in surgery. But the truth was, I felt like a scared young boy in that moment.

Chris and I unloaded Randolph and brought him into the house, getting him all set up on the tree stand when my phone rang again. I listened to Mom's latest update and knew that our plans for the day needed to shift.

"The surgery didn't go well, Chris. I need to get back to Arkansas as soon as I can."

"I'm sorry, Charlie."

"He's still with us, but he's not doing well at all."

"Can we get a ticket for you to fly down there?"

"Two last minute tickets to XNA? Do you think there are even two seats available?" I asked as she looked on her phone.

"There aren't. There's one that leaves in an hour and a half which give you just enough time to pack. Charlie, you need to get there in a hurry. I can drive you to the airport and then drive the truck down later."

"Chris, we travel together."

"Charlie, your family needs you there."

"You are my family, Chris."

"I'll get there as soon as I can, sweetheart. I promise I will."

I knew she was right, but it didn't make the situation feel any less stressful. I threw some clothes in a bag and met her at the truck.

"How did you, get in the truck? I have the key fob in my pocket."

"You gave me the spare."

"I sure did." She was three steps ahead of me.

Dr. Chris drove us to the airport and I was able to make it with time to spare.

I didn't know what to say, so I blurted out everything that came to mind. "I prepped the ingredients for chili. It's in the fridge."

"Okay, Charlie."

"The ornaments from your house are in the back seat of the truck. I packed those in there as I left the condo yesterday."

"Okay, Charlie."

"There's fresh fruit in the fridge for your juices."

"Thank you, Charlie," she was patient with my stalling.

"I don't know why I'm telling you all of this like you can't figure it out."

"It's okay, Charlie."

"Okay, I'm gonna go in here so I can go through security."

"Okay, Sweetheart."

"I'll call you when I get there, okay?"

She nodded, "I love you deeply, Charlie. Call me whenever you need me and we'll figure out what's next together."

I leaned across the truck and kissed her temple, "I love you so much, Chris." I hopped out of the truck and grabbed my bag from the back, knocking on the window as I remembered one last thing. "The Christmas Star.

We're supposed to chase it tonight since we forgot to yesterday."

"We can still do that, Charlie. You need to go!"

"How?"

"Call me when you get in and I'll tell you, okay?" she urged. I nodded and walked towards the doors of the airport, looking back to watch as my bride drove off in my truck.

When my flight landed in Arkansas, I called Dr. Chris. I was on the phone with her as I saw my Dad pull up curbside. I promised her that I'd call her again as soon as I got settled in back home. We went straight to the hospital and my family gave me the chance to sit alone with and talk to him. I told him I was there in the room. I held his hand and asked him to squeeze it if he was willing to fight for his life. There was no response, but I wasn't willing to settle for that.

"I'm getting married next week, Grandpa, and I need to know that you'll still be here to celebrate with me and my bride." I felt the slightest amount of pressure on my hand. "Are you going to fight?" Again, pressure. I told him that I loved him and left his room feeling hopeful.

Dad drove us to the house as mom followed in her vehicle to take him back to the hospital. He gave me the keys to the truck so I could have a vehicle until Dr. Chris joined us later in the week. I gave her a call to let her know what was going on as soon as I settled in.

"Charlie, what direction does the 2nd floor balcony face?"

"South, why?"

"Good, are you able to go up there right now?"

"I can." I hustled up the creaky wooden steps in my

parents house and found my way to the balcony, noting the missing glider that now had a new home with us. "I'm up here."

"I want you to look towards the southwest."

"What am I looking for? Oh wow!"

"Do you see it?"

"I do."

"We still got to see it together, Charlie. I'm still with you."

"Chris, I wish you were here."

"I know. I wish I were too, but you needed that time with your grandfather and your family."

"It's so beautiful. Where are you right now?"

"I'm sitting on our glider, pretending that I'm leaning into your arms."

I turned my head towards the spot that the glider used to call home and spied the wooden one. I was still able to see The Great Conjunction from there, so I sat and glided with Dr. Chris for a while. The two of us chatting about everything and nothing at the same time, miles and miles apart in space, but not in heart.

"Hey Chris?"

"Yes, Charlie?"

"Thank you for today."

"It's no problem, Charlie."

"No really, I fell to pieces today and it's only because I felt safe enough to do so with you. Thank you for that."

"You're welcome, Sweetheart. Thank you for trusting me to catch you."

"Mmm hmm." Silence carried the conversation as I heard the familiar squeak of our glider piping up in the background. It seemed to get louder and louder as my emotions began to well and swell until I couldn't hold them in any longer.

"Chris?"

"Yes, Charlie?"

"I loved you yesterday. I love you today, and I promise I'll love you tomorrow."

Through the silence I heard a sniffle and my heart longed to be in Kansas City with my bride.

Chapter 13
Christmas Eve

Dr. Chris:

Charlie had promised me that he would love me everyday and it nearly broke my heart that I wasn't sitting beside him on his parents' balcony. I knew it was a hard thing for him to see his grandpa in grave condition, but he had the support of the rest of his family to carry him through. For that I was grateful.

The holiday jubilee for Hope Gardens was supposed to be held virtually this year, the same way the Halloween party was. Charlie had asked if he could still play Santa from Arkansas. I told him that the virtual party definitely made that possible. He apparently had packed the Santa Suit before leaving Kansas City, so he was ready. I dressed as Anya, but set up the kitchen as a cookie workshop. So the children got to watch me create from the kitchen while Charlie, had hunkered into his Dad's garage, pretending he was in his own private workshop. It was one of the cutest things I'd seen in a while. I loved how much he enjoyed making children happy and I saw a flickering vision of him as a Dad.

We had the chance to speak that night again, as I joined Charlie on the glider still from two separate states.

"How's your grandfather doing, Charlie?"

"About the same today, but he squeezed a little bit harder when I asked him if he was fighting."

"That's hopeful. How are your parents and grandma?"

"It is. Mom and Dad are doing well, excited to see you tomorrow. Grandma looks a bit weary though. I can tell this is hard for her and honestly, I understand why. I tried to put myself in her shoes and imagine what it would feel like for your partner to be unresponsive. I'd feel helpless if something like that happened now. Imagine how amplified that would become if you'd spent more than 70 years together."

"I just wish I were there to hug her, Charlie."

"She'd love that, Chris. But you'll get to do that tomorrow."

"I will," I said, thinking about all that I still needed to do to before hopping on the highway to head south for Arkansas. Before I knew it, an hour had passed and I was starting to get cold. I offered to call Charlie before I went to bed.

"Alright, my dear. What's the weather supposed to do tomorrow?"

"I'll check and let you know before I go to bed."

"Sounds good. I'll talk to you soon."

I created a list as soon as we got off the phone so I could remember everything I needed to pack and do to secure the house before I left. I ran through the list pretty quickly and showered before hopping in the bed to lay down for the evening. I sent Charlie a text, "Video or phone?" Before I could set the phone down beside me it rang. I answered the video chat and let out a contented sigh as soon as I saw Charlie's face.

"Hi, Charlie!"

"Hmmmmm, hey Sugarplum. It's good to see your face."

"Yeah, likewise. Are you in bed?"

His voice softened, "I am." He studied my face, "I miss you, Chris."

"I miss you too, but I'll see you soon."

"What time are you leaving tomorrow?"

"I was planning on leaving in the morning so I could get there mid-afternoon."

His face perked up. "I just realized how excited I am to hold you again."

"I can hardly wait. So, the weather is supposed to be cold and dry throughout the day."

"You know how to work the seat heaters, right?"

"I do, Charlie. Would you prefer I drive my car down there?"

"No ma'am. The weather can turn at any moment in the winter. I'm not saying your car isn't safe. It's one of the safest on the road. But I want you in something that can take any type of weather."

"Got it."

He snickered, "I love it when you do that."

"What did I do?"

Shaking his head from side to side, he refused to tell me. I yawned.

"You sleepy, Sugarplum?"

"Mmm hmm."

"Okay, I'll let you get some rest. I know you'll be on the road for a while tomorrow."

"It will fly by in no time."

"I hope so."

"Me too," I chuckled. "I'll see you tomorrow. I'll text you when I leave so you have a better idea of when I'll arrive."

"Sleep well, love. Be careful on the road tomorrow,

okay?"

"Will do!" I smiled in his direction. He blew me a kiss which I caught with my hand and placed over my heart.

"Hmmmmmmm," he moaned as he smiled.

"Goodnight sweetheart."

"Goodnight Sugarplum. I love you."

"I love you deeply, Charlie."

The next morning I packed up the truck with my bag and the gifts that Charlie and I had bought for his family. I added water to Randolph and double checked all of the windows and doors before grabbing my backpack and pillow and heading into the cold. I said a quick prayer for traveling grace, sent Charlie a text so he knew I was on my way, and thanked Chief in advance for getting us to Arkansas safely.

The highway was fairly open. Not many other vehicles on the road as I was traveling, so Chief and I had a smooth and uneventful ride down to Fayetteville. Because there weren't many other vehicles, my mind had the chance to wander and reflect on the year that had passed. I found myself feeling grateful to have a chance to appreciate life. So often, before Charlie, I found myself flying through a year and wondering how we'd already made it to Christmas, when it felt like we had just celebrated the New Year. This year though, I was more intentional about celebrating the small things and being mindful of each day as it passed by. Love and loss will cause you to reevaluate your priorities and I'd experienced both that year.

Before I knew it I was in Arkansas pulling into the Hughes' driveway. Charlie came bounding out of the front door and through the courtyard to greet me. He opened the door of the truck and helped me out. I melted into his arms and let my head rest on his heart.

"Is this real?" he asked me.

"It's real, Charlie," I said squeezing harder than I knew I had the capacity to do.

He kissed my temple and lightly rubbed my back. "I've really missed you," he said wiping a tear from the corner of his eye. There was so much to appreciate this year, and it's not that I didn't already have a great appreciation for Charlie. It's just that this time apart really helped me to understand and value his presence.

I leaned my face back so I could look at him. I mean really see him. His eyes twinkled the same way they had last year. There was little stress on his face, unlike what I had seen the night before. I felt more relaxed, and more like myself with him than I had at any other time.

"Hey," I greeted him.

"Hey," he returned before leaning down and planting a seed of affection on my lips.

"Okay, you two!" I heard his dad exclaim. "What will the neighbors think?" he joked.

"Not my concern, Dad." Charlie chided before leaning in to kiss me again.

I pulled back. "Don't get grounded now, Charlie. I just got my visiting privileges restored." Both father and son laughed heartily in the same pattern. The apple didn't fall far from the tree here. I turned around to hug his Dad, and then heard his Mom's voice. I greeted her as well and noticed a figure standing in the doorway. It was his Grandmother. Before I could wave, she had already moved elsewhere in the house.

Charlie and his dad unpacked the truck and carried all of the stuff inside, while his mom and I moseyed our way towards the house.

"It's so good to see you, Chris. I'm so glad you

came. You didn't hear this from me, but Charlie's been a disheveled mess. I thought it was worry over his Grandfather. But when he got up this morning there was a different pep in his step."

I smiled, unsure of how else to outwardly respond as we found our way to the front door. Charlie, must have run upstairs to drop off the bags, because he was bounding back down the stairs as we entered the house.

"What can I get you, Sugarplum?" he asked as he gazed lovingly into my eyes.

"A bathroom," I joked as I leaned my shoulder into his chest.

"You know where to find it," he laughed.

Not long after I arrived, we found our way to the hospital to visit Grandpa Charles. We all waited outside his room for Grandma Elizabeth to spend some alone time with him. Charlie's parents went in to check on her after a half hour or so, and out she came, begrudgingly. She sat down in the chair beside me and I extended my hand for her to hold. I could feel the gratitude and exasperation as she tenderly held on to me. I didn't say a word, just comforted her through my touch.

It wasn't long before she spoke, "Don't ever stop loving each other. Charlie, you hold her heart everyday. Do you hear me?"

"Yes ma'am."

"Everyday."

"I will, Grandma," he said, looking into my eyes with a promise as sweet as a sugarplum.

"Everyday, Charlie," she adamantly replied.

"Yesterday, today, and tomorrow; every single day, Grandma," he told her, still gazing into my eyes. I mouthed the words, to him.

"You too, Chris. Say it out loud. Let him hear it."

"I love you deeply, Charlie."

"That's right. Everyday, you two. Don't take time for granted. It moves swiftly and old age will sneak up on you before you know it."

The two of us nodded in reply then sat in silence until Charlie's parents came out of Grandpa Charles' room, motioning for us to head inside for our visit. I followed Charlie in quietly, waiting for him to take the lead. He sat near the bed, his head bowed low. I found a seat in the chair on the opposite side of the bed and greeted Grandpa quietly.

"Hi Grandpa Charles. Thanks for letting us sit with you today," I whispered. He squeezed my hand and I looked at Charlie.

"Did he squeeze?" he asked me. I nodded rapidly and a smile breached Charlie's face.

"Grandpa, it's Charlie. It's Christmas Eve. We're going to Christmas Eve service tonight, and-" he looked up at me. "I forgot to pack a suit."

"I packed one for him, Grandpa." He squeezed again.

"I know you always tell me to sing so the Lord hears me, so tonight, I'm going to sing loud enough that both of you hear me."

I nodded across the bed at Charlie.

"I need you to know that I'm glad you're fighting, but I was selfish to ask that of you. If you need to go, Grandpa, if it will release you from the pain, if it's your time to go, I understand. We'll continue to take care of Grandma and will love her everyday just the way you did. Well, we'll try to love her as much as you did. Between Chris and I, we might be able to get halfway there, but we'll take care of her."

Tears began to well in my eyes and I squeezed Grandpa Charles' hand. No words would escape. I just continued to hold on as Charlie spoke to his grandfather. He squeezed with every sentiment.

"We'll see you tomorrow, Grandpa," Charlie said as he stood to his feet. "Merry Christmas." I leaned over and whispered into his ear, then followed Charlie out of the room.

After the Christmas Eve service, Charlie drove Grandma Elizabeth and I around the city for a bit before heading back to the house. I found out later that Grandpa Charlie always took her for a spin to see the lights on Christmas Eve. Charlie was doing what he could to maintain some sense of normalcy and tradition for his grandma, and that made me love him even more. She attempted to have me sit in the front with Charlie, but I wanted her to be able to see everything. So, in the back I sat. It was the first time I'd rode in the back of the crew cab, and I noticed a few items back here that I wasn't privy to when I rode in the passenger seat. When we got back to the house, Charlie helped his grandmother out of the truck and then opened the back door for me. Apparently the child locks were on for Jax, and there was no getting out without help.

His grandma went straight to the kitchen when we got back and I attempted to follow her. She still ushered me out of the kitchen, just as she had last year on Christmas Day. Charlie and I headed upstairs to rest for a minute before coming back downstairs when dinner was ready. He looked emotionally exhausted and it was starting to leak into his physical well-being. Things were a bit more quiet this Christmas Eve, than last year, and understandably so. Grandpa Charles had such a big presence and his love for Christmas trickled down to everyone else's Christmas spirit. In this season of love and understanding, it was tough to feel so disconnected from the moment. I prayed for a bit of levity for their family. We sat around the tree, looking at the ornaments in silence before Charlie began singing.

"Little Christmas tree, no one to buy you. Give yourself to me. You're worth your weight in precious gold you'll see, my little Christmas Tree."

Grandma Elizabeth joined in and before I knew it, I was playing along on the piano as every one of us was singing together with tears in our eyes. It was a song of love to give, a song that gave us peace, a song that hope, and a song that brought Grandpa Charles home to us.

I turned to look at Charlie for the last line of the song, "You're big enough for three." The twinkle returned to his eye.

"Hey Chris, you're really good. Do you know how to play, "The Holly and the Ivy?" Mr. Hughes asked me. I instinctively began playing the introduction and told him that this was my Dad's favorite Christmas song. He stood beside the piano and sang as I harmonized with him. We all sang the night away until there were no more requests, but I had one more song in me.

> "This is my winter song to you. The storm is coming soon. It rolls in from the sea. My voice a beacon in the night. My words will be your light to carry you to me."

By the time I got to the second verse, Grandma Elizabeth was singing along to a song I later found out she'd never heard before. It was a gift that was reminiscent of the time I spent singing at the piano with my own grandmother. I hugged her with all the love I could muster, and received the same in return.

We all headed to bed that evening with hope for what tomorrow could bring.

Upstairs in the office bedroom, Charlie stretched out across the Murphy bed as I changed into my pajamas. "I listened to that song on repeat last year, Chris."

"What?"

"Yeah, when I saw you with Marlo. I was at home like a sad puppy, zoned out, looking around at my empty house, listening to that song on repeat."

"Charlie."

"I did."

"Me too," I chuckled.

He looked at me like he saw into my soul and I returned the intensity, which changed his breathing. He looked like he was about to spring out of the bed, but before he could get up there was a quiet knock at the door.

"Come in," Charlie hollered.

Mr. Hughes opened the door gingerly, peeking inside, "Good night, you two."

"Goodnight Dad," we said in unison.

"Y'all need anything, you know where to find it."

"Yes, sir," I said through a slight chuckle - thinking about this same conversation that we'd just had a year prior.

Turning his attention back towards his only son, who still lay stretched out on the bed, resting his chin atop his fists, "Don't get grounded now, Charlie."

"We'll see, Dad," he laughed."

His dad snickered, "Mary's in labor, walking around town lookin' for room at the inn right now. Tonight is the night Jesus was born. Y'all can wait a day."

"I won't let him get grounded, Mr. Hughes," I offered.

"You better not, Chris. We'll ground you too daughter," he said with an ornery smile. Charlie winked in my direction. "Sleep well children."

"You too Dad," we echoed. His dad closed the door and we heard his footsteps trailing down the hallway. We honored our promise that night. Opting not to be grounded and deciding together to wait until the New Year.

I awoke the next morning with Charlie beside me. I could smell breakfast being made and my stomach was eager to rise for Christmas morning. I kissed Charlie on the forehead and woke him up.

"Merry Christmas, Sweetheart!"

He pulled me close and kissed my temple, "Good morning and Merry Christmas, my bride. Can you believe this time next week you'll be waking up as a married woman?"

I hadn't realized that it was that close, but he was right. Panic started to sink in. Had we taken care of all of the details that were left to manage? Every question, every detail that crossed my mind, pushed its way to my forehead in a wrinkle or furrowed brow. Charlie ran his fingers through my hair.

"Hey, none of that worrying. It's Christmas."

"How did you know I was," before I could finish, Charlie had mimicked the look on my face. I couldn't help but laugh. In fact, we both did. We were laying in bed having a good laugh when the door cracked open slightly and Grandma Elizabeth peeked her head inside.

"Are you decent?" she asked us.

"Yes, Grandma," Charlie affirmed.

"Merry Christmas!" she shouted jubilantly as she entered the bedroom and kissed us both on the forehead. "Breakfast is almost ready, sleepyheads."

"Yes ma'am!" Charlie said.

"Chris, I could use a hand in the kitchen," she said.

"I'll grab my slippers and follow you down," I told her. Charlie winked at me and promised not to fall back asleep.

That morning, Grandma Elizabeth and I got to chat as we worked together to finish preparing Christmas breakfast. She spoke about her 70+ years of marriage with Grandpa Charles. Their relationship, she said, was full of ups and downs, but they chose to start over anew each day. It took her 10 years to get to a place where they were both taking each day as the only moment we have. It was wisdom that I'd heard from my parents before and wisdom that I definitely took to heart. Seventy plus years is a testament to patience and loving in a way that was both felt and heard.

I got the honor of ringing the breakfast bell, which brought Charlie and his family downstairs to join Grandma Elizabeth and I to eat. Mr. Hughes asked Charlie if he would do the honor of blessing the Christmas Breakfast in his grandfather's absence and what followed was enough to pull tears from the eyes of even the meanest, grinchiest, scrooge that might exist.

"Heavenly Father, we thank you on this day for the presence of family both seen and unseen. In this challenging year we are humbled to have been given an opportunity to continue to live out Your will on this side of eternity. May we continue to keep Your Son in the center of all we do and reflect His love in our service to others. Fill the hearts of Grandpa Charles and those who are sick with hope. Remind them that nothing is too difficult for You because all power and might are in Your hands. May they run and not grow weary, may they walk and not faint. May they remember that their presence here on earth has a tremendous impact on others whether noticed or not." I felt Charlie's grandmother squeeze my hand. "Lord, we are grateful for time spent together and the memories we'll create and keep throughout the years to come. We thank you for the food we are about to receive. Let it nourish and strengthen us today and in the days to come. These things we pray in Jesus name, Amen."

We ate breakfast and got cleaned up to visit Grandpa Charles in the hospital before exchanging any gifts. Same visiting order as Christmas Eve. Unexpected results. By the time we visited Grandpa Charles, he was squeezing a little bit stronger than the day before and his blink was a bit stronger than I'd seen as well. Charlie spoke to him and we sat in silence before he finally wished him a Merry Christmas and told him that we'd be visiting once more tomorrow before we headed home on the 27th. I asked Charlie if he could leave me with him for a moment. I waited for the door to close before I spoke.

"Grandpa Charles, when I think about this family, I think about how you welcomed me in as a member from the very moment we met. I look forward to our children having the chance to get to know you. Charlie doesn't know it yet, but he's going to be a daddy soon." I felt him squeeze my hand and I squeezed it back. "Merry Christmas, Grandpa. I love you and I'll see you tomorrow."

Much like last year, we video conferenced with my family after opening presents and Charlie and I snuck up to the balcony again.

"What did you and Grandpa talk about?" he asked me as we got in a bit of time on the glider.

"That's between Grandpa and I, Charlie."

We spoke about the travel plans for the 27th and the two of us continued to glide in silence until Mr. Hughes came up to ask for a charger. I was trying to figure out how to tell Charlie that he was going to be a Dad. I knew that I wanted it to just be the two of us. But in the truck as he drove might have disastrous consequences. So maybe once we got back to the house. I knew I'd figure it out.

That evening we watched a couple of classic Christmas movies together, then called it a night. I went to sleep unaware of what tomorrow would bring, but an energy was brewing inside of me and I knew something different was stirring.

We were called to the hospital on the 26th. Everyone moved quickly and quietly, as we raced to receive the news they refused to share with us on the phone. Charlie and I waited outside of his room, as his parents and Grandma Elizabeth went inside to meet with the doctor. They were in there for about 30 minutes before anyone joined them. They all came out soon thereafter and the doctor called in Charlie and I.

"Which one of you was with him last on Christmas Day?" the doctor asked stoically.

"I was." I raised my hand.

His head turned in my direction. "Are you Chris?"

"I am."

"He opened his eyes and asked for you right after you left."

I sat down in the chair beside Grandpa Charles

while Charlie stood still, his feet cemented in place and his hands fidgeting and massaging his scalp.

I looked at the doctor and leaned towards Grandpa, "Can I?" The doctor nodded.

"Hi Grandpa Charles. It's me, Chris. I'm here with Charlie." We all waited patiently. Charlie asked the doctor a million questions, and I listened to his answers to see if there was something I could do to help.

As the two of them were speaking, a weary voice spoke my name. "Chris?"

My head turned sharply towards Grandpa Charles. I cupped his hand and replied, "I'm here, Grandpa. I'm here."

His eyes opened and Charlie stepped outside to grab the rest of his family.

"Chris, Merry Christmas," he nodded in my direction. "Merry Christmas," he said again as he squeezed my hand.

"I haven't told him yet," I hurried the words from my mouth before Charlie's return as the doctor stepped closer to Grandpa Charles who nodded weakly.

His eyes lit up as Charlie entered the room, "Merry Christmas!" They all gathered around to wish him the same and wait to see what was next. He didn't have much to say, but he kept making eye contact with me. Every time we locked eyes, I would nod and smile, and he'd do the same.

That night as we lay in bed preparing to rest before leaving in the morning, Charlie asked me again what I'd said to Grandpa Charles on Christmas Day. I made him promise that he wouldn't make a noise.

"Not a peep, Charlie."

"Promise, Sugarplum."

"Swear it, Charlie."

"I swear, not a sound, Sugarplum." I studied his face

to ensure he was serious.

"I was hoping to tell you when we got back to Kansas City, but today was unexpected."

"You're telling me."

I lowered my voice and leaned near his ear. "I told him that you were going to be a Daddy, but that you didn't know yet." Charlie's face froze.

His words were hushed but his breath and facial expressions danced with wild abandon. "Can I ask a question?"

"Yes, baby. I just didn't want you to yell excitedly."

His eyes narrowed. "Are you serious? That's what you told him? Is it true? You're not playing the what if game we were playing before are you?"

I whispered. "Yes, Charlie, that's what I told him and yes, it's true. I took a test before I left Kansas City."

"Holy Sh...!!"

"Shhh..." I said trying to cover up his expletive.

He caressed my face then whispered, "I couldn't love anything more than this moment."

I continued to whisper. "I love you, deeply Charlie. You're going to make a great Daddy for whomever is hanging out in here with me."

Then he kissed me; on the nose, not on the temple and not on the lips. He kissed me on the nose, and it was different than any I'd ever received from him before. It was tender and sweet, loving and nurturing, intimate and affectionate, all at the same time. We were more deeply connected that day than the day prior, only because Charlie had confirmation that we were building a family. I went to sleep that night feeling hopeful that our tomorrows were going to be filled with the type of love that his grandparents, and our parents had. And then my anxiety kicked in. We were going to be responsible for someone else's life.

Chapter 14
New Year's Eve

Dr. Chris:

The closer we inched to New Year's Eve, the more my anxiety began to quell. I only had a few questions on my mind really. If rain on your wedding day is supposed to bring good luck to your marriage, does the same hold true for snow? If so, just how much snow is considered a sign of luck and what if we received enough to shut down the city...again? I'm asking for a friend. It's me. I'm the friend. The trip home to Kansas City was beautiful. It snowed the entire drive back. Thankfully the roads were too warm for it to stick. That was another issue entirely over the next two days, as we were trying to move the rest of my boxes into Charlie's house. We'd pack up the pickup as full as we could and add boxes to my car, both of which were adding much needed weight for traction. Thankfully we weren't traveling very far, but unloading those boxes and the remaining furniture was a different story. The tenant in my womb was slowing me down. I was so thankful for Steve and Sabrina. Even Jax pitched in to help us.

We tried not to trek a sloshy mess into the house, but it was hard not to. Even though we'd shovel between trips to and from the condo, we still had snow greeting us when it was time to move the boxes inside, which is another thing entirely. We didn't put the boxes anywhere specific because it was so cold. We were literally bringing them inside the doorway, then turning around to go grab another load.

The evening of the 29th and the morning of the 30th, we spent unpacking as many boxes as we could. It wasn't quite what I had envisioned for my last days as a single woman, but unpacking boxes with Charlie was calming, especially considering that we'd be legally intertwining our lives for the foreseeable future on the 31st.

Family was calling to congratulate us and wish us well. As the hours progressed, more and more of those calls also included regrets that they would be unable to make it. This was a storm that would not stop. It had dumped 10 inches on us already over the course of four days, and the evening of the 30th the forecasters were calling for the same amount in a matter of hours. Charlie and I had a talk about whether or not to postpone, as the two of us were concerned about the safety of those who were traveling to celebrate with us.

His parents were included in that count. They had initially planned on driving in on the 29th, but their plans kept shifting with the weather. Soon the 29th became the morning of the 30th, then the afternoon of the 30th. Eventually after we had given them the latest forecast, their arrival shifted to the early morning hours of the 31st. Charlie was worried. I was too. So we offered a video conference to them as an alternative. We sent the link to all who were unable to join us, and hoped that we would have the opportunity to party with them at a later date.

In spite of the snow, I still had plans to spend one final night in the condo by myself before getting married. So, the night before my wedding, after our virtual rehearsal dinner, Charlie and Chief - who was fitted with snow tires and chains that chomped through the snowpack, dropped me off in the circle drive of the condo. I met my groom in the middle of the truck's cab, sealing the evening with a doting embrace and leaving him with the promise that I'd meet him at the altar.

"You be safe tomorrow so I CAN meet you at the altar," he said with worry in his eyes.

I nodded. "You too Charlie. Call me when you get home. Okay?"

The two of us got in one more glimpse of each other as single folk, before I headed inside to greet Ralph as a resident, one final time.

"Big day tomorrow, Chris!"

"Big day indeed, Ralph!" I replied.

"You and Charlie are going to make some beautiful babies." What a creepy thing to say to someone. I mean, I had no doubt that we would. But what on earth would possess someone to say such a thing without knowing whether or not people were able to have children or if they even wanted them at all?

"Thank you, Ralph." I realized that he probably had no idea what he was stepping into, so I ignored it all together and instead returned to get my rest because my tiny passenger was wearing me out.

That evening I received a call from Vonne, checking in to see how I was doing. I let her know that I was fine with the exception of the worry I held for our traveling guests. The snow had become relentless in its pursuit to cause gridlock, and I wasn't ready for the reality of people who were involved in accidents because they were trying to get to the church to celebrate with us. She and I were on the phone for at least 30 minutes when it occurred to me that I hadn't heard from Charlie yet.

"Hey Vonne, I have a phone call or two that I need to make."

"Are you okay, Chris? There's a lot of anxiety in your voice."

"I am. I'm not. I will be?"

"Call me back, sis and let me know what's going on."

"I will. Love you!"

As soon as I heard her reply I ended the call and dialed Charlie's number. The phone rang and rang, eventually rolling into voicemail. I waited another 10 minutes before calling again. I figured maybe he was driving and unable to answer the phone the first time. Again, the phone rang and rang before his voicemail picked up. I left a message explaining that I was concerned because of the snow. After waiting 20 additional minutes, I called again and left another message asking him to call me back as soon as he was able. Call ended. Another call began. Sabrina.

"Hey, Chris, how are you holding up this evening?"

"Hey Sabrina, I was doing okay, but I haven't heard from Charlie since he dropped me off here at the condo. That was well over an hour ago. I was hoping maybe he had stopped at your place to visit Steve. I'm just worried with the weather, that's all."

"Charlie!" Sabrina shouted. "Chris, did you leave him a message?"

"I did. Is he there?"

She wasn't talking to me, "Where is your phone?"

"He's there?"

"Mmmm hmmm. Check those pockets. All of them!"

"I'm so glad he's okay."

"Yeah, maybe it's in Chief. Go check! Sorry, Chris. He's here and I'm going to kill him for you."

"No need, Sabrina. I'm just glad he's safe."

"He hadn't intended on coming by here. I think he's a little nervous."

"Go easy on him, sis." I laughed.

"Never. Looks like he found his phone in the truck. He'll probably call you in a minute."

"Thanks, Sabrina. I'll see you tomorrow."

"You bet!"

She was right. Less than 60 seconds after getting off the phone with Sabrina, my cell phone rang.

"Hello?" I answered as nonchalantly as possible.

"Hey Sugarplum, I'm sooooooooo sorry!"

"Charlie."

"I was on my way home and I was just gonna swing by here to chat with Steve for a minute, but I lost track of time."

"I was worried you'd gotten into an accident or something."

"I'm sorry, I'm fine. Sabrina is giving me the stank eye right now, but I'm okay. I'm about to say goodbye to them right now."

"Charlie, I don't care how long you stay there. I just hoped the snow hadn't caused an accident."

"No accident. I'll be headed home shortly. I promise I'll call you when I get there. In fact, I'll text you when I leave so you know when I've left."

"If that works for you, then whatever sir."

"Meet you at the altar?"

"Of course. Are you okay?"

"Just nervous energy, Sugarplum. I'll be fine."

"Okay. Love you deeply, Charlie."

"I love you, Chris."

I called Vonne back and explained what happened so she wouldn't be busy worrying about me, then shuffled through the last stack of mail that was waiting for me on the kitchen island. Hiding out amongst the bills and Christmas Cards was the envelope from Colorado that Charlie had set aside just a week or so before. I vaguely recall seeing this arrive in May, but like all of the other mail I had received, I just stacked it on the island and grabbed what I needed in that moment before jetting and leaving it for later. Now, there I was, the night before my wedding, thinking about all who wouldn't be able to physically join us in the same space, but could attend because of technology. I wished that same technology offered the option to transcend astral planes. I knew that they would be spiritually present, my Grandparents and Marlo. But I wanted to see them just the same. I yearned for a sign that they were there to celebrate with me.

I held that letter in my hands and contemplated leaving it sealed. Without knowing what was inside, I could retain the peace that I had come to know. Once I opened it though, regardless of what the letter said, there was no turning back. I couldn't unknow what his final words were to me. I needed to know that he understood my hesitance. I wanted a sign. I asked for a sign, and then my phone rang.

"Hello?"

"Hi Chris. It's Janae." Marlo's intended. If ever there were a sign from the Universe, I took that as it.

"Hi Janae, how are you?"

Her voice was upbeat. "I'm okay, I made it to the hotel!"

"I'm so glad you could make it. I wasn't sure, with the weather and all, that anyone other than Charlie and I would be there." I laughed.

"I wouldn't miss it for the world. I feel like Marlo moved mountains so I could be here. There were so many things that could have gone wrong, but didn't."

"I'm sure he did!"

"Anyway, is there anything you need before tomorrow?"

"I think I have everything I need, but if you could pray for the safety of those who are going to try to travel to the church and reception venue that would be helpful."

"That I can do! Do you have something blue yet?"

"Oh shoot! I sure don't. I bet I can find something around-"

"Chris, I had picked out a garter to wear at our wedding. I brought it with me in case you needed it. Also, Marlo asked me to hand deliver his gift to you before your wedding. He said you were supposed to open it before you walk down the aisle."

I didn't know where the words came from, but I blurted them out before I could stop them. "Janae, would you like to stand in for Marlo tomorrow? It would mean a lot to us if you would."

"Chris, I don't know how comfortable I'd be doing that."

"I understand. Please know that you can change your mind at any point though."

"Noted. Is it okay if I meet you before the wedding begins?"

"Absolutely. I'll text you some details of my schedule. Does that work?"

"It does. Have a good night and I'll see you tomorrow."

After our call had ended I sent Janae the details I promised via text before it slipped my mind. I took a breath, studied his handwriting, then opened the letter from Marlo. Before I could unfold it, I received a notification on my phone. I assumed it was from Janae, but it was Charlie, letting me know that he was on his way home from Steve and Sabrina's.

"Be careful, love." I replied, then picked up the letter again.

Marlo was old school. Any memos at work were handwritten. His Christmas cards, handwritten. This letter. Handwritten. For that I was eternally thankful. It felt like he was still here. That part of him remained with me. I had him here, as long as I had this physical reminder of his existence on earth. I was grateful for Janae's phone call because it gave me the courage to read this letter instead of locking it away in a vault somewhere. It was dated May 24, 2020.

"Chris – my younger sister,

Congratulations!! I can hear you now – I'm only 6 months younger!' I'm so excited for you and Charlie. I've been rooting for him since we called him, mystery man. I have never seen you light up the way you do when he's near, or even at the sound of his name. Everything has a way of working out for our good. The heartache you suffered before him was there to help you appreciate Charlie even more. He is your person. I wish the two of you decades and decades of good times, laughter, and challenging each other to grow in love.

You and I have done a lot of living by each other's side. I've seen you push through your fears and cry thousands of tears. I have watched you prove other people wrong, and more importantly prove yourself right. I have had the chance to watch you stand up for others and for yourself and I truly am a better person because of your friendship.

I'm sad at the thought that I won't be able to see you get married or become a mom, because the two of us have shared just about every other milestone possible together. As you know by now, that virus is traveling fast through the globe and the doctors here in Colorado are trying their hardest to figure out how to attack its pathogens so they can treat people once they contract it. They're not so sure that the

METHOD THEY'VE USED TO TREAT ME WILL WORK. THEY'RE TRYING TO REMAIN OPTIMISTIC, BUT I KNOW IN MY GUT THAT I'M NOT GOING TO MAKE IT. SO, I'VE GIVEN JANAE SOME INSTRUCTIONS ON WHAT'S NEXT FOR MY PHYSICAL BODY. I'M NOT SURE WHAT'S ON THE OTHER SIDE. BUT, IF IT'S MY TIME TO FIGURE IT OUT, THEN I'LL BE READY.

I DO WISH I COULD HUG YOU ONCE MORE, BUT THIS IS ONE TIME WHEN THE RISK IS NOT WORTH THE REWARD. CHRIS, I KEEP THINKING OF ALL THE THINGS I WAS GOING TO DO. ALL OF THE THINGS I WAS GOING TO SAY. THE WEDDING GIFT I WAS GOING TO GIVE YOU. WHERE WE WERE GOING TO TRAVEL TOGETHER ON OUR COUPLE'S VACATIONS.

I MISSED SO MUCH LIFE, PLANNING WHAT I WAS GOING TO DO AND MISSING OUT ON THE MOMENT I WAS DAYDREAMING THROUGH. PROMISE ME THAT YOU'LL DO THINGS DIFFERENTLY. LOVE HIM NOW. CALL THEM NOW. SING TERRIBLY (WE BOTH KNOW THE TRUTH) TODAY. NOTHING IS PROMISED TO ANY OF US. NOT OUR HEALTH, OUR WEALTH, OR OUR HAPPINESS. ONE THING THAT'S CRYSTAL CLEAR TO ME IS THAT WE ARE CO-CREATORS IN THE LIFE WE LIVE. SO LIVE, CHRIS. LIVE THE LIFE YOU'VE DREAMED OF SINCE WE WERE LITTLE KIDS PLAYING BACKYARD DOCTORS WITH YOUR DOLLS.

I PROMISE I'LL BE THERE TO CELEBRATE WITH YOU, WHETHER YOU CAN SEE ME OR NOT AND I'LL FIND A WAY TO SHOW YOU THAT I'M THERE. IT MIGHT FEEL LIKE SOME OF THOSE NOTES WE USED TO PASS IN SCHOOL AND THOSE ADVENTURES WE CALL OURSELVES HAVING THROUGHOUT THE NEIGHBORHOOD. BUT YOU'LL KNOW IT'S-A-ME, MARLO. I COULDN'T END IT WITHOUT AT LEAST ONE WHACK JOKE.

YOU ARE A SPECTACULAR HUMAN BEING AND I'M SO GRATEFUL TO CALL YOU FRIEND. YOU DESERVE A UNIVERSE OF LOVE AND YOU WILL ALWAYS BE MY FAVORITE CHRIS.

I'LL LOVE YOU FOR ETERNITY, FRIEND.

MARLO

P.S. TELL THAT CHARLIE GUY, IF HE HURTS YOU I WILL HAUNT HIM UNTIL HE APOLOGIZES. I'M KIDDING - KIND OF."

How do you wrap your mind around the end of your

own existence and think enough of others to leave something behind for them as well? That was Marlo for you. I can only imagine what he must have done for Janae, if he thought enough to lift me up once more in a letter.

I lay on the floor, looking over each word, wishing there were more and trying to keep those tears of mine from staining the paper. I felt myself sink into the carpeting when a blanket of peace felt like it was draped over my head and shoulders.

"Thank you," I spoke out loud to Marlo just before my phone rang. I didn't look at the screen. I just answered it.

"Hello?"

"Hey, Sugarplum. Are you okay?"

"Charlie, I just read that letter from Marlo. I'm okay."

"You sure? I can come sit with you if you want."

"You miss me?"

He laughed. "Yes. A lot."

"Starting tomorrow, we'll share every day together."

He whispered, "I can't wait."

"Are YOU okay?" I asked after hearing the wistfulness in his voice.

"Yeah, I'm safely back at the house. Steve and Sabrina are ready for tomorrow."

"So is Janae."

"Is she here?"

"Mm Hmm.."

"In Kansas City?"

"Yeah, I asked her about what we had discussed."

"What did she say?"

"She was a little uncomfortable, just as we thought she'd be. But, I told her she could always change her mind later."

"Good."

We continued to chat about what was on our mind and what we were looking forward to on our wedding day.

"On the way home I had a random flashback of the vision I saw when we almost got in that accident. Two boys and a girl, Chris. Do you remember that?"

"I do."

"Were they twin boys in yours?"

"They were."

"Yeah, mine too. Can we name one of them Marlo?"

"Charlie, I would love that."

We stayed on the phone until I was too sleepy to filter what was coming out of my mouth before I spoke, which always made Charlie laugh.

"You need to get to bed ma'am. I'll meet you at the altar tomorrow."

"In my white dress. We ain't gettin no younger man, we might as well do this."

"Oh my. Goodnight, Sugarplum."

I giggled. "Goodnight Sweetheart."

"Hey. I loved you yesterday. I love you today. I'll love you tomorrow."

"I love you deeply, Charles Lane Hughes. I can't wait to marry you tomorrow."

"Are you sure you don't want me to come sit with you?"

"I'm sure. It will make tomorrow that much sweeter."

"You're right. I'm blowing you a kiss."

"I just caught it."

"Where did you place it?"

"On my heart. Are you stalling?"

"Absolutely."

"Goodnight sir."

"Goodnight, Beautiful."

I woke up the next morning excited about the day, until I looked outside. It seemed like there was more snow than they had predicted, and I wasn't sure what that meant for the day ahead.

The pastor called around 10 that morning to let me know that the church was in good shape and that he would be there and ready to go when we were. The limo company was running behind schedule, but promised to be there within an hour of my pickup time. The good news was, I had budgeted far more than the one hour cushion that they were absorbing. Steve and Sabrina were clear and ready to go. My parents, sister and family were all ready to go. I'd received a text from Charlie, his Dad was going to drive up that morning and I said a prayer for his safety.

Janae, met me at the condo around noon. She told me she was bringing lunch, the garter, and the wedding gift from Marlo.

Ralph called up when she arrived, and I asked him to send her on up. When she knocked on the door, I was eager to greet her with a hug, but that would prove to be much more difficult than I imagined.

"Hi Chris!"

"Oh Janae, you're pregnant!"

"I am. The baby should be here sometime in February."

"Seven months along already?"

"Seven months. I don't know that I'd add already though." She laughed. I didn't have any furniture to offer her a seat and I couldn't imagine her trying to get up off of the floor at seven months pregnant. I apologized profusely.

"It's quite alright, Chris. You didn't know."

"Hold on, I'll see if Ralph can bring up a chair." There was a knock at the door before I could get to the phone to call him. Ralph was waiting patiently outside with two chairs, one for her and one for me. He was truly the best.

We talked over lunch about how she found out after the funeral that she was pregnant with Marlo's daughter. A girl! He would've made such a great girl dad. I told her that I hadn't been to a doctor yet to confirm it, but that there was a strong chance that the child I was carrying was going to be born about 6 months after hers. We cried in the kitchen, then cried in the living room.

"We've got to stop all of this crying. No puffy eyes today. Today is a joyous occasion. Speaking of which, here's your something blue, and Marlo's gift."

"Thank you." I rushed to the kitchen to cover a paper towel with cold water in an attempt to shrink down any puffiness that might be lingering from the previous night's tears or those from that morning. When I returned, I opened the present from Marlo to find a photo of the two of us that perfectly captured the moment I punched him in the stomach during our Tom Thumb wedding. I didn't understand why they had children all dressed up and pretending to get married to each other. I also didn't understand why they tried to make my friend kiss me. So I punched him and ran down the aisle to the laughter of the adults who were present, save for my parents who ended up chasing after me. "I never apologized to Marlo for that." I laughed at the memories that came flooding back.

"Turn it over," Janae said.

I turned it over to find an inscription on the back of the photo from Marlo, "I KNOW YOU'RE SORRY FOR PUNCHING ME IN MY GUT. REMEMBER TO KISS CHARLIE WITH YOUR MOUTH – NOT YOUR FIST. LOVE YOU FOREVER, SIS."

I laughed and cried, and Janae did the same. "That husband of yours was one in a million, Janae."

"He was."

"If you ever need anything, you know I got you."

She nodded and barely managed to squeak out a thank you. Before I knew it, 2:00 had rolled around. The limo was supposed to get me around 1 to take me to the church, which meant they should've been close to the condo. I checked my phone. There were no messages. My dress was with my parents, so it was already at the church. The only thing I needed to do was show up ready to get my hair done, then get dressed.

The plan was for Janae to ride in the limo to the church with me, but after another 30 minutes of waiting, I decided to call the limo company myself.

"So it seems they've gotten stuck. They're sending another limo to get us. It should be here in 30 minutes."

"The wedding starts at 5:00?"

"Yes. I know, we're cutting it really close. I'll call my Mom and let her know what's going on."

Everyone at the church was on pause, waiting for my arrival. But they'd have to wait much longer than the 30 minutes I had projected. I received a call that the second limo was also stuck in the snow and they wouldn't be sending out another. Their vehicles all had low ground clearance. I called Mom back. Dad was personally escorting relatives to the church in his SUV.

"We'll figure it out, Chris." She urged me to stay calm. It was the only reaction I felt in my body.

I called Charlie to let him know what was going on.

"Are you in your dress?"

"No. My dress is at the church."

"I'll pick you up in 20 minutes."

"Charlie, you're not supposed to see me before the wedding."

"At this point I don't trust anyone else to deliver you there safely. I'm coming to get you."

In 20 minutes, Janae and I met Charlie and Chief in the circle drive. He was just as surprised to see what she was carrying as I was when I opened the condo door.

"Put Janae in the front, Charlie. There's more room up there."

Charlie helped her into the truck, then turned to help me up into the crew cab.

"Are you in?" he asked me before shutting the door after I said yes.

He put the truck in drive and away we went. I waved goodbye to Ralph and turned to watch the condo get smaller as we drove away from it. It was like closing the pages of a book I had thoroughly enjoyed reading over and over again but had put on a shelf in hopes of the new adventure that awaited me on the other side of the bookcase.

We arrived at the church a little before 4:00, which meant that I'd need to hurry up and get ready. The women in my family, Sabrina and Janae included, surrounded me and lifted me in prayer as they began the process of dressing me and fixing my hair to be wedding ready. In less than 30 minutes we were all ready to go. I received a letter from Charlie, delivered by my nephew Corbin. They urged me to read it out loud. It probably kept me from crying, but it sure didn't stop their tears.

"Chris, I'm so excited to step into our life together. I am a better human being because of the way you love me and I vow to return that love to you ten-fold. There's nothing we can't conquer together and I'm grateful that you've chosen to walk through life with me at your side. One adventure each day, no matter the size. I'm looking forward to growing in love with you. Meet you at the altar! Charlie"

I sent Charlie a text, "Love you, deeply Sweetheart.

Meet you at the altar."

His reply was one emoji, "😍"

Before I knew it, I was handing over my phone to my sister and we began to line up in processional order. I said one quick prayer of thanks for the day that I was able to experience when I felt a light hand on my shoulder. I turned around to find Mrs. Hughes, wearing the same champagne colored dress as my mother, holding her corsage in hand and asking for me to pin it on her. I hugged her with all the strength I could muster.

"You look beautiful Chris!"

"I didn't think you'd make it, Mom!"

"We all did!"

"All of you?"

"Grandpa's out there too. Charlie hasn't seen him yet. Grandma Elizabeth is going to walk him down the aisle."

I tried my hardest not to cry, but there was no stopping the joy that flowed from receiving that news. I pinned on her corsage and hugged her once more before watching her head to the front of the line with my Mom.

Dad snuck in from who knows where and quietly asked me if I was ready. I nodded.

"It's not too late to change your mind." A smile rose upon his face.

"I know, Dad. No changing my mind. I'm ready."

"I know you are, kiddo. I'm so proud of you." He stuck out his left arm for me to hold and with his opposite hand, delivered my bouquet, and away we went.

I heard the music echoing through the sanctuary. and assumed there wouldn't be many people present. I assumed wrong. Between my Dad and his family, they had picked up as many local guests as possible to ensure they could be present for the wedding. I caught a glimpse of them as the doors opened for our wedding party to walk down the aisle. The next time the doors opened, my eyes were glued on the handsome man that was waiting patiently for me at the altar. I'd never been so sure of someone in my life.

Charlie:

I walked into the sanctuary with the pastor, who shook my hand and then took his place. There I stood, at the altar, waiting nervously in front of faces I recognized and some I didn't, trying my hardest not to lock my knees. The doors opened and in walked my grandparents, with my father trailing closely behind them for safekeeping. I was so overjoyed to see them that I teared up. It was at that moment that I knew I was going to be a weepy mess during this ceremony.

I knew Grandpa had been discharged from the hospital on the 29th, but I didn't think there was any way that he'd be here in Kansas City for the wedding.

In walked our Moms behind my grandparents. They lit a candle for all who were missing, including my groomsman, Marlo. The wedding party was next, Steve and Sabrina, Vonne and Janae, followed by Jax bringing the rings, Christina dropping the flowers, and Corbin excitedly announcing to all that, "The Bride is coming!" The doors closed behind the children. My stomach was anxiously awaiting her arrival and though I had just dropped her off at the church, I was ready to see her, to hold her hands and recite those vows. *Don't lock your knees Charlie.*

When the doors opened again, my eyes were locked on her. Her soul was gorgeous and waiting for her to walk down the aisle was the hardest thing for me to do. On the outside I may have looked cool, calm and collected, but inside I wanted to run to her. Her smile was directed at me and I raised one eyebrow in her direction, like the tip of a cap. We didn't take our eyes off of each other. I don't think an army of children could have made me lose my gaze. I could feel them welling in my eyes the closer she got to the altar and I could feel the love being poured into me as she neared the end of the aisle. *This woman.* By the time her Dad went to shake my hand, the tears fell out like they were exhasperated from trying to hold onto my eyes.

He pulled me near and whispered to me, "I love you, Charlie. Take good care of Chris for us. It's okay to let them fall. Don't try to hold in those tears of joy."

I nodded at all of it and squeezed him tight. I barely recall what was said. I waited to take Chris' hand until it was presented to me by her Dad. Then in an instant, with the touch of her hand, I was transported back to the Fresh Grind where I caught her. It was like looking at her for the first time all over again. The warmth that was ever present when she was near, seemed to be stronger, or maybe it was my nerves that made it feel that way. Either way, there was that magnetic pull again. I had never felt so certain that I was supposed to be connected to someone in all my life.

Dr. Chris:

Dad had given me away and Charlie held my hand. It was like I was instantly back at the Fresh Grind being caught by the man who was standing in front of me, only now, he was waiting to marry me. I didn't have the words to tell him how much I loved him, so I pushed that energy through my body and hoped he felt it. He moved closer towards me and the two of us found our way to the altar.

"Hi," he said with a wide grin.

"Hi," I said, returning his smile with one of my own.

Our guests laughed. The pastor walked us through the traditional ceremony and a very special guest performed a reading.

Marley had been doing exceptionally well at each of her 6 month incremental visits, and I asked her parents if they would be okay with her being part of our wedding ceremony. Once I had their approval, I asked Marley, who was over the moon with excitement. She quietly approached and lowered the microphone, cleared her voice, and began stoically reciting the first of two passages.

"Mawwage." Her giggle induced laughter within all of us. "Mawwage is what bwings us togeder today. Mawwage, that bwessed awwangement, that dweam within a dweam. And wove, twue wove, wiww fowwow you fowevah...So tweasuwe youw wove..."

She waited for our guests to stop laughing before starting her second passage, which was a bit more serious in nature.

"As you hold the hands of your beloved, remember that there's more to love than the feelings of passion that pull you in close on this day. Love is helping each other up when you fall. Love is communicating why you're angry and coming to a resolution together. Love is holding each other through grief and walking beside each other in joy. Love is supporting each other's dreams and never allowing doubt to creep in or settle in place. Love is creating individual pieces that fit together to build something greater. Love is walking together in the same direction every single day, not because you have to, but because you need to, you want to, you choose to, you promise to. Love is unspoken tenderness that adds light and life to others with each passing hour. Choose love today. Choose love tomorrow. Choose love, always."Jax's eyes fixed on Marley, were full of adoration.

Charlie and I marveled at Marley as she recited her passage. He squeezed my hand with each passing sentence, and nodded in affirmation when she was finished. Tears rolled softly down his face and mine. I reached up with my left hand to wipe them away and our guests cooed at my outward expression of love.

We recited traditional vows before the sand ceremony and exchanging of the rings. The pastor pronounced us husband and wife and Charlie cupped my face like I was a precious gem.

"Can I kiss you?" he asked, then bit his lip, anxiously awaiting my answer. I nodded.

There felt like a million eyes on us in that moment, but none of that mattered. I was completely swept away as his left hand traced down my spine, coming to a rest on my waist, cradling me softly as he slowly dipped me backwards. My heart felt like it was about to beat out of my chest before the feel of his lips on mine caused my knees to wobble. I was glad he was holding me, because I surely would've collapsed. But if love was helping each other up when you fall, I would've been okay. So much electricity surged between our lips as I thought about the fact that I was kissing my life partner. I curled my fingers around his forearms to steady myself, and for the first time in my life, I wasn't shy about showing everyone else how I felt. There he was, steady and stoic, full of warmth. Home. I kissed him like tomorrow wasn't promised and I wanted everyone to know how much I loved him that day.

I don't remember much after that. I do remember seeing a big charter bus parked in front of the church. I'm assuming it took people to the reception which was being held at the place where we met, The Fresh Grind coffeehouse, not Arrowhead Stadium. I remember taking very cold pictures in the snow and Charlie's warm body, keeping me from freezing. I remember the way he looked at me as if there weren't anybody else on earth he wanted to be with in that moment. I remember him driving us to the reception and kissing at every stoplight. I remember walking into the reception with the wedding party and I remember sitting down to eat. There were guests we greeted, those who called him by his new nickname, Sparky, and a dance floor was created. But before we danced, there was the toast.

Every guest received a champagne flute filled with sparkling cider and one sugarplum nestled at the bottom. Forks clinked on glasses, prompting us to kiss each other. As I stood beside him, Charlie raised a glass in the air and thanked everyone for braving the elements to join us. He thanked our parents for loving us into the people we were on that day. He thanked our friends for standing with us on one of the most important days of our lives and then he turned towards me.

"Chris, I wouldn't be the man I am today without your love and support and I promise on every sugarplum in our glasses that I'll magnify that love and return it to you and others. I promise I'll cherish and live each day. I promise I'll choose love, always."

We danced the night away and at midnight during the countdown to take us into 2021, Charlie with his forehead nuzzled on mine, asked me what the best part of that year was. I smiled and kissed his nose.

"It will always be you, Charlie. Every year, from this point forward. The best part of my year, each year, will always be you."

He was everything that I wanted in a partner. He was everything that I needed. And I - I felt like I was everything I wanted to be in that moment. I was enough. He was enough. We were enough, and we were about to step beyond any place we'd ever been before.

"Is that why you and Dad make a sugarplum promise, every New Year's Eve Mom?" our Son asked after I finished telling his bride the story of how his father and I met.

"It is, Marlo," I told him before he turned to his twin brother, Chuck for confirmation. "Ask your younger sister, Vonnie if she knew while you're at it," I said as I watched them head towards the row of gliders in the snowy backyard.

I felt abundantly blessed to have built a family with the man who was snoring away in the easy chair. I tapped him on the leg and handed him his coat, hat, gloves, and the trusty red and white fair aisle printed scarf that I had wrapped around his neck so many years ago. "Let's get in some time on the glider, Sweetheart."

"As you wish, Sugarplum."

My life had forever been changed by sugarplums, by the spoonful, those that shimmer, and those we made promises on every year. When Charlie and I met, I had no idea what the future would bring us, but I was continually encouraged to stay open and in the moment. His presence in my life added more value than even my wildest imagination could have conjured up. And while our life together was far from smooth sailing, the choppy waters we experienced together taught me more about myself, about life, and about love. For that I was exceedingly grateful.

AUTHOR'S NOTES & ACKNOWLEDGEMENTS

Author's Notes

So here we are, at the end of the story of Dr. Chris and Charlie. Of all the books in this trilogy, this was the most challenging one to write. I've changed the middle, and the ending, but never the beginning. I knew in my gut that Marlo's death was going to be tough to write, and much like the people I've personally lost in the last two years, his life was one I learned a lot from. It is not in our words that our lives are lived but through our actions; in how we pour into others, in how much we embrace the unknown, in how much we charge ahead towards our dreams.

Our actions leave a wake that ripples far beyond our immediate circles. Marlo's death in this book is a symbolic reminder for us to embrace life for all of its beauty, simplicity, and inifite possibilies. The loss of what we once knew as reality and thought to be normal has shaken many of us back to the core foundation of who we are as human beings. Indeed it has caused us to question what's really important in our lives.

My hope in losing Marlo, is that through Dr. Chris'

example, you can still see the opportunity to find yourself, and love hard and deep, so others will never question what they meant to you.

This series was an unexpected detour from my path as a children's book author, and one I have learned to embrace over time. They say authors write the stories that they need, yet I doubted that I needed a romance novel in my life. I was wrong.

These books were about so much more than Dr. Chris, Charlie, Marlo, Steve, Sabrina, Marley, Jax, and any of the other characters who were included. They're far bigger than romance. They're about the sweet fruit that comes from nurturing healthy relationships; romantic, friendly, familial, collegial, whatever form.

Even when we think we have the answer, we only really possess a tiny fraction of knowledge compared to all the information there is to obtain. Through these books I've had the chance to connect more interpersonally with readers and friends, and while none of it was something I predicted for my life, I am grateful for every ounce of it.

Only time will tell whether or not I continue to write romance novels. But, the stories within the Sugarplum series have had a profound and indelible impact on my life. They've taught me more about myself, about life, and about love. So I guess I did write the story that I needed afterall. For that I am exceedingly grateful.

Acknowledgements

To the Beta Readers, your patience, quick follow through and time is truly invaluable. I appreciate your willingness to ensure that the third and final book for Dr. Chris and Charlie lived up to the expectations left by the first two books in this series. I appreciate you more than you know.

To the friends and family who encouraged me to stick it out through the end of the series, I appreciate you and am tremendously grateful for your support. My most sincere thanks to Herston, Kelsey Haynes, Kelly Williams and Tanesha Ford for risking potential spoilers to help me sift through the silt to find the gold. I appreciate your time, your honest critiques, and the humor you leant to a book with such heavy expectations.

To Coach D, thank you for holding me up through my grief and for bringing Charlie to life in a way that helped me envision the finish line of this story (*ahem* unabashed plug - y'all go check out the audiobook version of this series!). Forever grateful for your light.

To my parents, thank you for openly displaying your love for all who are present to witness it. It is because of how you love each other and others that I was able to write such a powerful example of long lasting relationships. Happy 50th Anniversary!! Hope the love scenes don't embarrass you too much. 😇

To Grandpa James, who encouraged me with quiet nods and your one of a kind smile, thank you for giving me a glimpse into who you were as a human being. One of our last conversations on this side of eternity was about how you had been thinking more about your late wife, Grandma Elizabeth. I could see the love you still held for her in your eyes during that chat. As heartbreaking as it was to lose you, that one brief moment was encouraging. In it, you showed me that there is at least one thing exists without beginning or end. Love is eternal.

Finally, to the enthusiatic readers of the Sugarplum series, thank you for sharing your love of Dr. Chris and Charlie. I hope the final installment fills your soul with love in action.

About the Author

C. L. Fails is an Author, Creative Architect, and an Accidental Educator; having served pre-school through college students in her hometown of Kansas City. An agent for equity, she has dedicated her career to helping others learn to follow their internal compass, and thrive despite challenge. Cynthia is currently Founder & CEO of LaunchCrate Publishing - a company created to help writers launch their work into the world while retaining the portion of profit they deserve. Outside of LaunchCrate she is an active advocate for education, serving as a former Girls on the Run Coach, on the Board of Directors for the Children's Campus of Kansas City and Junior Achievement of Greater KC, on the K-State in KC Task Force, as well as Chair Emeritus of the Multicultural Alumni Council at Kansas State University.

She is author and illustrator of the Ella Book Series, The Christmas Cookie books, and her latest series, "The Secret World of Raine the Brain." She also penned the interactive modern memoir, "So, Okay..." documenting the life stories of her then 94 year old Grandfather. All are fun books that inspire us to be bold, take risks, and learn from our mistakes. When she's not helping clients, hosting a podcast, speaking with audiences or working on her latest book about building community, you can find her doodling on whatever object may be nearby.

Her favorite work is documenting personal narratives through the Modern Memoir service, and serving as a Story Shepherd to writers, working to launch their work into the world through Idea to Editor. Both services are offered by LaunchCrate Publishing. Check out launchcrate.com for more detailed information.

CPSIA information can be obtained
at www.ICGtesting.com
Printed in the USA
LVHW031139071121
702657LV00010B/1636